WRECKED BY LOVE

BY LOVE SERIES

MARY O FLOURNOY

COPYRIGHT

Publisher: Captive 8 Publishing
Editor: Holly Atkinson, Evil Eye Editing
Cover Design: Rose Miller

Ebook ISBN-13: 979-8-9874444-0-5
Paperback ISBN-13: 979-8-9874444-1-2

DEDICATION

To my daughters, Kyler and Nya, who asked me every day for the last six years - is your book done? I hope me finally reaching my dream sets your own ablaze.

To my husband, Marleaux, who was always there for me with his encouragement, love, support, and what my girls and I like to call his Marleauxisms. I owe you more than what is describable and none of it would hit the mark. I love you.

ACKNOWLEDGMENTS

Mary E. Thompson. I do not know how to thank you for the countless hours of texting, talking on the phone, and flying across the states to collaborate. You patiently and generously offered your years of wisdom on all things writing, romance, publishing, and so much more. Without your continued support, this book would not have been possible. I hope you truly know what a precious gift of friendship and mentorship you have given me. Thank you.

CONTENTS

CHAPTER ONE

Bella

I WASN'T IN THE WOODS AT MIDNIGHT BEHIND MY BROTHER'S HOUSE to have mini orgasms caused by Dean Cannon, my brother's best friend, from merely breathing in my ear.

When I grabbed his wrist to dislodge his hand from my mouth, I noticed a few things.

One, I couldn't even wrap my hand around his wrist. Two, he was unquestionably all muscle. He was solid. There was no give under my hand. None. Three, he didn't move the slightest when I pulled on his wrist. Not *even* a millimeter. Four, he had to have some sort of electrical suit on because the currents were expanding.

Through my hand.

From his wrist.

To decidedly specific body parts on me.

Oh boy.

"It's me, Bella. Don't scream."

Scream? I was having trouble breathing.

"Are you okay?" The sparks tingled even after he removed his hand from my mouth. Only to place both hands on my waist.

In an attempt to divert attention away from the fact I was *not*, I snapped, "Dammit, Dean! You scared the crap out of me."

"Bella, you *are* running *in* the woods *in* the middle of the night." Dean's disbelieving tone clearly pointed out the obvious stupidity in my statement.

"Yeah, but I'm not lurking behind trees scaring people."

"Bella."

Not sure what he meant by that Bella, I remained quiet and focused on controlling my rampaging hormones. An extremely challenging task, even when we had a room separating us. But with this proximity? Prayers were in order.

"Wait. Why *are* you lurking behind trees in the middle of the night?"

Dean continued to hold me as he scanned my face. "I just left Alex. We knew you'd be out running tonight, so I told him I'd check on you on my way out. Save Alex the trouble."

"What? Why?"

He gently squeezed me. "I wanted to avoid bailing you out of jail and Alex the headache of having you detained, again."

My eyes widened. "What?"

Dean smiled.

My stomach dipped.

"Bella, a year ago you thought you had a clue and broke into Old Man Harper's cabin looking for it. Alex and Trent had to finagle his kids into not pressing charges." He shook his head. "Every time you think you figured out something new about the accident, you and Rocky take off on some wild goose chase that leaves either Alex, Trent, or me cleaning up after you. Since tomorrow marks ten years, it's not that difficult for me to assume you'd up your sleuthing game."

"How were Rocky and I supposed to know they had an alarm installed on the premise?" I stomped my foot and grumbled.

Chuckling, Dean pulled back, grabbed my hand, and led me down the trail. "I don't know. Maybe breaking into someone's house isn't the way to go."

"It was vacant, so technically we didn't break into anyone's home."

I couldn't ignore the sparks emanating from his hand anymore and tugged mine free. "Where are you taking me?"

"I'm walking you back home."

I stopped in my tracks and replied, "Who said I was done jogging?"

One of Dean's eyebrows lifted. "You were *standing* behind Alex's house"—minor detail—"and there is no way in hell I'm letting you walk around at night by yourself."

Of course, he wouldn't. Dean's protective ego wouldn't survive my womanly independence.

"What about you? I mean, after you verify I'm secure in my apartment, *you'll* be all by yourself *at* night." I stood in the universal pissed-off woman stance—hands on my hips.

Dean's response? He crossed his bulging arms across his massive chest.

I threw my hands up, turned around and marched away harping, "You do realize women have been taking care of themselves for centuries, right?"

He ignored my question. "Did you have another nightmare? Was it the same as the previous ones?"

My next step faltered as my feminine outrage vanished to be replaced by shock. After Alex had admitted me to the psychiatric ward at Granite Creek Hospital ten years ago, I'd learned to hide the nightmares from everyone. How did Dean know I still had them?

"No nightmare," I readjusted my ponytail as the lie poured from my mouth. "It's ten years tomorrow. Tonight. It's understandable I'd have trouble sleeping."

Dean grabbed my elbow, and those damn sparks ignited. His voice was gentle but firm. "Hey. Don't lie to me, Bella."

Looking over at him, I saw he was serious and a little—hurt? Of course, he wouldn't take me lying to him, but Dean wasn't someone who had earned the right to my nightmares, no matter how much my sappy heart demanded otherwise.

"Sorry, Dean." Hedging on what I could reveal without Dean rushing to Alex, I gave a little. "Both. It's the same and not."

I was grateful to see my apartment complex and hoped Dean would take it as a sign not to push for more. Because while the nightmare was the same, the woman's voice was not. And her yelling *"Oh my God! What are you doing?"* was absolutely different. I didn't need or want the pitiful look that was sure to come from Dean as he reminded me *again* that it was *just* an accident.

"You should have turned your outside light on before you left." Dean focused on my entryway.

"I did."

His expression plainly called bullshit.

"I did. I bet the light just burned out." I hoped.

Dean removed my keys from my hand. "Wait here."

After years of Alex and Dean's protective streak, I knew my best course of action was to wait while he ensured my apartment was safe, and since I lived in a small space it wouldn't take long.

Sure enough, Dean returned quickly. "Do you notice anything different?"

"What?"

"Anything look different?"

My stomach dropped as I glanced around my apartment. "Was someone in here?"

Guilt flashed across Dean's face as he made it to me. "Shit. Sorry, Bella." He rubbed my arms. "No, no one was here."

I thumped his chest once and bit out, "Dammit, Dean. Give a girl a heart attack, why don't you!" I did my best to ignore his hands caressing my arms and how good it felt.

"I'm sorry. I didn't mean to scare you." He watched me. "Are you okay?"

Taking a step back and out of his reach, I bumped into the door and blindly reached for the doorknob. "I'm all good." Not really. "Thanks for walking me home and making sure my apartment was safe." Please stop touching me. Actually, touch me *everywhere.*

"Are you sure?" His eyebrows met.

"Yup. All good." My erratic nodding a twin for an active bobble head.

Dammit, where was the freaking doorknob?

He leaned forward and grabbed my hand. "What's going on?"

Those damn sparks started back up. "I'm just tired." I licked my dry lips as another lie slipped out, but I couldn't tell him his proximity was driving my body insane.

A brief but gentle squeeze of my hand followed by, "Why don't you want to tell me about the nightmare?"

I rarely got away with anything. Between my brother and Trent, one of his best friends being police detectives and Dean, rounding out their trio of friendship, being a private investigator, they always figured out when I was lying. This was one of those moments I wished Dean sucked at his profession instead of using what he knew of my past to call me on my bullshit.

More importantly, I didn't want him to tell me for the umpteenth time that the accident that killed my parents was *just* an accident. That what I *thought* I remembered while in the car with my dead parents wasn't what truly happened. I'd had years of Alex and Dean, even if it was cautiously and irritatingly gentle, telling me my brain injury altered my memories from that night.

"I..." I cleared my throat. "I'm not ready."

"Okay, Bella, but when you're ready, I'm here for you." Dean drew small circles with his thumb on my hand.

I plastered a smile on my face. The one where you try to hide what you're feeling? That's the one that was losing purchase on my face as I answered him. "I know."

Just not the way I want you to be.

He dropped his hand and opened the door. "I'll be back tomorrow to change out your light. Make sure to lock this behind me."

"You don't have to do that. I can call management and have them replace it."

"Not a problem." He ignored my veiled request as he leaned forward, cupped my face, and pressed his lips to my forehead.

I froze. Dean hadn't kissed me since we were kids and holy freaking cow, his lips were going to be permanently emblazoned on me.

He stepped back and pointed to door. "Lock it."

Forcing myself to move, I closed the door, locked it, and through the pounding of my heart in my ears, I heard his footfalls as he walked away.

Dean Cannon had kissed me.

CHAPTER TWO

Dean

I STARED, UNSEEING, AT THE FILES ON MY DESK BECAUSE THE thought—*I fucked up last night*—kept repeating through my head.

The second I'd touched her face I knew I messed up. I never should have kissed Bella. She was so unbelievably soft and her fucking smell. All woman.

Jesus. Playing it off had been torture as I'd turned away from her with a fucking hard on—all from a simple kiss on her *forehead*. The whole time I fought myself not to demand she open the door so I could finish what I'd started.

All of this made me feel like the biggest asshole. It was the tenth anniversary of Bella's parents' death. A death she had been a party to and still reeling from as her midnight run demonstrated, and here I was lusting over her.

Having her in my arms after the last few years of self-imposed physical distance, I'd slipped. No, more like years of watching Alex and Bella torture themselves over that night, my subconscious had demanded I give Bella the littlest bit of comfort.

That one fucking slip strained my restraint to paper thin. Any more careless mistakes and it'd evaporate completely, leaving nothing but heartache. For Bella and me.

So, I had to make sure it never happened again. Distance was vital and no touching. Absolutely no damn touching.

Unfortunately, the case in front of me didn't provide me with answers on how to go about that.

"Dean, do you need anything before I head out for lunch?" Lily's head popped around the edge of my office door.

Lily'd been my office manager almost as long as my private investigation doors had been open. To say she was the best would be a gross understatement. Something that asshole she was seeing didn't get.

"No. I'm good."

"I'm heading over to Harper's. Want me to grab you something?"

I shook my head. "Thanks, but I'll grab something when I step out. Enjoy your lunch."

"All right. I'll see you later."

When the door closed behind her, I refocused on the file in front of me. It was my latest case—a cheating husband who thought he could get away with banging his oldest daughter's best friend while dipping into his children's college funds to spoil her with luxuries he wasn't even providing his own family. How the fucking dick could sit next to his family at the dinner table while his college-aged mistress gave him a handjob—yes, I had the pictures to prove it—I couldn't fathom. More importantly, I didn't understand how someone who had it all—a loving wife and family—would throw it away.

Twenty-two years later and my dad still mourned my mother. He cherished every moment he'd had with her, even the times she'd sassed him. Looking back now as an adult, I knew he'd riled her up on purpose. To see the spark in her eyes, the flush in her cheeks.

"Dean? You here?" Trent bellowed from the front.

Just in time to get me out of my head because now I was romanticizing my parents' relationship like Bella and Rocky did. We had enough of them waxing on about it growing up, I didn't need to do it on my own.

"Back here."

"Lily at lunch?" Trent asked as he walked through door in his usual detective uniform of jeans, button down shirt and blazer.

"Please tell me she didn't go see that jackass," Alex demanded to know as he followed Trent into my office dressed in the same manner as Trent.

"Harper's as far as I know. As for the jackass, I think she may finally be coming to her senses. She's been sending a lot of personal calls to voicemail, staying later to work. Small things like that." I leaned forward, forearms on my desk as Alex and Trent sat across from me.

"Did you offer to have a conversation with him?"

"Yeah. A few times. She's refused every time and I don't want to push the issue."

"She's a smart girl. She'll come to you if she needs to," Alex's sentiment mirrored my own.

"Yeah, I'm hoping she doesn't have to, but you didn't come here to discuss Lily and her problems. What's up?"

Alex started, "This goes without saying, but this stays between us."

I nodded my acknowledgment even as my gut warmed at the warning.

"Looks like Richard's death may not be as simple as driving while under the influence."

My eyebrows shot up. Richard was always inebriated. There wasn't a time I remembered, high school included, when Richard had been sober.

"Yeah, we all expected Richard to kick it behind the wheel with the way he drank, but Richard's been drinking since he was a kid. It was his water and his body couldn't not handle it." Trent stretched his legs out in front of him.

Alex picked up where Trent left off. "It made us look into Richard's happenings before the accident occurred. Nothing unusual about it. Well, at least for Richard."

"Yeah." I tensed, bracing for their response.

Alex leaned his forearms on his knees. "We were right. Richard's blood alcohol level was too high. He was likely incapable of walking, much less driving."

Uneasiness trickled through me. "Richard was an alcoholic. He could handle his liquor, more than the average Joe."

"True, but Richard wasn't just drunk. His blood alcohol level was four times the legal limit." Trent's tone stated there was more to it.

I still wasn't surprised. "And? The man bathed in alcohol."

"His blood was saturated in it. He wouldn't have survived the night with all that alcohol in his system. So why would someone put him behind the wheel?" Alex fisted his hands.

"Someone used the fact Richard was a drunk to kill him. Why?" I leaned back in my chair blowing out the suddenly bitter breath in my lungs.

"No clue." Alex flexed his fingers in attempt to regain circulation after the white-knuckled fist he had them in earlier.

The hairs on the back of my neck stood up. "Are either of you bothered by the fact that we know someone who was murdered and that we may even know the murderer? Especially here in our small town?"

"Yeah." Alex sighed and rubbed the back of his neck. "I always expected to find Richard dead, but by his own doing. Not by someone we might know."

"It's difficult not to suspect people's ulterior motives with our line of work." Trent shook his head. "But this puts a whole new spin on things."

"So, who do we know who would want Richard dead *and* would be willing to kill him?" I asked.

"Besides the usual suspects?" Trent's grim question only confirmed the suspect list was way too long. "I have no idea."

Alex continued, "And, whoever did it did enough research to stage it to look like an accident."

"Interesting considering his usual pool of associates aren't known to be the intellectual type. So, that really begs the question—who wanted Richard dead?" Because all of the above clearly showed someone was after Richard specifically.

"We're hoping Bruce will be able to give us some insight. He's our next stop." Alex settled back in his chair.

"Do you think he'll actually give you anything?" Doubt colored my words. "My guess, he's probably a party to whatever Richard was messed up in considering they were locked at the hip since kindergarten."

"We don't think he'll intentionally give us anything. We're hoping he'll slip up or at least involuntarily lead us somewhere." Trent drummed his fingers on the arm of his chair.

"Is that where you need me? To follow him?"

"Yeah. He'll be looking for Trent or me." Both Alex and Trent stood as Alex continued, "Besides we want him to think we're taking his word that he doesn't know anything."

"Let me know when you've finished speaking to Bruce."

Alex and Trent lifted their chins and stepped out of my office.

"Alex?" I called out.

He stopped. "Yeah?"

"How you hanging in there? Anything you need from me?" Besides closing the gap on the missing pieces in Bella's memories from the accident. For years I watched her struggling to piece them together with no luck.

"Nothing you aren't already doing. I'm more worried about Bella and how the ten year anniversary is going to affect her. She still beats herself up trying to remember anything from that night." He paused. "Now knowing she may have been right all these years." He sucked a pained breath. "I don't have the heart to get her hopes up without knowing for sure. Without proof. Without concrete evidence. Because right now all we have is Richard, of all people, drunkenly mouthing off at Shackles about my parents' accident. I need more before I say anything to Bella."

"Don't beat yourself up. We all believed the same thing – justifiably. We had no way of knowing any better."

It didn't matter that what Trent said was right. It would take Alex a long time to get over dismissing his sister's beliefs regarding their parents' deaths.

"It'd make me feel a whole lot better if I could prove whether or not it was truly an accident or not once and for all. Until then, I'm meeting up with Bella later, so I'll get a better feel on how she's doing then. Hopefully her damn stubborn ass hasn't done anything I'm going to have to get her out of."

Trent and I chuckled.

"You're looking in a mirror," I yelled at Alex's retreating back.

He flipped me off as he continued to walk away.

Trent flicked his hand out as he took his departure too.

Looking back down at the papers on my desk, I mentally added checking out Bruce to my to-do list.

CHAPTER THREE

Bella

"WHAT IS YOUR FAMILIAL RELATION TO BRUCE EVANS?"

I barely held my frustration in check before responding to Nurse Booby, "I'm a close friend." Sort of.

"We don't give out patient information to close friends." Her crossed arms and tapping red fingernails all lent to her unspoken command—*fuck off.*

"I know, but Bruce's brother is my good friend. I want to be here for him—to offer him moral support." I pulled up a friendly smile, hoping to play on the strength of the sisterhood. "You know how guys are. They'll never ask for help, but in times like this, they need it. They need us women." I glanced at the male emergency room technician next to her hoping he didn't take offense.

"No." She didn't budge an inch.

"I..."

"Excuse me. Can you tell me where Phillip Hudson is?" Tall, Dark, and Handsome interrupted.

The male attendant didn't even have an opportunity to do his job because in a blink of an eye, Nurse Booby transformed into Nurse Helpful.

"Well, I'm not supposed to give out patient information unless you're family and I wouldn't want to get in trouble." Nurse Booby leaned forward, assets on full display, and all but invited McHotterson to give her his number as she completely ignored me.

And, yes, he took the bait.

Arms on either side of Nurse Booby, McHotterson closed the gap between them and murmured, "I wouldn't want to get you in trouble. Of course we're family."

"I won't tell if you don't," she purred while stroking his arm.

Her coworker—the one supposedly working the emergency room desk—studiously inspected the papers on his desk, ignoring the mating dance happening in front of him.

Turning to the side, she bent over—you guessed it, ass up in the air —to the computer to get McHotterson the data he needed.

I desperately needed another shower after this.

"Excuse me." Not one single eyelash of hers fluttered at my words, but I wasn't deterred. "Since you're searching your database, would you please look up Bruce Evans?"

"Ah, here you go."

She slid him a piece of paper that obviously had more than a room number on it and completely ignored me. Again.

McHotterson held her hand and murmured, "Since you've been such a doll, would you mind giving her what she wants?"

The venom that punched out of her sideways glance at me would have been lethal if McHotterson didn't carry the antidote.

But the seductive smile she gave McHotterson was an open invitation to assist him in *any* manner he'd like. "Anything for you."

Bitch.

The word shot through my mind as I walked away from Nurse Booby at the information desk at Feldspar County Hospital. I tried not to demean my fellow sisters. It was tough enough being a woman, but when the sisterhood shit on you as well? Yeah, bitch *was* nice.

I knew my ponytailed hair and make-up free face were a convenience for my work at the FeldsPaw Clinic. I received one too many kisses from my furry patients to justify putting it on, and why bother dressing up when I knew at any minute, I would end up with animal debris on my clothes.

Even if I wanted to wear something more revealing, it wasn't like I was overly endowed to begin with. No, my B-cups were barely a handful, and until this moment, I hadn't disliked them; having smaller assets suited me well when dealing with my patients.

But, to have a fellow sister who was heavily endowed in *all* of her feminine assets make another female who was *not* feel invisible or worthless?

Bitch.

It was on that thought, I reached the surgery waiting room and was immediately confronted with Alex and my good friend, Leonard, toe-to-toe, in each other's face ready to... I didn't want to find out what.

"What's going on?" Although I directed my question to Alex and Leonard, I scanned the room, noting Dean was in attendance. A few other officers were huddled in conversation and seemingly oblivious to the tension between my brother and my friend.

I wasn't surprised to see Dean there. As a private investigator, Dean often consulted with Alex on his cases. However, after last night's kiss and Dean's stopping by this morning to change my light bulb, my body was on a hormonal short fuse.

Dean headed toward Alex and Leonard, in what I hoped would be his attempt to prevent an argument. However, the second our eyes connected, Dean changed his trajectory toward me. Meanwhile, both Alex and Leonard focused their attention on me. I didn't know what to make of this, and I prayed my body didn't give my wanton hunger away.

However, it was Alex and Leonard's heated expressions that held my attention. Not once in all the years I'd known Leonard had they ever had a disagreement. So many times after school, we'd hung out at my house doing homework, eating snacks, and goofing off. Not to mention all the dinners Leonard had stayed for just so he could enjoy a home-cooked meal and not once in any of those encounters had they ever raised their voices in anger to each other.

"You shouldn't be here." Dean looked down at me.

At the same time, Alex bit out, "What are you doing here, Bella?"

I chose to ignore Dean even if my body screamed at me to rub against him. Instead, I aimed my attention to Alex. "I'm here for Leonard."

"Why?" Frustration laced the word.

"Because I'm his friend."

"I know that, Bella. How did you know to come here?" Alex growled when his patience disappeared.

I gentled my voice before addressing Leonard. "After I completed my rounds tonight, I saw the local news report about an attack on Bruce. According to the reporter, you found Bruce beaten and unconscious in his hunting cabin. From their initial assessment, it looked like he had been there since yesterday."

I directed my next comment at Alex. "More importantly, the reporter stated Bruce was rushed to Feldspar County Hospital where the doctors were performing emergency surgery. I came as soon as I heard."

The already heated air in the room blistered.

"Shit," Dean pushed past the tightening of his lips.

"That's just fucking great." Alex vibrated with renewed anger.

Leonard echoed Alex's temper. "What? Pissed off you're being exposed?"

Alex shifted the barest inch forward at Leonard's words.

My nerves took flight inside me. How would any of this expose Alex? Leonard couldn't believe Alex was associated with Bruce's attack. It just wasn't a possibility.

Then I noticed the room had quieted.

Not good.

"I don't understand. What do you mean?"

Leonard did not hesitate. "It means I don't trust the police. Always after Bruce, never giving him a break. One damn toe on the line, and they're all over him. And, you—" He stared at Alex. "You don't leave any fucking stone unturned." Leonard squeezed his neck and began pacing. "And then, you got Castor walking around like a fucking peacock with his minions trailing behind him doing his bidding."

"Nuh-uh. Bruce doesn't do toes," Alex ground out. "He's one

hundred percent vested in whatever shit he's doing. As for that other crap you just spewed about minions—fuck you. I do not do anyone's fucking bidding."

Leonard swung around to face Alex. "Bullshit. Just last week at Coop's, Brooke threw Bruce out when he chatted with another customer. Brooke didn't even hesitate to toss Bruce out, but Blake King?" An angry shake of his head. "No, he got to sit back and enjoy his meal. Talk about keeping it all in the family."

Alex jabbed his finger at Leonard. "Watch your mother fucking mouth. Bruce has, on numerous occasions, destroyed Coop's. Brooke has every fucking right to protect herself and her business."

"Protect?" Disbelief etched on Leonard's face. "Bruce minded his own fucking business when Blake got all up in his face. Bruce *also* had every right to protect himself, but it wasn't fucking Blake she kicked out."

"I'm sure Brooke must have had a good reason for her actions. What were Bruce and this Blake King arguing about?" I interjected before Alex moved any closer to Leonard.

"Bruce Evans' family?" The doctor had horrible timing.

Or perfect timing.

All the apprehension in the room redirected to him.

Leonard stepped toward the doctor. "That would be me."

The doctor eyed everyone in the room before settling on Leonard. "May I ask your familial relation with Mr. Evans?"

"I'm his brother, Leonard Evans." The tension in Leonard's body didn't abate.

The doctor beckoned Leonard, "If you'll follow me, Mr. Evans."

Alex flashed his badge as he walked up to the doctor. "I'd like to know when I can speak with Bruce Evans, and I'll want a detailed report of his injuries."

The doctor hesitated, looking around the room once more. "Please stop by the nurse's station, and I'll be with you shortly."

Leonard stiffened but didn't say a word before following the doctor out of the room.

Alex turned to me and clipped out, "Isabella, go home."

"This isn't the best time for you to be here." Dean echoed Alex's sentiment.

I felt like I was back in grade school when they did whatever they could to get rid of Alex's annoying little sister. Dammit, at twenty-six, I was beyond being a kid, and it was time they treated me like an adult. "No, not until one of you tells me what the heck is going on."

"Not going to happen." Alex's barely controlled frustration rang through.

Alex never told me anything about his cases, but this was different. This involved Leonard, my friend, who'd been there countless times after my parents' death. Who hadn't outright dismissed me when I ranted about there being more to the accident than everyone kept telling me. Being here now for Leonard was the least I could do to repay his kindness.

"What I know is none of this makes sense. What was Leonard referring to? Why does he not trust you?" I persisted.

"Oh, boy," Dean muttered.

Alex blew out a breath and rolled his shoulders. "Bella, I can't tell you what's going on. You know that."

"Doesn't mean I have to like it, and this is different." This was my friend.

Alex drew me in for a hug. "You're going to stick around for your friend, aren't you?"

I held onto the sides of his shirt and nodded.

"There's no way I can convince you to leave?"

I shook my head.

"You do realize Leonard probably won't leave Bruce's side. You'll be sitting here, twiddling your thumbs for hours."

"Then I'll sit here for hours, twiddling my thumbs." I didn't budge.

"I don't like it, but I have to stop at the nurses' station then meet Trent at Bruce's cabin. Promise me you'll stay out of whatever this is." Alex's frustration seeped through.

I squeezed my lips shut because I knew from experience a non-answer was the best way to go. I couldn't make that promise when Leonard, who had been there for me countless times, needed me now.

"Promise me, Bella." Alex stared down at me.

"I'd be lying if I did." And I'd learned a long time ago not to lie to Alex.

He sighed. "Sorry our plans got canceled. How are you doing today?"

"I understand, and I'm hanging in there. You?"

"Same. Rain check?"

Our sibling bond became stronger, deeper after our parents' death and because it was, I knew Alex's response was somehow—off. Was it because of Leonard's comments, Bruce's attack, the ten year anniversary of our parents' death or was it something else?

"Absolutely."

Dean interrupted our moment. "I'll stick around with her, make sure she doesn't get into any trouble."

I pushed away from Alex and argued, "I don't need a babysitter."

"Works for me." He bent down and kissed my cheek. "Love you, Bella."

"You know that doesn't work on me anymore." Ever since our parents' deaths, Alex would routinely pull out the brotherly love to guilt me into cutting him some slack. "I can take care of myself."

Sincerity danced in his eyes even when his lips twitched. "Doesn't mean it's not true."

Okay, maybe his affection did work. "Fine, but don't think I'm giving up that easily. I'll just pester you tomorrow." I smiled, indicating I was only partially joking.

"I was afraid of that." Alex didn't sound like he was joking.

Like all little sisters, I ignored my brother's annoyance and stood on my tiptoes to give him a peck on the cheek. "Catch whoever did this."

"I'm working on it." Alex called to Dean as Alex made his way out, "Swing by the station tomorrow."

"Will do."

NOT THAT I would admit my brother was right, but we stayed in the waiting room for hours, and Leonard never came back out. Which wouldn't have been so bad if I had been by myself.

But I wasn't.

Instead, I had six-foot-three and two-hundred-twenty pounds of deliciously solid muscle sitting next to me. And his voice? It was as if his voice had a direct connection to my uterus. Each syllable in his baritone tone caused fresh juices to soak my panties, and my nipples ached they were so hard.

Squeezing my legs together hadn't relieved any of the pressure. No, the slightest movement begged me to disappear to the closest bathroom so I could find some relief because sitting next to a sex god was torture. If rumor were anything to go by, the majority of the women in Feldspar could attest to this.

Except for me.

I tried to focus on the currently horrible and confusing situation so my hormones would stay off of Dean's lusciousness.

It didn't work.

No woman ignored Dean.

So when Sheriff Castor stepped up and said, "Good evening, Dean and Isabella." I practically leaped off my seat to greet him.

"Good evening, Sheriff." Yes, it came out breathy.

Dean's "Sheriff," was calm and collected, unlike mine.

"I'm sorry to break the news to you, but I just spoke with Bruce's doctor, and Leonard is refusing to leave Bruce's side."

I stared out the waiting room door as if I could see Leonard through the walls. "How is he doing?"

Sheriff Castor lowered his voice. "He's upset, but that's to be expected. Bruce is still unconscious, so we won't know anything until he wakes." He leaned forward and gently squeezed my hand before he releasing it. "You both should go home and get some rest. I'm leaving an officer outside Bruce's room. They'll be safe, Isabella."

"Thank you, Sheriff." It was the best I could hope for at the moment.

Dean took my hand and tugged me toward the exit as he bid farewell to the Sheriff. "Evenin' Sheriff."

Now, I was entombed in the elevator with Dean and drowning in his intoxicating scent. Not to mention the delectable image of Dean was visible on every *single* reflective wall. Literally surrounding me with him. There was no avoiding him. I desperately needed out of the elevator and away from Dean.

The second the elevator doors opened, I bolted out and ran right into a hospital orderly. If it weren't for Dean's quick response, we both would have ended up sprawled across the floor. Instead, I was wrapped in Dean's arms, face buried in his chest, inhaling his scent up close and personal.

Someone hated me.

"Oh my! Are you okay? Can I get you anything?"

I knew that voice. Nurse Booby.

Slowly, I turned my head, torturing myself with Dean's physique, and came face-to-face with her perky melons.

It felt as if I moved in slow motion when I raised my head to find Nurse Booby giving Dean a come-hither smile and ignoring the fact I was *in* Dean's arms.

See? Total bitch.

What hurt more than the fact another woman would kick a fellow sister while she was down was the fact that I knew Nurse Booby fit Dean's type. Tall, blonde, buxom, and willing.

Everything I was not. Well, except for willing. No way I was going to stick around and watch them hookup.

Dean's grip tightened around me as I attempted to remove myself from the situation.

"Bella, you all right?" Dean's voice reflected his annoyance. Probably directed at the fact I was currently hampering his booty call.

God, I had to get out of there.

"Yeah. Yes. Yes, I'm fine."

In my attempt to escape Dean's embrace once more, I placed my hands on his firm chest and pushed. To no avail.

Nurse Booby huffed away in anger as she realized her offer was being rebuked by my presence.

Dean slid his arm around my waist and moved us toward the exit.

I knew Dean was doing his protective duty, ensuring I arrived at my vehicle safely before he returned to the hospital to take the nurse up on her invite. That was one hassle I could save him and another heartache I could save myself.

"Dean, it's okay. I can find my way to my truck. You can go on back, and you know..."

Dean stopped in the middle of the parking lot.

"What did you say?"

"I said, you don't have to walk me to my truck. You can go on back and connect with the nurse." I said it and didn't combust.

Small miracle.

Dean ground out, "There is no fucking way I am *connecting* with that woman. Jeez, how could you even think that?"

"What?"

"Shit, Bella, I *do* have standards."

I stared at him.

Standards? Tall, check. Blonde, check. Abundance of cleavage, check. Willing, check. *What did I miss?*

"You're messing with me, right?"

"I may like female companionship, but I do not appreciate being accosted." Dean's eyes narrowed and his mouth flattened into a thin line.

Accosted? Yes, Nurse Booby had intimately pressed into Dean, but I wouldn't categorize it as accosting. Invitation? Absolutely.

It was Dean who looked confused now. "How were you in my arms and missed the whole thing?" A shake of his head. "Bella, no woman should hit on another man while he is with another woman." This shake of his head was in disgust. "I'm surprised she hasn't been outed from whatever universal group you women have."

I burst out laughing.

He was right. Every woman should have the freedom to be who they truly were. But, in my opinion, our friendly neighborhood nurse was a little *too* friendly.

I quieted and wiped the tears from the corners of my eyes. "Thanks, Dean. That felt great."

"Glad to be of service." His smile—as usual—knocked the breath out of me.

God, he was so beautiful. His thick, jet-black hair made his blue eyes pop, and his cheekbones looked as if they'd been chiseled on his face.

Every inch of him was delectable.

I had to stop thinking of Dean in that manner. I wasn't doing myself any good.

"Since your virtue is at stake, you can walk me to my truck."

"Smartass." The humor in his word matched the twitch in his lips.

"That's me, the pesky younger sister." I attempted to keep it light. To keep us on the easygoing road we've always been on.

"I wouldn't say that."

I stopped at my truck and unlocked the door—all while purposely ignoring his odd comment and what it could possibly mean. "Thanks for walking me to my truck." I folded into the driver seat and then looked up at Dean. "Have a good night."

"Bella, I know it goes without saying, but be careful."

I sat in my truck and looked at him. "I always am."

But if you want to be my personal bodyguard and guard my body all night long, I wouldn't object.

CHAPTER FOUR

Bella

As I made my way to my darkened apartment, again, Dean's cautionary words filtered through my brain, making me doubt my safety.

A day earlier, my shadowed entryway would've had me guessing it to be more kid shenanigans. It was little things like the pool chairs scattered throughout; the sprinklers turned outward, so they sprayed the walkway instead of the grass or light bulbs exchanged with strobe lights.

Kid pranks.

When I looked at my darkened front porch for the second night in a row, the hairs on my arms stood up. A warning that whatever was going on wasn't kid pranks.

I was debating what I should do next when headlights from an approaching car and my neighbor's opened doorway lit our joint entryway. And the broken glass on the ground.

Definitely not kid pranks.

Peering at me through his thinly wired spectacles, my aforementioned neighbor, Mr. Stewart, said, "Good evening, Miss Hall."

"Good evening, Mr. Stewart."

He glanced at the broken glass and promptly returned his attention to me. "I'm glad to see you're finally home. Please make sure to remove this safety hazard promptly. It has created an inconvenience amongst your neighbors and shows poorly on our living environment."

At least this time, Mr. Stewart hadn't threatened to report the infraction.

"Of course. I will rectify the situation immediately. Please accept my apologies for any inconvenience this may have caused you."

A prim nod in acceptance and a terse, "Good evening," and Mr. Stewart retired to his apartment.

I hurried inside and grabbed the broom and dustpan. It had been a long day, and all I wanted to do was soak in a hot bath while I enjoyed a cold beer, not stand out in the cold sweeping broken glass. I figured if I moved quickly, I'd be able to—"Aaah!"

Dean stood outside my door, looking from the broken glass to me.

"Bella, you didn't check the peephole before you opened your door. That's *not* being careful."

"Dean! You scared the bejesus out of me." My heart beat thunderously inside my chest. "What are you doing here?"

At the same time, Mr. Stewart opened his door. "Miss Hall, please keep your evening festivities private." Mr. Stewart glanced from Dean to my opened door to the broken glass still on the ground. "And remove this debris expeditiously."

Mr. Stewart didn't wait for my response before retiring back into his apartment.

I stared at Mr. Stewart's closed door. *Private* festivities *with* Dean?

Immediately, images of Dean naked in my bed flooded my brain. All his smooth, golden skin laid bare for my view, my touch and taste, while his rigid cock stood erect, imploring my attention.

Just as quickly, my panties grew soaked, my nipples pebbled to hard peaks, and my breaths became pants.

Visions of a naked Dean dissipated as he snatched the broom and dustpan out of my hand. "Bella, go pack a bag. You've got ten minutes before we head out."

Taking a deep breath, I attempted to gather control of my rioting body and focused on Dean's comment.

"Why do I need to pack a bag, and why am I leaving?" I shook my head to clear the cobwebs. "Wait, why are you even here?"

Dean paused in the middle of his sweeping and looked at me. "I wanted to make sure you were okay, and I thought maybe you'd want to get some dinner. You know, so you're not alone tonight."

My heart fell in a puddle of love. Normally, Alex and I spent the anniversary of our parents' passing together, but with the recent events, our plans were sidelined. So for Dean to step up and want to soothe my pain almost made me go for a hug. Almost. Anymore contact with Dean and I wouldn't be liable for my actions.

"That's sweet, but I'm going to just stay in and unwind."

He scanned my face. "Humor me."

"I'm fine. Really." And I'd be better if he left. Any more time in his presence and my resolve to keep my distance would crumble. "As you can see, I'm okay, so you can go now." I held out my hand for the broom.

"I will after you pack a bag."

"What? Why?"

"You're not going to be here tomorrow."

He *was* losing his mind, and my grip on my temper was slipping.

"Yes, I am. Aside from work, I plan on being here"—I pointed at the ground—"tomorrow." I might have leaned toward him slightly on the last word, but really, what did he expect, telling me where I would be?

"Bella, get your shit." Dean, broom and dustpan in hand, made his way toward me.

"Don't order me around." I took my own step toward him, the grip on my temper lost.

In one step, he was toe-to-toe with me, looking down at me from his considerable height. "Bella, either you get your shit, or I do."

I sucked in a breath. "You go through my stuff and we'll have problems."

No way did I want him to see my lacy undergarments or my Dean Toy.

"Got something to hide?" Heat flared behind his eyes.

Yes. Yes, I did.

"You can't just go through my things. They're *personal*."

His smile was slow, wicked and knowing. "I bet they are."

Oh, God. How did I end up discussing my sex toys with Dean?

Dean Cannon knew I had sex toys and was smiling about it.

Shoot me now.

Or fuck me.

"I'll just give you a hand with packing." He made as if to move past me.

I flew to my bedroom, locked the door, and yelled, "I don't need your help!"

His chuckle seeped through the door as my head plopped against it.

"Really, someone shoot me," I muttered.

Dean

I stood on Bella's stoop and swept the broken glass to keep myself preoccupied. Mainly, so the images of having *private* festivities *with* Bella inside her apartment would leave my head. A challenge since her pebbled nipples strained against her T-shirt, letting me know she liked the idea too.

It took more control than I wanted to admit to not act on our shared desires.

The other reason didn't help either. No, it threatened my control even more because *fuck me, Bella has toys.* I really didn't need to be thinking of sex toys and Bella in the same thought, but once there, all I could think of was how could I get her to play with me. The image of Bella with her head thrown back, her thick silky hair wrapped around my hand, while I rode her from behind, and drove her toy in her from the front played out in my mind. All the while, I would admire the smooth line of her back and her heart-shaped ass tipped up to me—for my taking.

Shit, I had to be careful. I was going to make myself come in my jeans like a teenager.

Rearranging myself, I forced my thoughts to the broken porch light I was sweeping. A second malfunctioning light—coincidence? I didn't think so, but what exactly did it mean?

Pain sliced through me at the thought of Bella being hurt. To not having her in my life, even if it was at arm's length. I'd rather her remain Alex's baby sister—off limits, but here, unharmed.

Then I'd received Alex's text asking me to keep an eye on Bella since he'd found something at Bruce's cabin, and there was no way he could get to her tonight. Hence my lame excuse about dinner and pushing her to pack an overnight bag. Instead, I stood sweeping a broken light bulb in Bella's entryway in an attempt to assuage my need to do something—to protect.

Needless to say, after everything, there was no way I was going to leave Bella alone.

No doubt it would be torture on us both, but until I replaced her light bulb—again—and checked into her security a little more, I'd fucking handle having her close without indulging myself. While I had her under my roof, I would *not* have her under me. So, no holding her, no kissing her, and absolutely no fucking.

Shit. Forget torture—this was going to kill me.

Forcing my mind off Bella's body, I mentally created a to-do list. The first order of business was to replace her light bulb, again. Next, I'd contact Wyndham Terrace management to retrieve footage of their video surveillance. With any luck, whoever caused this would be captured on camera.

Next up, a conversation with Alex about all the shit he'd found at Bruce's cabin and how that equated to Bella needing protection. Did it have to do with Richard's comments at Shackles? Bella's accident? And did Leonard have anything to do with it? Shit. Add Leonard to the mix, and Bella was destined to place herself directly in the middle of this shit storm. I couldn't stand by and watch her meander through danger without doing something about it.

I dumped the broken glass in her trash, returned the broom and dustpan to their spot as Bella walked out of her bedroom. She was breathtaking in snug blue jeans and a tight white T-shirt that drew my eyes to her breasts and ass. Which made me want to wrap her silky ponytail around my hand and bend her over for my pleasure.

Bella interrupted my inappropriate thoughts.

"I'm ready. You can drop me off at the clinic on the way to your house."

She was too fucking cute. So fiercely giving and utterly oblivious to her draw. But there was no way she was going to spend the night at the clinic or anywhere without me to protect her.

She just didn't know it yet.

Making my way to the front door, I started, "Do you have—"

"Shut it."

"Just making sure you don't forget anything you might need." I chuckled.

She flounced by me, halting in her open doorway as she shined her sweet smile at me. "Thanks for sweeping the glass."

Bella

I utilized the time I gathered my overnight bag to wrangle my rioting hormones under some sort of control. The precarious ledge of arousal I straddled barely made it bearable to sit a confined space with Dean.

The fact I only had fifteen minutes before we reached the clinic helped me keep my sexual frustration in check. Fifteen minutes next to Dean before I could take a deep breath of air not accentuated by his manly scent.

"Dean, I *am* capable of driving myself to the clinic." I bit out for the umpteenth time in the last ten minutes. "You don't have to drive me."

Standing next to my truck at my apartment, Dean and I had argued about him driving me to FeldsPaw Clinic. Until Mr. Stewart's porch light came on, and I'd promptly climbed into Dean's truck. I'd already tested Mr. Stewart's equanimity twice tonight. I knew the third would result in another complaint lodged with management, something I did not want or need.

Dean ignored my comment. "Have there been other random events around your apartment complex like the broken light bulb?"

"Yeah. It's just kid pranks." Goosebumps erupted on my arms, reminding me that maybe it wasn't *all* kid pranks. I swung my gaze out the side window and sighed.

"What kind of kid pranks?"

"The usual. Turned sprinkler heads, lounge chairs in the swimming pool, strobe lights in place of porch lights. Kid pranks." I chuckled. "My favorite so far is when Mr. Stewart was taking his nightly swim and swam into a bar of Snickers. Oh my God, I don't think I ever saw Mr. Stewart behave so inappropriately. I thought he was going to drown in his attempt to get out of the pool quickly."

"Now, *that* would have been something to see." Humor lit Dean's words. "All right. All jokes asides, anything else that *didn't* seem like kid pranks occur? Anything that at the time you thought wasn't quite right but labeled it as part of the pranks?"

"What's going on?" I turned back to Dean as I warmed at his questioning.

He quieted. "Hopefully nothing."

Uneasiness spread through me. "The sprinkler prank happened the same time I found my doormat moved. I found it two feet away from the door like it had been tossed backward. At first, I thought the kids were trying to get everyone's mats wet with the sprinklers, but my mat was the only one moved. At least down my line of sight." I pushed the thought out of my mind, doing my best not to let fear overtake my sensibilities.

"What about in your apartment? Anything out of place? Off?" Dean glanced at me.

I fully turned to Dean and quietly told him, "You're scaring me."

"It's not my intention to scare you." His voice gentled. "Bella?"

"No. I haven't noticed anything peculiar inside my apartment."

A nod from Dean. "That's good. Get any funny vibes while you're out and about? At work? With friends? Leonard?"

"Okay, now I'm officially scared. What's going on?"

At the stoplight, Dean turned to me. "I don't know—yet. But, Bella, I'm making sure nothing will happen."

"This has to do with what happened to Bruce, doesn't it?" All of Dean's questions, his unexpected appearance at my apartment, his invitation for dinner, and his insistence that I pack an overnight bag were all beginning to make sense. Neither Alex, Dean, nor Trent would leave me in a potentially unsafe environment.

At the change of the light, Dean returned his attention to the road. "Yes, it has to do with Bruce's attack. His brother is your good friend. That's too damn close for my comfort, for Alex's."

"Are you saying Leonard has something to do with what happened to Bruce?" My disbelief was evident in my voice. "I can't believe that. Leonard wouldn't harm his brother."

"I'm not saying that." He didn't deny it either. "What I am saying is you are Leonard's good friend, and you'll do what you can to help him, thereby inserting yourself in whatever mess is swirling around Bruce and Leonard."

"Leonard was there for me after my parents died, you know that."

"I know. But whoever attacked Bruce is still out there and knows he survived. They'll be gunning to get him again. With Leonard standing vigilant at Bruce's bedside and you attempting to stick to Leonard's side." Dean shook his head. "Just because he was there for you then doesn't mean you have to place yourself in danger for him now—or ever."

"You have no idea. Leonard more than supported me during that time. He was there when I—" I stopped before I admitted just how much of a difficult time I'd honestly had after returning from Granite Creek Hospital. Alex had been tormented by my inability to recuperate fully after the accident; therefore, I'd vowed when I returned from Granite Creek Hospital to protect him just as equally as he had me.

If it wasn't for the medication, the night terrors would not only have plagued me but Alex too. Instead, I was able to keep from screaming. The constant replay of the accident and the images of my parents' dead bodies—day or night—it didn't matter. That night haunted me.

My stay in the hospital gave my brain a chance to heal, but my mind said there was something I was missing. Leonard listened to me when I talked about how I just *knew* the accident was more than that. That something else happened that night that was always out of my reach—brain injury or not.

Without Leonard's jokes and quiet presence, I don't know what I would have done back then. So many times I thanked my lucky stars I'd run into him that first night I went running trying to escape it all. I don't know who had been more scared—Leonard or me. Looking back, how we met was kind of funny. Both of us lying flat out on our butts staring at each other, turned into hours of us talking in hushed tones or just sitting in silence. We met several nights a week after that—both of us doing our best to soothe each other's internal demons.

So, no, I wouldn't clue Dean in on how much Leonard's friendship meant to me. Dean just needed to know that whatever I could do to help Leonard through this, I would.

"It doesn't matter what you think. Leonard *was* there for me. *I am* going to be there for him now."

A sigh from Dean. "I know."

He didn't sound happy about it either.

CHAPTER FIVE

Bella

"YOU MISSED THE TURN." I LOOKED OVER MY SHOULDER AT THE street we just passed where the clinic was located.

He didn't acknowledge me.

I looked back and pointed to the upcoming street. "If you take the next right, you can swing back around."

Again, he didn't acknowledge me.

He kept driving.

Right past the next street.

I whirled back to him. "Dean, you missed it again."

The streetlights skimmed Dean's face, showcasing his keen focus on the road.

"Dean!"

His eyes shifted toward me for a split second. "We're not going to the clinic."

"I can see that," I snapped. "Why are we *not* going to the clinic?"

"It's safer at my house."

I froze. *Safer at Dean's house?* There was definitely more going on than Dean was willing to admit, but there was no way I could stay at his house.

His home.

No way. No how.

I couldn't sleep under the same roof as Dean and pretend all was normal.

"I'm not staying at your house." My voice came out steady and nothing like the panic internally clawing at me.

He didn't answer. Just kept driving.

"Dean, I'm serious. I'm not staying at your house."

No response.

I was a second away from losing my burger we grabbed for dinner when my body swayed with the truck's turn, forcing me to look away from Dean to his gravel driveway. He lived ten minutes outside of town in an area densely populated with beautiful trees, which created a vast canopy around his property. It looked and felt like a cabin getaway where your worries disappeared and your soul was replenished with nature's beauty.

Breathtaking.

But it didn't matter that I loved where Dean lived or that I would take being there *any* time, *any* day, over *any*thing else. I couldn't stay there tonight—not after I'd been in his arms. There was only so much I could endure.

I wasn't willing to commit the ungodly amount of time it would take me to walk to the clinic in the dark with my overnight bag. I knew enough to know a woman out alone in the somewhat deserted woods was screaming for trouble. Plus, I was pretty sure that between Bruce's attack and Dean's odd behavior that this wasn't the time to take off by myself. Even with Rocky's untarnished best friend record I knew I couldn't call on her because she was working late. Then I wondered which would be worse—walking at night in the woods by myself or facing Dean in his home, alone.

Before I devised an escape plan, Dean had us securely in his garage and on our way into his home.

Every time I walked into his kitchen, my breath caught. It was stunning in an "I am man and this my cabin" kind of way with stone countertops, river rock backsplash, stainless steel appliances, and log back-supported stools tucked around the island. Yeah, it screamed cabin, but yet it also stated home. A home where a family gathered around, prepared meals, talked, laughed, lived. All of Dean's remodeling told me he was considering a future with a family.

The idea of him with a family hurt more than I was willing to admit because it meant he was thinking of settling down.

With a woman who was not me.

Tearing my eyes away from the kitchen, I forced myself to take in the rest of his house. He kept the cabin theme throughout with its rustic appeal, and it had all the warmth of home, family.

From the kitchen, there was a step down to the central living area where the massive sectional faced the enormous, mounted television and a wall of windows that showcased the beautiful woods. You were a part of nature but removed at the same time.

It was absolutely breathtaking.

When you ventured farther in, you encountered a full bath, a weight room, and a bedroom Dean turned into his home office. These rooms continued to follow the cabin motif. But the main attraction wasn't the view, rather the semi-spiral wooden staircase that looped around the wood-burning stove in the center of the room which was ensconced by river rocks. When lit, the warmth already inherent in the home complemented the heat of the stove.

I could stay there forever. A crackling fire, the view of the woods, a book, a glass of wine—I'd be set. Okay, all I really needed was Dean, but if he weren't there, I'd settle with the other.

Dean didn't seem to realize I was glued to my spot in the kitchen, taking in his home. He went straight to the staircase and climbed it.

With my overnight bag.

"Dean, I'm not staying here!"

He ignored me and kept going.

I hurried up the stairs after him. "Dean!"

He kept walking to the room at the far end of the hall, past the three guest rooms.

"You passed the guest rooms."

Dean continued to ignore me all the way to his room.

The angst built up in me turning my breaths turned to pants as I watched Dean disappear to the left in his room, toward his closet. That couldn't possibly mean what I thought it meant.

My fear pushed through and I breathed, "Dean."

He walked back out and immediately his face softened when he saw me freaking out.

"Bella, it's a precaution. Everyone will expect you to be in the guest room. They won't expect you in my room." His gentle tone reiterated he thought my freak out was due to some unforeseen danger.

The fact no one would be looking for me *in* his room burned a hole in my chest. No one would ever expect it, and *that* killed. Dean and me, that was funny. No way would someone like Dean desire someone like me. I clearly did not fit his build of a woman. Add in the fact I was his best friend's little sister.

Yeah, no one would ever think to look for me in his bed.

Ouch.

"Hey. I won't let anyone hurt you. You're safe here." He was in front of me, both hands on my biceps, doing his best to reassure me.

Safe from everyone but me and my lifelong dreams of being with Dean. Dreams he had no idea bounced around in my head. I should be thankful he'd misinterpreted my expression for fear and not for what it truly was.

Small miracles.

"You need a dog." Yes, I blurted that out. The multiple emotional hits I endured in the last few hours finally caught up to me. My random comment was an indicator I needed to regroup before I spilled what was really on my mind.

The look on his face was almost enough to make me laugh, but I kept on with my inane commentary.

"Your backyard"—if you called a forest a backyard—"is a doggie heaven—tons of room to run and chase the woodland creatures. Although, there is a lot of yard so maybe you should get two dogs. That way, they can keep each other company. But I guess when you have kids"—my breath hitched—"they could keep the dogs company, and you should have kids soon. I can ask around and see about getting you one or two."

I stopped speaking because I knew I was rambling. Rambling and sounding like a complete nitwit. Although Dean seemed like he didn't mind. No, he looked like he was doing his best not to chuckle. However, he didn't do a good enough job of keeping the humor out of his eyes or the smile from his face.

"You can get me one or two?"

"Sure, but if you want more than two, it might take me a little longer to get them."

Dean threw his head back and laughed.

I waited because he was a sight to watch when he laughed.

Handsome.

Confident.

Magnetic.

Dean straightened and sucked in several deep breaths in a quest to gain control of himself.

"Dean, I'm not sure why me offering to get you puppies..." Oh, I *was* an idiot. "I meant I could find you puppies, not kids. You don't need help making children. I'm sure you can handle that fine by yourself." Someone shoot me. "I meant not by yourself. Obviously, you would...you know...with someone. You know..." Really, someone help me.

He gave a slight shake of his head and a barely-there smile graced his mouth. "Bella, when it's time for children to run rampant in my home, I'll make sure to let you know."

What did he mean by that? Did he mean I would participate in that specific endeavor or would I find out by proxy because of his friendship with Alex? Either option didn't help because he would be naked—with me or with someone else.

I had to get away from him before I said something else more horrifying. Angling my head toward his room, I blurted, "I'll just go to bed now."

His smile changed; it was no longer amused. No, it was a *whole* lot more. His eyes heated and I felt the pull toward him. Just a nibble. That wasn't much to ask for, was it?

The pink of his tongue peaked out to moisten his bitable lower lip as he got closer, and I knew I was finally going to get to know what Dean Cannon tasted like.

Dean stepped back, and his face closed down. He no longer looked at me like he wanted to devour me. No, he looked like he wanted to be as far away from me as possible.

"What time do you need to be at work tomorrow?"

Cool and calm. That was how Dean sounded.

I cleared my throat. "Six."

"Works for me. Good night, Bella."

Dean didn't wait for my response.

No, he left me standing in the hallway.

BECAUSE IT WAS the ten-year anniversary of my parents' deaths, I expected my sleep to be fitful. What I hadn't taken into account was sleeping *in* Dean's bedroom, *in* his bed. Since his house was more secure than Fort Knox, I wasn't able to go on one of my nightly runs. One of the better remedies for my sleepless nights.

Counting sheep behind my closed eyelids—no help.

Counting the knots in the wood beams in Dean's ceiling didn't help either.

Tossing and turning—*that* slowly reignited my sexual frustration. Each time I adjusted, Dean's scent permeated into my lungs, filling me. His sheets, smooth and textured, brushed against my beaded nipples and intensified the carnal ache in me. The tangled sheets around my legs lightly rubbed against my clit, giving me glimpses of release.

I wanted, *needed* release.

I looked at the clock next to Dean's bed—three-thirty in the morning. Aside from my tossing and turning, I hadn't heard any other sounds in Dean's home. He *had* to be asleep.

It wasn't a difficult decision to retrieve my Dean Toy. Dean had been joking earlier with me about packing my sex toys, and because I believed I would spend the night at the clinic, I hadn't hesitated to bring it with me.

The first vibration against my clit had me moaning.

Yes, this was *precisely* what I needed.

I imagined Dean kneeling above me, cock in hand, slowly gliding it back and forth on across my folds as I guided my vibrator in the same action. Juices flowed from me, coating his cock, my toy.

I couldn't suppress my next moan.

He'd back off to ensure I didn't have an early release. I withdrew the vibrator in the same manner.

Never too soon, always prolonging the pleasure.

After coating his penis with more of my juices, he'd glide it back down to my rear, circling my opening, teasing me with the possibility of more. I applied more pressure, letting the vibration pulse through me, imagining Dean tapping me with his cock.

With each vibration, each slide, I pulsed closer and closer to my release.

My gasps quickened and the sounds that escaped me matched in tempo.

It wasn't enough.

I closed my eyes and spread my legs open farther, pressing my Dean Toy harder against my folds with each glide but never entering myself. Dean would enter me partially, giving me hints of fullness, but pulling back before I could have it all.

My moans quickened as I reached for more.

I smoothed my left hand up to my heavy breast and cupped it, imagining Dean's calloused hand molding it. The contrast in sensations —his solid smooth cock and his rough hands—had me soaked.

My breaths were nothing more than puffs of air. The noises I made incomprehensible, but Dean would not allow me my release yet.

He'd bend over me, cup my breast in his hand, and offer it to himself. Slowly, as he kept his eyes locked on me, he'd blow a single breath on my peaked nipple, causing it to distend further in its plea for more.

I looked down at the hand, holding my breast, the crested nipple, and couldn't control my breaths, creating the same effect. My nails bit down around my nipple, and I envisioned Dean holding it between his teeth, hinting at another kind of pleasure. Just as quickly he'd release it.

I was so wet. I knew my release was close, and Dean hadn't even entered me yet.

Oh yeah, Dean inside me. I wanted that.

Slowly, painstakingly slow, I pushed my Dean Toy inside me, imagining it was Dean's cock. I was so wet my hand shook with restraint. I wanted all of it, all of him. Then finally, finally, he'd plant himself fully in me.

Filling me.

Consuming me.

My moan was slow and long.

He'd hold himself like that. Not moving. Pulsating inside me. I wriggled with the need to move. To finish what he'd—I'd started.

Then slowly, he'd gather my nipple between his two fingers and roll it. The feeling mirrored the pulsing inside me. I flowed around his penis, dripping for him and coating my hand.

Then he finally, *finally* moved inside me. Unhurriedly, in and out. Building the pleasure and the whole time, rolling my nipple with each stroke.

I bit my lip, trying to smother my moans and imagining the teeth there were Dean's.

Our combined efforts increased. Dean's rhythm accelerated nearing his release as my movements became erratically brisk in time with his. I rammed my Dean Toy—Dean's cock—inside myself, at the same time Dean—I—released my nipple and slid my hand down to my clit. The barest pressure and the orgasm surged out of me. I shoved my face in Dean's pillow to suppress the moan I knew would wake him.

Several minutes ticked by before I got up and cleaned myself.

Of course, that meant changing the soaked sheets.

I HEADED out of Dean's laundry room the next morning, telling myself I was being a good guest by washing his sheets and hopefully he wouldn't notice that the wash was needed. Although it didn't help that my mind replayed, vividly, what I'd done the night before *in* Dean's bed.

"Mornin'."

"Good morning." I chanced a peek at Dean as I made my way toward the coffeepot next to him.

Dean stood next to the kitchen counter, sipping his coffee. "Bella, you didn't have to wash the sheets."

Blood rushed to my cheeks. To hide my face, I pulled the coffee carafe out of its stand, banged it against the coffee stand, and spilled the coffee in my rush to pour it.

"I know." I cleared my throat. "It's just common courtesy after I slept"—among other things—"in them."

My movements were jerky as I wiped the mess up and I tensed at the prospect of him finding out about my late-night activities. I kept my back to him hoping to prevent any revelations from his too-perceptive eyes.

Dean's hand stilled mine in its movement to wipe the spilled coffee. The heat from his body a wall against my back.

My heart jumped.

"I got this. Go sit down." His voice came out low and hoarse.

I wrenched away from Dean as if I'd been scolded.

"You okay, Bella?" Curiosity lit Dean's words. "Did you not get enough sleep last night?"

I looked at Dean. I figured the best tactic was avoidance. "Umm... yes, no. I was worried about Leonard. Have you heard anything?"

Dean leaned against his countertop, arms crossed across his massive chest, and shook his head. "No, I haven't heard anything." One eyebrow shot up. "You sure you're okay? You look a little...flush."

I knew if I touched my face it would be on fire with embarrassment. It was almost as if he knew what I'd done last night in his bed. On that very thought, I gulped the coffee, choking myself in the process. My hand shot to my mouth as I coughed uncontrollably.

"You okay Bella?" Dean's warm hand settled on my back, rubbing.

No, I wasn't, and could he please get his hand off me? Good Lord, I needed to get myself under control and away from Dean, pronto.

I backed away from Dean, cleared my throat once more, and counted to ten to wrangle my emotions and hormones under control.

"Yeah, I'm fine. I just drank it too fast. Sorry about that." I couldn't look him in the eyes yet. "I'm just"—a quick glance at him—"going to grab my stuff." I rushed toward the stairs. "I have an early appointment with Mrs. Dixon, so we should get a move on."

I didn't wait for his response and took the stairs two at a time.

CHAPTER SIX

Dean

I DID NOT SLEEP A FUCKING WINK LAST NIGHT. INSTEAD, I'D LAIN and thought about Bella in my bed. Imagined running my hands over her curves the entire night. Cupping her breasts, sucking her nipples to hard points while sliding in and out of her wet heat. The whole time I'd listen to her moan my name.

Then I had heard her; it had been low, needy, and cut off just as quickly. Initially, I'd thought I'd imagined it, but then I heard the muted humming and the moaning renewed.

Every ounce of my willpower had gone into *not* fucking barging into my room and taking over. To teach Bella to never use that damn toy on herself without me. Instead, I'd satisfied my need by stroking myself and allowed my imagination free rein on my Bella fantasy while I listened to her pleasure herself.

I went back to my fantasy, only this time, I'd include her fucking toy, sliding it in and out of her, her juices coating my cock and hand while I fucked her with it. I'd fist her hair, causing her back to arch. I'd bring her closer to the edge, over and over but never allowing her release, wanting her fucking begging for it.

Because I was a breast man, and I loved every*fucking*thing about Bella, I would in no way ignore hers. I'd glide the vibrator up to her breasts, circling one on low—just enough to send the vibrations radiating outward, getting closer and closer to her nipple but never touching. Then I'd take her nipple between my fingers and lightly roll it, tug it, all while continuing the torture of the vibrator.

Her moans greedier, she would beg desperately for release, mirroring my own need, only to have me back off again.

I'd watch her panting, imploring me not to stop while I pleasured her. Her plump lips parted, making the *fuck me* noises that drove me crazy. Flipping her onto her knees, I'd wrap that silky hair around my hand and fuck the sweet depths of her mouth with her toy, forcing her cheeks to hollow with the effort she'd use on the toy.

Her hands glided over my thighs, one taking hold of my cock, the other my balls, rolling them while stroking me, massaging my pre-cum up and down my shaft. I'd fuck her hand as her thumb glided over the tip, squeezing out more. To repeat the process over and over, all the time, never allowing my release.

Driving me fucking crazy.

When I couldn't hold out anymore, I'd finally lay her down and sheath myself in her wet core. The whole time I rocked back and forth, I'd watch her. See the pink in her cheeks as she flushed near her orgasm, the juices on her plump lips and the glazed look in her eyes.

Finally, as I was beginning to re-enter her, I'd reach down and press my thumb on her clit. Her entire being would squeeze down on me, forcing my release.

I'd blown right along with my imagination, doing my best not to let Bella overhear me. It hadn't mattered; I'd heard her release. It was such a fucking sweet sound, it had ramped me back up. Squeezing the tip of my penis, I'd forced myself to envision grotesque images—anything not related to Bella naked, satiated, or ready to be fucked.

It had taken a long time, but I'd finally been able to hold myself at half-mast. And I'd stayed that way the whole night, alternating between wondering if Bella's difficulty sleeping was due to the anniversary of the accident or if she'd imagined me when she made herself come. Mostly I'd fought myself the whole night from dreaming of fucking Bella.

Fuck.

My cock was standing at attention again.

I felt like a teenager who had just realized a girl's body contained far more treats than met the eye. And as for the waking up with an erection and having to take myself in hand to abate my need, *and* still remaining at half-mast? Only with Bella did that teenage problem remain.

Yup, a fucking teenager.

In repayment for the suffering Bella had instilled upon me last night, I'd teased her a little that morning. The blood that had raced to her face, her jerky movements, avoiding eye contact—all of it made me want her more.

Sucking in a breath, I pulled myself away from that train of thought and reminded myself Bella was Alex's baby sister. A huge fucking no-go.

I watched Bella make a quick exit, her rambling excuses of having patients early bringing me back to the here and now. To the here and now where I reminded myself to maintain my boundaries with Bella. To remember Alex'd have my balls in a vise if he even knew where my thoughts were going with his sister.

The text I received from Alex while Bella was upstairs gathering her items reinforced my vow to stay away from Bella and helped me refocus on the matter at hand. Alex wanted to meet at the police station to discuss what they'd found at Bruce's cabin and to verify I was still watching over Bella. My libido cooled at the reminder of the possible danger around Bella.

So, yeah, the text I received from Alex did not help my mood one bit.

"I'm done in your room if you need to use it." Bella didn't waste time getting herself ready.

"Thanks. I won't be long."

I mirrored Bella's speed and raced through my shower and had us out the door in ten minutes.

"What's on your plate for today?" I glanced at Bella while turning onto the main road.

"The usual—work, lunch, and I'm going to call Rocky later. I'm hoping she can come over tonight for a girls' night." She turned to face me. "You?"

"The same but without meeting Rocky."

Her soft and too-short laughter floated toward me. "Do you ever tire of your job? I mean, you deal with some ugly things, and I don't know. Doesn't it ever make you sad that you see the sucky side of people all the time?"

"You could say the same thing about Alex." I looked over at her before turning my attention back to the road.

"Yeah. I asked him that too when I was younger, but I'm curious about you."

I hesitated. This was my opportunity to draw a line in the sand with Bella safely on the other side. Opening up meant letting her in, which was a risk I couldn't take. Instead, I found myself saying, "It only bothers me that people suck to begin with, but I like to think I'm helping people too. Without me, some of them would continue to be used or hurt in far more devastating ways. I hope that I at least bring them some peace."

Another quick glance and my gut clenched at the look in Bella's eyes. That was why I'd opened up. To have Bella look at me that way.

Shit. This wasn't keeping her at a distance.

Her voice was soft when she spoke. "I'm sure the people you've helped are grateful for everything you've done."

Something inside me eased at her words. Something I didn't know I needed until I heard her words. Something that I knew only Bella could conquer.

Shit.

My knuckles were starkly white as I squeezed the life out of the steering wheel.

This was *absolutely* not keeping Bella at a distance.

I knew she meant to comfort me but my body, my soul, my every-thing reeled at the smooth warm hand she placed on my arm. My bones pushed against the skin of my hands at the death grip I maintained on the steering wheel. Because the only thing I wanted to do was yank the truck over so I could finally get my hands on Bella.

She pulled her hand back and a quick uncomfortable laughter bubbled out of her. "What's the funniest case you've worked on or the most bizarre?"

I slowly released a breath letting go of the rioting emotions strangling me and focused on the awkward transition Bella gave us.

"I'd have to say it was the case where an older couple kept hearing the animals in the barn making a ruckus or they'd find them out of their pens. They tried to set up video cameras, but it kept glitching on them. After a few weeks of this going on, they called me." Remembering my shock at what I found tugged a smile out of me. "My surveillance is a bit more complex than theirs, so the first night out I caught their granddaughter in the barn. She'd been staying with them during the summer to help them out on the farm but was bored out of her mind." My laughter wasn't like Bella's. Mine filled the truck as the images from that case filtered through my brain.

"What? You can't leave me hanging like that." Bella's smile was full of anticipation.

"She'd dress the farm animals up as her favorite cartoon characters —and I mean she'd literally dress them in her costume clothes and have tea parties with them. She also believed animals should be free and that we didn't have the right to hold them in captivity. So after the tea parties, she'd let them out so they could be free."

Bella's mouth opened and closed in surprise before laughter erupted from her. "Get out! You're joking."

I shook my head. "No, I'm not. Her grandparents didn't know whether to laugh or send her back to her parents. She was so adamant in her belief and stood her ground when they confronted her."

"That is priceless!" Bella clutched my arm.

My cock stood at attention and I slowly blew out a breath, hoping Bella didn't realize the effect her touch had on me. I forced my mind on the images of the pig with a cape and tiara or the horse with a mask and fake mustache. None of it worked to deflate my rising cock.

Pulling into FeldsPaw's parking lot, I worked on calming the hell down before Bella noticed.

"Thanks, Dean. That was hilarious." She moved her hand away from my arm to wipe at her eyes.

"Glad I could make you laugh."

Bella jumped down from my truck. "Thanks for the ride."

"Anytime."

I watched her walk into the clinic before backing out and making my way to the police station. The whole time I mentally fought to deflate my erection.

It wasn't going to help anything if I walked into the police station with a hard-on and tried to explain to Alex it wasn't because of his sister.

"Good morning, Dean. How are you this fine day?" Ms. Folgers beamed at me from behind the police check-in counter.

"Mornin', Ms. Folgers." I bent and kissed her cheek. "Not too bad." I pointed to the flowers on her desk and asked, "What did Bobbie do now?"

With a shake of her grandmotherly white head, she said, "Nothing."

"Seriously?" My eyebrows shot to my hairline.

She leaned forward and whispered, "Yeah, and that has me worried."

"Why? I thought you wanted him to behave."

She shuffled the already-organized papers on her desk in her nervousness. "I do. It's just—I know Bobbie's not ready to tame the wildness in himself yet." She stared at the flowers. "So, he's either buttering me up for something big or he already did it and hasn't been caught yet."

"Your grandson is lucky to have you."

More shuffling of her papers. "Thank you."

"And, while Bobbie is sowing his wild oats, he knows he holds a treasure in you." I nodded to the flowers. "Appreciate your good fortune while you have it. The bad will be here soon enough, if it comes."

Ms. Folgers wiped at her eyes. "I thought at my age, I was supposed to be giving you the words of wisdom."

I straightened. "I'm returning the favor. Those were words you gave me."

"Well, it seems you were only half listening to me then." She sniffed daintily.

"What? I am enjoying my life."

She looked at me over the top of her black-rimmed librarian glasses. "Oh, yes, there's no doubt you're enjoying yourself." A small shake of her head as worry etched her face. "But, Dean, are you really truly happy?"

"What's not to be happy about?" Not wanting to get into this conversation with her, or anyone, I nodded toward the inner pen. "I'll see myself to Alex and Trent."

I didn't wait for her response and took the steps two at time.

There was a time when I believed in what Ms. Folgers had told me. Until I realized the one woman I wanted to be intimate with I couldn't. My friendship with Alex halted any possibility between us. So, I'd protect Bella like Alex asked me to.

Without fucking her.

No matter how blue my balls got.

Hitting the top of the stairs, I ran into Alex, who was carrying two coffee cups.

"You're just in time. Follow me."

"What's going on?" As I fell into step with Alex, I noticed the exhaustion pulling on his face. "Did you get any sleep last night?"

Alex shook his head as he opened the door to the conference room. Inside, spread across the conference table and walls were newspaper clippings and pictures. Tagged above each one were dates and a makeshift timeline connecting each.

Trent looked up from the folder of pictures he was skimming. "Dean."

"Trent." Taking in the room once more, I asked, "What do you guys got?"

"Before we tell you, tell me what you see." Alex handed one of the coffees to Trent even though Alex looked like he needed both of them more than Trent did.

I took my time, walking the perimeter of the room, looking at the articles, pictures, and anything else pinned up or laid out. I turned back to them and asked, "Where'd you get this?"

"Bruce's cabin."

"What? Is this what you were talking about in your text?" Shock rooted me where I stood.

"Yeah, but it wasn't in open sight. I wouldn't have found it either, but the floorboard sank down when I stepped on it." Alex sat and waved his hand around the room. "A box full of this crap stopped my foot from going straight through."

"What the fuck was Bruce doing with all of this?" I sifted through a folder with pictures. "What's his interest in..." I grabbed the pen and paper next to me and saw the list Trent made of everyone in the articles and pictures. "The sheriff, his daughter, Blake and Ava King, Richard's arrest at Shackles but not any others?" My head shot up to meet Alex's eyes. "You and Bella?"

"Great fucking questions." Alex's tone dropped reflecting his frustration.

"Who are Blake and Ava King? And is that the same Blake Leonard mentioned at the hospital? The one Bruce got kicked out of Coop's for talking to?"

"We don't know yet. Notice anything else?" Trent asked as I took a seat next to him.

"Yeah. The earliest article dates back to the night Alex's parents died." I stared at Alex. "Do you remember Bruce anywhere near the accident?"

"No." He sipped his coffee. "I do know Leonard became friends with Bella after she returned from Granite Creek Hospital." His voice muted in his contemplation of the past.

Not liking any of this, I kept my cool, trying to figure out how all these pieces fit. "So whatever happened that night set Bruce to tracking the lot of you."

"Yeah, but what the fuck does my parents' death have to do with Bruce? In everything Bella's told me about that night—the look on my parents faces, my mom's shout of 'watch out!', my dad's hard brake, the light—she's only ever mentioned the sheriff." Alex pointed to the papers and said, "Even with her unbendable belief about that night being more than it appeared, none of them ever came up."

"Wait a minute. Bella was in the backseat, behind your dad, right?" Trent asked Alex.

"Yeah." Alex watched Trent flip through the papers on the desk.

"It was dark out. So how could she see the looks on your parents' faces *and* lights? If the lights were coming from the front then she would have been blinded and unable to see anything. Instead, it sounds like everyone was lit up from behind." Trent kept shuffling through the papers.

I stilled at Trent's train of thought.

"Shit," I whispered.

Trent yanked a folder out and flipped through it. "According to Bella and the report, she said your mom was turned around listening to Bella tell her about the dance right before the accident. That's when she saw the look on your mom's face right before she yelled *Watch out!* The next thing she remembers is being yanked to the left. Meaning your mom had to have seen something while looking over her shoulder at Bella." He looked up at us. "What if they were clipped from behind?"

None of us said anything as we let the implications of what Trent was saying penetrate.

"Fucking shit," Alex bit out.

"I thought they cleared the debris as part of your parents' vehicle?" I asked for clarification.

Alex stared at the report in Trent's hand. "They did."

"Yeah, they also stated some of the debris was from an earlier accident." Trent mumbled flipping through the report. "But it wasn't confirmed. We need to check that it's still in evidence and run it through to system to corroborate our assumptions. I'll also reach out to the investigating officer, who has since retired, to see if I can't jog anything from his memory that he didn't put on the report. And does whatever Richard was talking about Shackles have to do with this or is there something else we're missing?"

"Fucking shit." Alex repeated himself. "All this time I kept putting everything she said off as a result of the injury to her head."

"Don't. We all did and beating ourselves up over it won't help us solve anything. And all of this still doesn't answer anything. We don't have any connections. Just more loose ends." I reminded not only Alex and Trent but myself as well. I picked up an article dated two weeks ago. "Looks like Ava's in town to help the mayor with his birthday party and Blake's assisting with the old gym across town. Have either of you spoken to this Blake or Ava King?"

"Not yet." The breath Alex blew out complemented the exhaustion in his words.

I glanced back down at the article. "They don't look familiar to me. Are they from around here?"

Trent nodded. "Yeah. Blake was in the same year as us and Ava, a year younger than Bella."

"Really?" Even I heard the disbelief in my voice.

"Same but different." Alex slid the yearbooks from the cumulative mess toward me. "Take a look at the pages tagged in blue."

After placing the recent articles and yearbooks side by side, I confirmed Alex's statement. Ava's adolescence had disappeared as she morphed into a knockout, but it was Blake who held my attention. His high school picture showed an insecure, gangly boy who was doing everything he could to disappear from the image. But, the man in the article? Not someone you would dismiss. It was evident Blake had taken the years since high school to shed the insecure persona and replaced it with visible confidence.

"Their transformation is not unusual. Most kids lose their gawky appearance after high school." Alex pointed to the article regarding the gym opening. "However, it seems Blake went a step further. MMA fighter and coach. Sounds like a man who needs to be in control of himself."

"Or maybe he's a man who just cares about his health." Trent flexed his biceps.

Ignoring Trent, Alex went on, "Why did Bruce track Blake all these years? Why did Leonard mention him at the hospital? What happened between Bruce and Blake at Coop's? Was it a recent thing, or did something happen back in high school? The night of my parents' deaths?" Alex burst from his chair and began pacing. "Fuck, too many questions."

I walked over to the wall with the most recent articles and focused on them. "Let's add some more. The only article Bruce has relating to Richard, his forever partner in crime, is the one where he was arrested at Shackles the night before he died." Scanning the other articles confirmed my assessment. "That wasn't the first time Richard was arrested. Why does this particular arrest matter? Besides the fact it was the last time Richard was arrested, and it occurred the night before he died?"

Trent made his way to the other wall. "Richard mouthed off the night at Shackles. Something about how Sheriff Castor didn't do anything or couldn't do anything because it's been almost a decade. And no way could he pin anything on him without proof. Maybe Richard's ramblings weren't ramblings to Bruce." Open speculation in his words. "And, after Donny mentioned it to us it definitely caught our attention."

Alex stood in the middle, gaze moving over the articles and pictures pinned up along the walls.

Trent turned back to us. "What if Richard and Bruce are the reason for the accident? It'd make even more sense that Bruce would keep an eye on everyone, especially you and Bella. But there isn't a statute of limitation on murder, so his comment still doesn't make sense. And how does everyone else fit in?" He lifted his chin toward the opposite wall and asked, "What I don't get is why he was tracking his own brother?"

"Maybe Leonard knows what Bruce did or Leonard's involved in it too? It could be Bruce was worried Leonard would reveal something to Bella." It was a logical assumption on Alex's part.

"I get that, but Bruce has pictures of Leonard without Bella. And why wouldn't Bruce just ask Leonard? I know Bruce was cagey, but it looked like he at least trusted his brother."

My gut heated. "But Leonard and Bella weren't friends before the accident. Leonard approached Bella when she came back from Granite Creek Hospital. Did he ever try for more with Bella?" The thought alone made me want to hit the nearest wall.

Alex shook his head. "Bella never mentioned it, although it was written all over him." His brotherly tone clearly stating he didn't like it then or now.

"Time to move this shit forward. Dean, you take Blake and Ava King. See what you can find out. I'll take Leonard. Alex, you look into Emily Castor and the evidence from the other unsolved accident from back then." Trent's barked out orders evidence that he was done guessing and was more than ready for answers.

"If you think I'm not going to have fucking words with Leonard, you're out of your mind. He knows something that could possibly put my sister in danger. I'm not sitting this out." Alex's quiet words belied the threat behind them.

"We're not asking you to sit it out," I interjected, "but Alex, Trent might get more out of Leonard if his face isn't being bashed in."

"Fuck!" Alex exploded.

"I'm going to swing by the hospital now, see if I can't get some answers out of Leonard." Trent headed toward the door.

"I don't fucking like this." Tension still radiated from Alex even though he let the Leonard situation go for the moment. "Let's meet after."

Trent shook his head. "Make it tonight, my place. I have to swing by Trudy's later."

I was surprised by that comment. Trent did everything he could to avoid his ex-wife. If it weren't for their nine-year-old son, he wouldn't look, much less speak to her. "Everything okay with Dusty?"

"Aside from the usual shit kids pull, he's great. Trudy, on the other hand, is working my last fucking nerve."

"Let me know if you need anything," Alex offered.

Trent lifted his chin in acknowledgment as they made their way to the door.

"Before you take off, do you know anything about the vandalism occurring at Bella's apartment complex?" I stopped them.

"Yeah, Wyndham Terrace has video cameras installed throughout the complex. I pulled the video and caught a bunch of high school kids goofing off. Already had words with them and their parents, but that was a few weeks ago. Why?"

"It could be nothing, but last night at Bella's apartment, her lightbulb was busted. That's the second time she's had issues with her light. Broken glass all over the ground. I'm going to head over there later today to pull the footage and replace the bulb."

"I'm not thinking that's a bunch of high school kids pulling pranks." Alex raked a hand through his hair as his frustration mounted. "Shit, what if it's related to all this bullshit?"

"When you pulled the footage, did you notice anything else out of sorts? Anyone taking pictures of Bella?"

Alex shook his head. "No, but I wasn't looking for more. Although I would have fucking noticed someone taking pictures of Bella."

"Mind sending me those?" I asked. "I want to take a second look."

"Not at all. I'll get those to you this afternoon. Let me know if you see anything."

"Absolutely. She mentioned she wanted to get together with Rocky tonight. I don't foresee any problems with both of them there." Whatever was going on, my gut told me, Bella would be safe if she stayed around people.

Trent spoke up, "I think as long as we can keep Bella occupied, we'll be okay to solve all of this before she's truly in any real danger."

Alex sighed. "I'm not going to hold my breath. Bella *not* help Leonard during all of this?" He shook his head. "I don't think so."

"One thing at a time."

I hoped it would be that easy.

CHAPTER SEVEN

Bella

I DID MY BEST TO FOCUS ON MY PATIENTS DURING MY MORNING rotations at FeldsPaw Clinic. It proved difficult with thoughts of Dean running through my head. None of it made sense.

In all the years I'd known Dean, he'd never shown the slightest interest in me. Not once. Part of me believed the hot-and-cold I'd received from him last night was only a figment of my imagination. All these years of wanting him had finally caught up with me, making me see what I wanted to see.

"Ouch!"

Sparky, Mrs. Dixon's spoiled Pomeranian, nipped my fingers, reminding me I had a job to do *not* related to Dean Cannon and his sexiness.

"Sorry, Sparky." I pulled her up for cuddles and smooches.

The tiny puffy caramel dog looked like a miniature bear with the disposition of one too. I'd warned Mrs. Dixon to stop spoiling the dog. Explanations that sassy attitudes and being overweight—the nip and real reason Sparky spent the night—weren't good for the dog bounced right off Mrs. Dixon. It was also the reason why the lovable little monster spent the night at the clinic while I ran various tests confirming she indeed *needed* a more restrictive diet *with* exercise.

"Want me to take the little puffball for a walk?"

"Arf." Sparky barked at Parker's deep voice and practically leaped out of my arms toward him. At first glance, his mammoth frame camouflaged his caring soul, but like the animals sensed—he was one big teddy bear.

"I don't think she wants to go for a walk. More like she just *wants* you," I teased.

Parker's slow sensual smile was the perfect example of why females loved him, Sparky included.

"Females, I love them all. Big, thin, short, tall, four legs. You can't go wrong."

"Yeah, the four legs get me every time," my deadpan response lost behind my smile.

"Smartass."

I shooed him out the door with Sparky. "You better take Sparky before she gets *more* annoyed you're not paying her enough attention."

Tipping his head to me, Parker turned with Sparky in his arms for the enclosed play area set aside for the visiting animals.

I took that moment to pull my cell phone out of my pocket and tried once again to reach Leonard.

I'm checking in again. I'm really worried about you. Text me. Please.

I'd already left him one voicemail and two other texts earlier in the morning. All had gone unanswered. Since he'd never not responded to me, I took it as a bad sign.

Buzzing from my phone startled me, and I said a quick prayer hoping it was Leonard.

Noon. Harper's Corner.

Not Leonard—Alex. It was such an Alex text, not a demand but not a request either.

Today I would take him up on his offer and question *him*. I wanted some answers regarding Bruce's attack and why Leonard didn't trust the police. There were so many questions bouncing around in my head, and since Leonard wasn't answering, I'd start with Alex.

See you then.

Until then, I'd try my meek investigator skills out on the computer. There had to be more news posted about the attack on Bruce by now. All I needed was the littlest clue. Anything to get the closure for Leonard that I'd never received for my parents' early death.

Ten years later, and that night still haunted me. The not knowing, the lapses in memory—that night always presented as a slide show in my brain every single day, never leaving me alone. Me jabbering away at Mom about the dance. Dad doing his best not to gag at the boy talk. The looks on their faces right before impact, their yelling, the pain of the seatbelt against my torso as my dad slammed on his brakes and then nothing.

Alex, Rocky, Dean, Leonard, the police, and the doctors all telling me what the evidence showed. The skidmarks were from an earlier accident. Same with the vehicular debris. Nothing pointed to any foul play. All of them doing their best to fill the missing gaps, and none of them really telling me a damn thing.

The doctors told me my memories might never come back. The psychological trauma I'd endured being stuck in a car with my dead parents for hours, coupled with the injury to my brain. They were surprised I remembered as much as I did. But it wasn't enough and didn't prove what my subconscious was telling me—it wasn't just an accident. Even if no one believed me.

No matter how much I reviewed old news articles, nothing stood out, no clue as to why Dad had swerved, to why they died.

Leonard deserved more than that, so, for now, I'd avoid looking at the whys. Unfortunately, I was afraid there were probably *many* reasons why his brother was hurt and all of them reasonably sufficient for the attack. Not that I thought attacking anyone solved anything, but Bruce more than likely had tested that theory. So until I hit a dead end on *any* other leads, I was going to ignore why someone would attack him.

It wasn't until I hit the sixth article by a smaller paper, *Small Talk*, that my investigative instincts started humming. They had reported Bruce's attack occurred one week after the accidental death of a one Richard Coleman, who happened to be Bruce's longtime friend, drinking buddy, and all-around partner-in-crime. It went on to state although Richard's death had been cleared as drunk driving, on behalf of Richard actually drinking *and* driving, Bruce's absence was noteworthy. They pointed out that Bruce had been becoming less of a staple in Richard's drunken escapades and questioned if there was discord between the longtime pals that could possibly have played in Bruce's attack.

Now, I wasn't a detective like Alex, nor was I a private investigator like Dean, but I was a veterinarian who *investigated* mysterious animal symptoms. In my line of work, sometimes random bits of information were just that—random. Other times, that randomness connected. I didn't want to jump to conclusions, but I was betting those two events were related. I just had to figure out how.

Searching further didn't give me any more insight. Richard had been drunk and drove off the road, crashed into trees and boulders, and hadn't survived. Besides the fact it reminded me of the accident my parents and I were involved in, nothing else jumped out at me.

Changing my tactics, I focused on the Castor family, considering that Leonard had mentioned them the previous night at the hospital. I figured I'd have more luck gathering information regarding Sheriff Castor rather than his daughter since he was in public service. I was right. There was article after article on Sheriff Robert Castor—everything from reelection campaigns, low crime rates under his supervision, to the community outreach programs he engineered for at-risk adolescents. All of them commemorating him on his tremendous community service for the citizens of Feldspar.

If I was honest, and I tried to be at all times, it was all just a tad over-the-top. All of it combined created the Sheriff as a righteously pious man. Outwardly, he appeared to be an upstanding civil servant and a doting, loving father to his only daughter, Emily Castor, especially after her mother's unexpected death.

More research informed me Peggy Castor had passed away when Emily was eleven. Peggy's unexpected death had been at the hands of a drug user who needed quick cash for a fix. The culprit had been apprehended, charged, convicted, and according to the follow-up article, was currently serving time at Granite Creek Penitentiary. Again, nothing out of the ordinary.

Emily was less interesting. She appeared in a few articles related to her father, her mother's death and was listed on Granite Creek Hospital's website as a rape counselor. Otherwise, Emily Castor was someone who did not enjoy the limelight. How she went without even one social media account, I had no idea. She was the opposite of her father.

I decided to look up Blake King since Leonard had mentioned him at the hospital. Blake was more visible than Emily Castor but not by much. Blake had several wins in the MMA field and was touted as someone to watch in the arena. The latest article in *Small Talk* indicated he'd recently joined the coaching center across town for MMA fighters. It went on to mention his sister Ava as an up-and-coming party consultant who had blown the waters on several prominent events. The latter had caught Mrs. Dixon's eye, who then insisted on acquiring Feldspar's very own Ava for her husband, the mayor's, sixtieth birthday bash.

Besides Sheriff Castor's overzealous community service and the connection between Richard and Bruce, I couldn't deduce what Leonard had been referring to the previous night. But knowing my friend, if Leonard believed there was something going on, then there had to be *something*.

Instead of beating my head on something I couldn't readily identify, I moved on to my next to-do on my checklist—touching base with Rocky.

Two rings later, and Rocky answered, "What's shakin' Bellalicious?"

"At the moment, nothing. What about you? Anything *interesting* happen lately?" Bubbles of happiness always took flight inside me when I spoke with her.

Rocky's trepidation vibrated through the phone. "Well, that depends on what you consider interesting. For me, interesting is *not* having Creepy Kevin come by the shop on multiple occasions asking me to a business luncheon that absolutely is *not* business-related. Or how about *not* receiving the five-hundred messages from, again, Kevin stating my presence is required at the city council meeting when it has *never* been required before. Or the fact he's RSVP'd to Mrs. Dixon's shindig stating *we* are beyond thrilled to join the mayor at his birthday celebration," Rocky deadpanned. "So, yeah, nothing interesting at all."

"Shoot. I hoped to get a hold of you before Kevin's assault started."

"How'd you know he was turning his eye"—Rocky's gag reverberated in my ear—"toward me?"

"Well, he *just* happened to be outside the clinic yesterday when I got off work, and oh boy, did Kevin have a plethora of questions for me about you. I did my best to dissuade him, but you know how he was when he was pursuing me—blinders on, tunnel visioned, and inflexible in his mission."

"Shit. I was afraid of that, but it makes sense now. I wish it didn't, but it does."

My curiosity piqued. "What makes sense?"

"The city council meeting Kevin wanted me at? Mrs. Dixon attended it and afterward advised me that good ole boy, Kevin, aka the vice mayor, stated there was an issue with the zoning surrounding my business. She kindly but firmly demanded I attend to this matter to cease any further inclinations from Mr. Reynolds." She paused. "As if I'd be okay with any of it. The jerk." The undercurrent of worry in her tone couldn't hide behind her usual sarcasm.

"No! What possible zoning issue could he have found? Sterling's Custom Auto has been in that same location for over fifty years."

"I have no fucking clue, but whatever it is, I'm going to have to play nice with Kevin until I get it resolved." More gagging from Rocky. "By the time this is over, I may actually lose the ten pounds I've wanted to lose."

"Don't you dare lose ten pounds. Those ten pounds are vroom, vroom."

"Did you just use a car metaphor to describe my curves?"

"I actually got this one right." I gave myself a pat on the back for finally getting anything vehicular correct.

I heard the pride in Rocky's voice. "I knew you could speak car. Talk about cars—did I tell you about the '67 DeVille that recently came in?" Rocky's whistle sang through the phone. "She may not have curves, but she's one sleek beauty. I stayed up last night, rubbing her down."

I couldn't help it. I burst out laughing.

"Laugh all you want, but I think I'm onto something. Think about it. She doesn't talk back. She doesn't lie. She won't cheat on me. I can give her my all, and she'll only ever appreciate it. It's a win, win."

"Rocky, not all guys are lying cheats like Carson." All humor left me.

"No, they're also like Josh, Ethan, Tim, and do I really need to mention Kevin?"

"Okay, okay. I get it. But don't close the door on them all." I rushed before she could interrupt me. "Take your time cracking it open, but don't seal it. I'd hate to see you do that."

Rocky's resignation was hard to miss. "Only for you, will I *consider* that option, but Bella? I can't make that promise. Not right now."

My heart ached for her. "It's a deal. As for Kevin, there must be something we can do that doesn't involve you placating him in *any* way. The littlest give on your part and Kevin will twist it to his liking. I hate to say this and don't say no out of pride, but it seemed to work in my circumstance, maybe you should have Ash speak with him. Kevin seems to actually hear it when men talk, even if it ended with Alex receiving a written warning from Sheriff Castor."

"My pride is *not* the reason I don't ask my brother for help."

I snorted. It totally was.

Rocky continued as if I hadn't interrupted her. "However, Ash is currently out of reach, so that means I need to placate the somewhat powerful slime-ball for the time being." More sounds of gagging. "And before you ask, I already contacted Mr. Quincy, who happens to be out on the east coast visiting his daughter, who just had his first grand-daughter. He's not coming back anytime soon, but he said his partner at their law firm, Mr. Lively, would be able to help me."

"Shit is right." I sighed. "Okay, new plan. We research the zoning issue ourselves. It can't be that difficult to figure out. I'll go to City Hall later today, gather all the data I can, then we can meet at Harper's to pick up Leonard's dinner. After we swing by the hospital to drop Leonard's dinner off, we—"

"At the hospital? Is he okay? What happened?" Her rapid questions were just as fast as her speech.

"Yes, no, maybe. Have you seen the news lately? About Bruce being attacked and Leonard finding him?"

"No! What the hell happened?" Rocky's disbelief rang out.

I relayed everything I'd found out about the attack, the scene at the hospital with Leonard, Alex, *and* Dean, and my online research on all the people mentioned during their squabble.

"So, I was planning on surprising Leonard with dinner at the hospital tonight, because you *know* he's going to be there, and hopefully I can get him to open up about everything that is happening."

"Wow, that *is* a lot, and we *will* break it all down tonight at your apartment *after* we drop Leonard's dinner off. Don't think I'm letting the whole Dean kissing thing slide either. That definitely requires beer time." Rocky's decree paralleled a king's but better because it was a best friend's proclamation.

"I believe it requires shots, not beer. Dean, flirting *with* me." I fanned my face. "Definitely shots."

CHAPTER EIGHT

Bella

I looked up at Emma Duncan, Old Man Harper's granddaughter, who was the beneficiary of Harper's Corner after whatever resolution had occurred from the Harper sibling dispute.

"Long night?"

She could say that again. "Yeah, I didn't sleep well."

"Why's that?"

Dean's deep voice surprised us as we turned to look at him. He stood there in the same jeans and black T-shirt from this morning with his hands on his hips, looking like the epitome of a model-turned-biker —complete and utterly drool-worthy.

"How do you do that?"

No way was I going to answer his question.

I felt my face heating with sexual hunger and embarrassment. I prayed Dean thought it was because of the heat pouring from the wood-burning stove next to me.

His gaze heated. "Naturally."

Yes, he did.

Emma cleared her throat, drawing our attention. "You sure about the coffee?" She glanced at both of us, her smile wide enough to shove a whole slice of pie in. "I can get you some water instead." Another glance between us. "Iced water."

I wanted to drown in it. Instead, I shot Emma a thanks-for-having-my-back look. "I'll take coffee, thank you."

Dean slid into the booth next to me, forcing me to move over or have him sit on me.

"I'll take coffee too." A twitch of his lips was the only indicator he was teasing. "Hold the ice."

Emma's laughter filled the air as she walked away.

Hoping to keep Dean distracted, I latched onto why he was there. "Did you get a summons too?"

"Yeah." He smiled the knowing smile of someone who'd been a witness to our sibling antics for too many years.

"Do you know what Alex wants?"

His smile disappeared proving once again that Dean was no rookie in our trio. "An idea."

"And that idea would *be*?" All these years and I knew he had more than an idea. I also knew it would be like pulling teeth to get the information.

Trent and Alex slid into the booth across from us, halting any response from Dean.

"Sorry we're late. Did you order yet?" Alex asked.

I looked at my brother and shook my head. "Just coffee."

"And water." Dean winked.

I ignored Dean. "Alex, you don't look like you slept a wink." I scrunched my nose up. "Sorry, Trent, but you only look slightly better."

"Bella said she didn't sleep well last night either." Dean's teasing tone begged someone to ask why.

Both Trent and Alex glanced between us, clearly missing the joke.

Alex, however, zeroed in on my blush. "Not that much." A question in his eyes as he answered my unasked question.

"I only slept more than Alex because Dusty ended up staying with me last night." Trent unknowingly saved me from answering Alex.

"Oh no! Is he okay?" My words were pitched higher and louder than I intended.

Trent's voice warmed when he responded, "Dusty's good." The warmth left him just as quickly. "Trudy..." Trent stopped before he spoke ill of his son's mother.

Smiling, I did my best to change the subject. "I'm glad to hear Dusty's great." Turning to Alex, I asked, "How's Bruce?"

"Bella, you know I can't talk about cases."

I didn't like the fact my good friend's brother was one of Alex's active cases.

"I'm not asking you about the case, Alex. I'm asking how Bruce is doing."

Alex stared at me for a minute. His gaze softened along with his voice as he replied, "He's not doing well."

I closed my eyes. This had to be so hard for Leonard. While it was true Leonard and Bruce weren't necessarily close, it didn't negate the fact Leonard loved his brother. Growing up in a home where foul, offensive language and behavior was the norm hadn't fostered a close, loving relationship. Even though they hadn't had the best role models, Bruce had stepped up to take the brunt of the verbal and physical abuse from their parents. Leonard never forgot that, never would.

I reopened my eyes. "How was Leonard?" My concern for Leonard softened my words.

"He's upset." Trent's jaw tensed.

"Leonard found his brother beaten and on the verge of death," I said. I knew at least Alex would understand what that could do to a person.

Alex blew a breath out. "I know. Bella, do you know why Leonard went out to Bruce's cabin last night?"

"Yeah. Leonard told me Bruce hadn't returned any of his calls or texts in a few days. Said he wanted to check in on him."

"The area around Bruce's cabin doesn't have the best cell reception," Trent reminded me. "It's not unlikely Bruce wouldn't have received Leonard's call or text to give him a call back in the first place."

I shook my head. "I know Bruce isn't the most...reliable, but he's different with Leonard. He knew Leonard worried, so he always made sure to call him back or send a quick text telling him to eff off." A ghost of a smile appeared and disappeared just as quickly. "Leonard would laugh when he got those because it's Bruce's twisted macho way of telling Leonard he loved him too."

Dean shifted slightly toward me. "When was the last time Leonard saw or spoke with Bruce?"

Squinting, I shrugged. "I want to say it was last Thursday. We just finished dinner, and Bruce called Leonard to tell him he was going to the cabin. Something about setting up a trap for wild game." I sat up straighter. "I thought it was strange since Bruce wasn't a hunter, and Leonard seemed really nervous about Bruce doing that."

All three of them tensed.

I looked between them and knew that Bruce's hunting trip meant something more.

"Did he say anything else?" Alex leaned toward me eager for more.

I shook my head again. "No, and I didn't have a chance to ask about it because I got an emergency call about one of my patients and had to leave. I should have asked him more, right?"

"No, Bella." Alex sat back shutting me down.

"Wait, haven't you spoken to Leonard yet? What's he say about all this?"

"Bella," Alex said in warning.

I leaned toward Alex, frustrated. "Dammit, Alex. You know I'm going to pester him for answers so you might as well tell me."

Alex's head shake was a show of typical big brother annoyance.

"Leonard's not returning my calls or texts. I'm worried," I whispered as I settled back in the booth.

Dean bumped my shoulder. "They're fighters, Bella."

I looked at him. "Sometimes fighters get tired."

The mood grew somber. They knew there had been a time when I hadn't wanted to fight anymore. The nightmares of the flipping car, the flashing lights, and the cold darkness hounded me continually and caused me to wake with screams locked in my throat.

Alex shot a hand across the table, squeezing mine. "Bella, I'm so sorry." Sorrow and guilt laced his voice.

I squeezed back. "You don't have anything to be sorry for." I didn't blame him. At the age of eighteen, in one night, he'd become my sole guardian, my only family, and the man responsible for our lives, ignoring the pain and loss of our parents to focus on my recovery. A recovery that was required because I *had* survived.

Alex nodded. "I do. If I hadn't—"

"Stop," I demanded. Granite Creek Hospital wasn't a bed and breakfast, but it also wasn't an asylum where patients were tortured. "You did the right thing."

Alex's, "Bella" was pained.

I held his hand tighter and leaned forward. "You did the right thing. I wasn't getting better. I was slowly deteriorating. My mind..." A short quick shake of my head. "My body was fighting itself, turning on me in an attempt to protect me from..." I tugged his hand as I implored him to understand. "That night killed Mom and Dad. It almost killed me. You *did* the right thing."

"Isabella, I should have been more patient. Being with Mom and Dad in the car accident. I...didn't know the flashes of that night were caused by memory loss, a traumatic brain injury. I shouldn't have pushed you for answers. I *should* have been more patient." Alex sounded uncertain, troubled and almost regretful.

"Stop. Don't do that. You are *not* to blame. What happened to me wasn't your fault." Looking back, I was thankful Alex had given me the help I needed. Without Granite Creek Hospital, I would have eventually died.

I pulled out my best little sister smile and teased Alex. "If you don't stop blaming yourself, I'll admit *you*. You need to learn to let go and be present in the here and now." Quietly, I said, "I survived. You made sure I did. Thank you."

Dean broke the heavy moment by chuckling. "I'd pay to see Alex strapped down."

Alex released my hand and gave Dean the one-finger salute.

"Here is your coffee and water." Emma winked at me. "Are you all ready to order?"

"I'm starved. I'll take the special for the day." Alex's smile borderline resembled a ravenous mountain lion if you didn't catch the amusement glinting in his eyes.

Emma didn't fall for his mischievous charm and tilted her head toward Dean in silent question.

"I'll take one of those too."

Trent piped up, "Me too."

"Bella, surprise?" Emma sounded hopeful.

"Oh yeah. Can't wait to try it."

Alex handed his menu to Emma. "How come we don't rate the surprise?"

"Because you're special."

We were still laughing when I noticed Emma hesitate. "Being here at Harper's Corner, with Bella being my willing guinea pig, I'm beginning to put my toe back in the kitchen. To experiment once again."

Dean caught onto Emma's discomfort. "Toes? That's definitely a *unique* spice."

I really wanted to kiss Dean for not making Emma uncomfortable. Instead, I used their laughter to place my *other* order. "Can I place a preorder for dinner? Rocky and I want to take Leonard dinner tonight before we get together."

Dean, Alex, and Trent immediately quieted.

"Absolutely. How is Leonard? Any word on Bruce?" Emma's concern touched me.

I pointedly looked at Alex. "I don't know." Returning my gaze to Emma, I continued, "It's been a little difficult to get a hold of Leonard. Understandable but difficult. Although, I'm sure a meal from you won't go amiss."

A soft look from Emma before she said, "When you see Leonard tonight, give him my best. Should I have that ready around seven?"

"That'd be great. Thanks so much." I continued to ignore the looks I received from the guys.

"Not a problem. I'll be back in a jiffy with your lunch orders."

Alex jumped right in, "You just can't help yourself, can you?"

"What?" I ignored Alex's resigned tone and put on my best innocent expression.

"What my ass. Bella, this is dangerous. Stay away from Leonard."

I latched onto Alex's slip. "Dangerous? Is Leonard in danger?"

Alex clamped his mouth shut so fast I heard the crack of his teeth meeting.

Before I could push for more, Kevin, Rocky's very own personal stalker, stepped up to our table.

"It seems with the recent events your time would be better served doing your civic duty and not chaperoning."

Civic duty? Chaperone? As if Alex and Trent were just kicking around drinking a beer with their friends at Coop's. The insinuation pissed me off.

"Even with the recent events, all city employees are allowed lunch breaks." Alex pointedly looked Kevin up and down. Alex's insinuation hard to miss.

Emma, bless her savior's heart, walked up to Kevin stopping any further response. "Excuse me, Mr. Vice Mayor."

"Of course. Good day everyone." Not waiting for a response, Kevin continued on his way.

Emma placed our plates in front of us with a chorus of *thank yous* all around.

She saved mine for last. "Bella, here is one country-fried sandwich with gravy and a few *special*"—a wink at Alex—"ingredients. Let me know what you think."

I leaned forward, closed my eyes, and took a whiff of my plate. Sweet and spicy scents combined with... I didn't know what, but I couldn't wait to dig in. "It looks and smells delicious."

Emma's joy lit up her face. "I'll be back later to check in. Enjoy!"

CHAPTER NINE

Bella

WE WERE HALFWAY THROUGH OUR MEAL WHEN ALEX ASKED ME, "Did you know Blake and Ava King? Emily Castor?"

I swallowed the bite of food. "No. Blake and Ava King don't sound familiar at all." Even after my online research confirmed they were locals. "As for Emily Castor—she was a little loud back in high school, so she was kind of hard to avoid, not to mention, everyone was always talking about the latest stunt she'd pulled. Otherwise, I don't know her."

Alex nodded. "What about Leonard?"

"What about him?"

"Did Leonard know Emily? Blake?" It was clear Trent and Alex were partners with the smooth transition of their questioning.

I took my own bite and thought it over. "Leonard is my age, so I want to say no. He didn't really hang out with anyone in your grade except for Bruce and Richard. Mostly he hung out by himself." I shook my head to clear it. "I can't say for sure. That time was a blur for me. Sorry."

"No apology necessary," Trent said.

"Why are you asking about them? Do they have something to do with Bruce's attack?" I asked.

An exasperated look from Alex basically told me, again, I wasn't going to get an answer.

"You can give me that look all you want, Alex, but Leonard mentioned last night at the hospital something about them. It's not hard for me to put two and two together." Okay, so I'd stretched the truth out a little bit. Technically, Leonard had only mentioned Bruce and Blake arguing at Coop's, but I was hoping they wouldn't catch it and spill something. "And, what did he mean you never leave any stone unturned?"

"You sure Leonard never mentioned Emily or Blake all these years? Not even concerning his brother? Did you ever see her or him hanging out with them? Hushed conversations with Bruce and Richard? Anything?" An assessing look from Alex.

I didn't miss he ignored my question, but I took a moment to think back to when Leonard and I had become friends. I'd kept my circle of friends small after the accident. Avoidance of the rumors, murmurs, and outright questions regarding that night—my priority had been in my recovery.

I learned quickly how people, who in the name of friendship, were not in reality friends. More like investigative reporters out to get the latest juiciest piece of information, to be in the know before anybody else.

After our meetups at night, Leonard had approached me slowly at school. He'd never pushed for information and had diverted attention from the whispers and finger-pointing to a joke or a discussion regarding a school project.

Through all this, I'd avoided Bruce and Richard because of their less-than-cheery dispositions. More importantly, Leonard had made sure to avoid them and I had minimal interactions with them too. So, no, I couldn't say I remembered a time where any of those guys had mentioned Emily, and since I hadn't mingled upon my return from my stay at Granite Creek, I couldn't say I remembered her, either.

"Well, you know when I returned to school, I wasn't necessarily

Miss Social, but I don't remember seeing them. But then again, I wasn't necessarily looking for them either."

The three of them exchanged looks.

"What's that look for?"

"What look?" Alex dug into his food, avoiding eye contact with me. Innocent, they did not pull off.

I attempted not to roll my eyes at them. "Don't you remember Emily? She was in *your* grade, and what about this Blake and Ava King? You guys know—knew everyone."

Quiet enveloped our table.

"What am I missing?" I looked between the three of them.

Dean blew out a breath. "Yeah, Emily was in our year, but we didn't know her either. Different crowd. Blake and Ava did attend Feldspar High. Blake's the same year as us and Ava's a year younger than you."

"Okay." That wasn't unusual. High schools had their cliques. "Who did Emily hang out with? What about Blake and Ava?"

"Blake and Ava—no idea." He hesitated. "Emily hung out with Richard and Bruce."

That was interesting because I'd never seen Emily with Richard or Bruce. I looked at Alex. "Did you ask Leonard about Emily? Blake?"

Alex met my eyes but didn't answer.

I kept up with my questioning. "Do you want me to? Did you reach out to her? To her dad, Sheriff Castor? You do work with him. What about Blake?" No need to tell them I planned on reaching out to Ava.

"Leave it be." Alex ordered.

"Sure. I'll get on that right away." The sarcasm in my agreement wasn't hard to miss.

Dean snagged a fry from my plate. "Bella, they moved away after your accident."

"Dean." A warning from Trent.

"I'm not telling her anything she couldn't figure out on her own."

Alex shook his head.

That was an interesting tidbit I'd found out during my research earlier. "He's right. I'm going to find out so you might as well tell me." Then it hit me. "Guys, the Winter Formal was that night too."

All of them stared at me.

But I wasn't deterred. "What if everything started at the Winter Formal, and then with Blake and Ava back, it spooked whoever attacked Bruce?"

Dean pulled my hair. I knew to get my attention. He just had no idea how much of my attention he got. "What makes you think the Winter Formal has anything to do with any of this?"

"I don't know, but most of them left after my accident, which was the same night as the Winter Formal." I looked between them. "I mean, it can't be the accident that sent them leaving, so that leaves the dance."

All three stared at me, and the hairs on my arms stood up. Shit, what if it was related to my accident?

My sisterly instincts blew up. They knew something—about that night—and they didn't want me to know. A low barely-there hum sang through me—a connection coming to life. Did that mean it was related to my accident and I'd been right all these years or was I wanting it so bad I was making something out of nothing?

Trent placed his coffee cup on the table. "Unfortunately, your assumptions aren't enough to go on. Nothing connects the Winter Formal to Bruce's attack or anything." He leaned forward. "We need more than that."

He needed more as an officer of the law. I did not.

Looking at Alex, I persisted, "Yeah, I know, but will you look into it anyway?" Because you all just unwittingly told me it could possibly be related.

Alex assessed my face. I'm sure wondering if I was going to do something he wasn't going to like.

"Bella, if we have time between everything else, I'll look into it." He partially gave me what I wanted.

And for the first time in years Alex didn't sidestep my inquiry into our past. For a second I was stunned silent and then everything accident related in me lunged to the front. Made me believe I wasn't just seeing what I wanted to see.

It gave me the courage to push my luck by asking, "Now, what was it you were going to tell me?"

Another look from Alex clearly stated he wasn't going to fall for my trick.

"Fine. Be a brat." I stuck my tongue out at him.

Dean easily caught and ate the fry Alex threw at me. "No wasting perfectly good food."

"You forgot to mention delicious," Emma interjected.

I knew my smile resembled the cat that got the cream but Emma's dish was that tasty. "That goes without saying. You have to make this dish"—I pointed to my empty plate—"a staple on the Harper's menu. It looked, smelled, and tasted unbelievable. It was smooth, sweet, and spicy, all at the same time." I kissed my fingertips and lifted them in the air. "Perfecto!"

"Oh, I'm so glad you liked it! I've been tinkering with the recipe for months now. I couldn't get it right."

I patted my stomach. "Rest assured, it's more than right."

"Thanks, Bella. Here's a slice of chocolate cream pie for trying out my dish and the bill for when you're done. No rush. Thanks for coming by."

I clapped my hands. "Yay! I love your chocolate cream pie. Thanks, Emma."

"No problem. You've been a tremendous help in fine-tuning my dishes."

As Emma turned to leave, I remembered where I'd seen Blake. "Emma, who was that guy at Toole's the other day? The one who helped you load the lumber onto your truck?"

Emma's face pinkened. "He said his name was Blake, but I don't know him. I only met him at Toole's that day."

Rocky and I had seen the chemistry between them, but I knew Emma's history was going to make it difficult for Blake to get near her.

But that didn't mean she didn't deserve some happiness. "Didn't he give you a promotion card for his gym? Did you sign up? I've wanted to get back into shape—maybe we can join together?"

All three guys turned their heated eyes to me.

Emma's face reddened further. "Um, I'm...not sure if I'm going to join." She gave a casual shrug. "With the restaurant and the restoration of my granddad's cabin, I don't have much time for anything else."

"Well, he did say we could try it out for a week before making a decision. I say we give it a try and see how it goes." I ignored the guys' looks. Emma was my way in to speak with Blake. I wasn't going to miss the opportunity.

"If you want to get in shape, I'll help you." Dean's growl hit me in *all* the right places.

"Thanks, but no. I'd rather work out with my girlfriends." A lie, but the workout I wanted with Dean was not in the gym. More importantly, I needed an excuse to see Blake, to get close enough to ask questions about the Coop's incident with Bruce.

The guys' questions regarding Blake and Ava made me wonder if maybe Ava was the voice I heard in my dreams. In order to find out, I needed an excuse to be around them both.

Dean didn't let it go. "Your girlfriends aren't going to kick your ass in shape. I, on the other hand, will." He leaned into me. His lips brushed my ear as he whispered, "And, I'll make sure you enjoy it."

My mouth parted as the ability to breathe left me. I no longer cared about questioning Blake. I wanted Dean as my personal trainer.

Emma cleared her throat, breaking the spell. "I'll let you know what I decide, Bella. Meanwhile, enjoy your pie."

Not able to quite speak yet, I nodded and picked up my fork.

My first bite had me closing my eyes and moaning in bliss. "Mmmm."

Dean

I couldn't make myself look away. The look on Bella's face as she ate the damn piece of chocolate pie tightened my jeans around my quickly rising cock. Then she had to moan. I needed to distract her and myself before I fucked her on the table in the middle of Harper's Corner *in* front of her damn brother.

Forcing my attention to Alex didn't help. I decided to ignore the look Alex and Trent gave me.

I cleared my throat. "I went to Bella's apartment before coming here and replaced the lightbulb again. I also spoke with the apartment manager to get a copy of the video footage for the last twenty-four hours. She's going to send it to me later today."

Bella swallowed a bite of pie before addressing me. "One, thank you for changing the lightbulb. Two, you know, I *am* right here. Three, I want to see the footage too."

"I'm well aware you're right here." The struggle to keep Bella at a distance getting more and more difficult. "I'll let you know what I find before torturing you with endless hours of boring video."

She looked up at me. No way she misunderstood the heat coursing through me. I wanted to take a bite of her.

"Bella."

She struggled to move her gaze to Alex.

"It's a precaution. If the kids are pulling the pranks again, then I'll need to make sure the message comes across more formally. It's a nuisance, waste of time and money, and the initial fun of the prank is over." Alex's police affectation didn't hide his need to protect his sister. Now more than ever.

"Fine, get all cop on me."

Trent chuckled.

"Do I need to do anything? File a complaint?" she asked Alex.

"For now, no." Alex paused, "Have you noticed any other pranks? Anyone stand out?"

Bella paused with the fork to her oh-so-inviting mouth, no doubt connecting my questions the previous night to Alex's questions today.

"No, why?" she answered.

Trent sipped his coffee and avoided looking at Bella.

"Just doing what you call my cop diligence," Alex responded in what Bella called his cop voice.

"Uh, huh." She laid her fork down on her empty dessert plate. "I need to get back to work *and* walk some of this food off."

I slid out of the booth. "That's our cue. Let's go."

CHAPTER TEN

Bella

"Thanks for chauffeuring me around tonight." I watched Rocky sniff the Harper's to-go bag in her hand. "I didn't have a chance to swing by my apartment to pick my car up since my sleepover at Dean's house."

"No problem." Rocky didn't break her stride while she opened and peered into the bag. "Do you think Leonard would miss it if I ate half his steak?"

The hospital's automatic doors swooshed opened as we approached. "Yes, I do." I snatched the bag from her. "He probably hasn't had any decent food since yesterday. Besides, we're going to Coop's after this, so be patient."

"I'm starving," Rocky whined. "I just need something to tide me over until we get to Coop's."

"You wouldn't be so hungry if you ate something besides chocolate all day," I quipped, watching the elevator numbers descend.

"Chocolate is a very important food group." Rocky's pout disappeared as her excitement took over. "Besides, I lost track of time working on the designs for the DeVille. I really hope the owners love what I'm coming up with. I believe it'll meet the history of the car and their family, something that is important to them."

"Careful, Rocky. You do have to give the car back."

Staring intently at the elevator numbers lighting up, Rocky mumbled, "I know."

"Don't sound so surly. It's not like you can't buy your own DeVille to lust over."

"I can't buy every car I want." Rocky scowled at me.

Laughing, I stepped out of the elevator before I responded. "Don't be such a sourpuss. You're doing what you love."

"Stop being so logical. It's taking the fun out of my pout." Rocky shoulder-bumped me as we made our way to Bruce's room.

And, that's when I saw her. I pulled on Rocky's arm drawing her in to me and whispered, "Oh no. Nurse Booby is talking with Gordon."

Gordon was a police officer who worked with Alex. I didn't know him very well, but he seemed like a nice guy. Cute too, with a lean runner's build, dimpled smile, and thick locks of untamed curls.

Rocky leaned into me too as she stared down the hallway. "Who is Nurse Booby? And is it a bad thing she's speaking with him?" She whispered.

"She's a barracuda in human form. We might be better off waiting until she leaves." I stopped us in the hallway, not sure what to do.

Rocky stood straight up, grabbed my hand, and marched us to them. I tried to resist, but Rocky was stronger than she looked.

"Hey, Gordon!" Rocky's cheerful greeting bounced off the walls.

Gordon leaped out of his chair and away from Nurse Booby.

"Hey, Rocky. Bella." The relief in his words echoed in the hallway.

"Hi, Gordon," I replied and the smile on my face stiffened as I murmured a "hello" to the nurse.

She mimicked my insincere greeting. "I'm sorry to inform you, but the patient in this room is not allowed visitors. You're going to have to leave."

She wasn't sorry. She didn't care about the patient or us. She only wanted access to Gordon or any other good-looking member of the male species she could get her claws into.

"Thank you, Nurse Fenton. I can take it from here." Gordon's cop voice resonated between us. "I'm sure you have other patients that require your attention."

Laser beams shot out of Nurse Booby's eyes at Rocky and me for interrupting her cock pursuit. The animosity in her glare was barely banked as she turned amorous eyes at Gordon. "You're right. I do have other patients to attend to."

Gordon stood frozen as Rocky, and I watched her walk away.

We looked up at Gordon, who hadn't moved from his spot.

"You okay, Gordon?" I asked him.

He jolted as he came out of his stupor. "I'm not getting paid enough for this."

Rocky snorted.

"I thought guys liked...loose women?" I giggled.

"Loose women, not parasites." Gordon's face hardened.

Rocky tapped a finger to her bottom lip as she contemplated Gordon's response. "Well now, I thought all guys liked women who were bloodsuckers?" How she kept a straight face I had no clue.

He didn't fall for Rocky's faux innocence. "What are you ladies doing here?"

"We're bringing dinner to Leonard." I lifted the bag of Harper's food. "We figured he'd need a break, and we wanted to check in on him."

"As much as I don't want to agree with Nurse Fenton, I can't let you in the room. Sorry, ladies." Gordon went back to his chair.

"I figured that much, but do you think I could just poke my head in and ask Leonard to come out? I promise I won't step in the room." I crossed my heart and gave Gordon the most innocent look I could muster.

He snorted. "Never play poker, Bella." He tipped his head toward to the door. "Let me get Leonard for you. Wait here."

"Thanks, Gordon."

I turned to Rocky. "I don't have that bad of a poker face, do I?"

"Why do you think you got caught all the time? Why you never got away with anything with Alex?"

"I thought it was because he's a *really* good detective."

Rocky's eyebrows shot up.

"Whatever." It was a lame comeback. I knew it, but it was all I had.

"Bella. Rocky. What are you two doing here?" Leonard followed Gordon out of Bruce's room.

"Saving Gordon from Nurse Booby." Rocky smirked at Gordon.

Gordon crossed his arms and stared at Rocky.

Ignoring them, I stepped forward and gave Leonard a hug. "How are you doing?"

"I'm hanging in there." He returned my hug with a big sigh.

I pulled back and lifted the Harper's bag. "We brought you some dinner. Why don't you come sit with us for a while? It might help."

"Thanks, but I don't want to leave Bruce's side yet." Leonard looked from the bag to me.

I squeezed his hand. "I know, but you're not going to be much help to Bruce if you don't take care of yourself too. Come on. We'll go down to the waiting room. We won't be long. I promise." I held my breath, waiting for Leonard to agree.

Leonard looked over his shoulder and asked Gordon, "You'll come get me if there is any change?"

"I can't leave Bruce. Sorry man," Gordon's contrite tone let Leonard know Gordon wished differently.

"I'll stay here with Gordon just in case the octopus tries to suction herself to him again. If there's any change with Bruce, I'll come get you." Rocky came to the rescue.

Gordon shook his head at Rocky.

I gave Leonard's hand a slight tug. "Come on. Take a few minutes to eat something. It's Harper's steak and biscuits—you can't say no."

"All right. Just a few minutes," he reluctantly agreed.

Our short walk to the waiting room was quiet, and I waited until Leonard had a few bites of dinner before I broke the silence.

"I'm really sorry about what happened to Bruce. What do the doctors say?"

"The doctors placed him in a medically induced coma to give his body time to heal, to recover. We won't know the extent of his recovery until he comes out of the coma. They've got him in ICU because of all the..." Leonard's Adam's apple bobbed with his swallow. "He'll live."

I reached out and squeezed his arm letting him know he wasn't alone. "Do you have any idea who attacked him? What was he doing up at the cabin? Did he piss anyone particular off lately? I mean more than the usual?"

Leonard dropped his fork on the food container and, with a small, sad smile, said, "Lots, unfortunately, and you know the last time I spoke with Bruce, he said he was going hunting. He said he wanted to do the community a favor and catch a big fucking predator that was hiding. Otherwise, I don't know much else."

Something about his words niggled at me, but my brain was unable to grasp it. "Anyone stand out? Did he have trouble at work? Girl problems? Money problems? Anything?" There had to be something that would help me figure this out.

He hesitated. "You know Bruce. He's lived the same life with slight variations. Some of those variances were longer lasting than others." He picked up his fork and took another bite and avoided looking at me.

"What?" I jumped at what Leonard wasn't saying.

He shook his head and mumbled around his food, "Nothing."

I scanned his face seeing his discomfort clear as day. What was it he didn't want to tell me? I tried another tack. "You mentioned last night about Brooke kicking Bruce out of Coop's. It's not the first time she's done that. Why was this time different? What were Bruce and Blake arguing about?"

"This time, Blake stood up to him." Leonard lowered his fork his again and stared at me.

What was significant about Blake standing up to Bruce?

Taking a leap from my conversation with the guys at Harper's, I asked, "Were they arguing about Emily? Did Bruce know Emily? Did they date in high school?" I felt the oxygen in the room being sucked out. "Was it a bad breakup?"

"Bruce didn't date." The intensity in his expression told me there was more there.

"Does it have anything to do the Winter Formal?" I continued with Alex and Trent's earlier line of questioning.

"What do you know about that night?" Sweat beaded on his forehead.

Butterflies took flight in my belly. "You know what I remember. I lost a chunk of my memory, and I was hospitalized for months, desperately fighting my way back. That my parents died." I paused, not sure how much I wanted to reveal. "I'm starting to remember things about the accident."

Surprise lit Leonard's face up. "What do you remember that's different from before?"

If I opened up and revealed the mystery woman, would Leonard do the same? I had to try. "I hear a woman shouting at me. I see shadows moving above us." I shrugged playing it off as unimportant. "Maybe she knows something about the skid marks, the lights, something."

Leonard stared off into space at my announcement. We sat in silence as I waited for him to reveal whatever he was thinking. Hoping he'd give me anything about that night—Bruce, anything.

"Have you told Alex about it? What does he think?" Years of friendship alerted me to the fact Leonard's questions weren't innocent. He was asking more than he was letting on.

"I haven't had the chance. He's been busy." I didn't see any reason to sidestep his question.

Leonard scanned my face, I'm sure wondering if he'd get anything out of me.

We were at a stalemate, but I wasn't giving up. "What did you mean last night when you said I had no clue?"

Leonard's face closed down. "I didn't mean anything. I was tired and scared."

"Don't lie to me." Quieter, I said, "Not me." We'd been through too much for lies.

"I'm not lying." Leonard's words came out harsh.

No, but he wasn't revealing everything either.

"Have the police told you anything about Bruce's case?" I wasn't going to give up.

"Nothing useful. They're looking into it. They'll let me know when they have something. We know your brother will look into every little thing." Even as he carefully moderated his tone, frustration and anger warred for dominance on his face.

"What about the doctors? Did they say if it was more than one assailant?"

A shake of Leonard's head before he responded, "One assailant."

That must have been a pretty big guy to subdue Bruce. Bruce was six-foot-three of construction muscle and beer fat—not an easy target and mean to boot.

"Who knew Bruce was going to be up at the cabin?"

He shrugged. "I'm not sure." He placed his fork down once again and carefully blanked his expression. "What do Alex, Trent, and Dean have to say? Do they have any leads, suspects?"

"You know how they are, tight-lipped on anything work-related." I stared at my friend and wondered who he was protecting.

"I don't mean to rush you, but I want to get back to Bruce." He stood and pointed to the food. "Thanks for that."

Surprised, I watched him head toward the door. I was hurt he hadn't opened up to me. He was purposefully pushing me away.

I blurted out, "Someone is watching me."

He froze at the door.

"They've busted my porch light twice and have been through my apartment as well." I fibbed on the latter—at least I hoped I did, but he didn't know that. I figured if it got him to open up to me, then it was worth the white lie.

Leonard turned toward me. "What?" It was barely audible.

"And the night of the anniversary when I went jogging, someone was watching."

A muscle ticked in Leonard's jaw. "Did you see them? Did you report it?"

"No, I didn't see anyone. I wanted to believe it was my imagination playing tricks on me, but when I got back, someone messed with my porch light." I stepped toward him. "Someone had to be there."

The indecision warring inside Leonard contorted his face. "Bella, I'm going to take care of this. Until then, promise me you'll stay out of it."

"I don't understand. Why don't you want me to help? And how are you going to fix this?" I didn't understand why he didn't want my help or why he was doing everything to keep me in the dark.

"Bella..." He stopped when Sheriff Castor walked in.

"Hello, Leonard. Isabella," Castor greeted us.

"Hi, Sheriff Castor." I returned his greeting, frustrated he'd interrupted our conversation.

"I apologize for intruding, but I wanted to check with Leonard on Bruce's condition."

"It's okay. I was just leaving anyway." Not really, and I didn't want to leave. I wanted answers. Instead, I made my way to them and said to Leonard, "I hope you change your mind."

Glancing up at Castor, I bid him a good night and made my way to Rocky, who was still waiting with Gordon.

"All done, Bella?" Rocky's undisguised hope rang through.

"Yup." For now. "I take it Rocky kept you safe?" I teased Gordon.

Gordon tapped the gun on his hip. "I do have a gun."

"That's exactly what the good ol' nurse wanted to see—how you cock your gun," Rocky needled him.

"How you two stay out of trouble is beyond me." Gordon's exasperated tone made me giggle.

Rocky tapped his arm. "Aww, come on. You know you've enjoyed my company."

Gordon looked at his arm and back to me. "Tell Alex he owes me."

"Bye, Gordon." I laughed even more as I pulled Rocky away from Gordon.

Rocky yelled back, "I'll swing by tomorrow and keep you company. You know—to protect your honor from the less desirables."

Gordon looked up at the ceiling.

CHAPTER ELEVEN

Bella

"THE GUYS UNDERSTAND I'M DOING MY PART IN THE INVESTIGATION while they do theirs." More like I'd purposely left out the tidbit where I was going to visit Ava during my conversation with them at Harper's yesterday.

Rocky turned to me in the kickass purple swivel chair she sat on. Avalon Affair's waiting room showcased Ava's ability to put together an appropriate affair. "So, in other words, you didn't tell them you were coming here."

Not meeting Rocky's eyes, I inspected the interlocking swirls on the painting across from me as if it required my undivided attention.

"Oww." Pain shot through my arm from Rocky's pinch. Scowling, I asked, "What was that for?"

"Ignoring me won't change the fact they're going to be pissed at you for not telling them."

Indignation shot through me. "They can get mad all they want. I don't answer to them."

A slow naughty smile spread across Rocky's face. "Oh, this is going to be fun."

"What?" I didn't trust Rocky's sudden mood change.

Rocky's Cheshire grin said it all.

"So, did you decide which outfit you are going to wear on your date with Kevin?" Two could play at that game.

Rocky's smile vanished. "Bitch."

Even as my own Cheshire grin spread across my face I said, "That's no way to speak to your best friend."

"Best friends aren't mean to each other, either." Rocky's voice was dry in her sarcasm.

"You know, as part of your avoidance tactic, you can get ready at my house, and we can go to the party together." I handed Rocky the magazine she pointed to.

Rocky swatted me with the magazine. "That's brilliant! I knew you were my best friend for a reason."

"I'm starting to think it's because I put up with your abuse." I rubbed my arm, again.

Her impish smile said it all.

"Isabella. Raquel. It's so lovely to see you girls," Mrs. Dixon said as she walked over to us.

Coming to our feet, we met Mrs. Dixon and Ava.

I bent and gave Mrs. Dixon a kiss on her cheek. "Mrs. Dixon, it's a pleasure to see you." It was true. The things that came out of Mrs. Dixon's mouth were sure to put a smile on your face.

Ava extended her hand to us. "Raquel, Isabella. I'm Ava. Sorry to keep you waiting."

"Not a problem," I said.

"Oh, are you girls planning a celebration? Ava's just the best. The surprises we have in store for the mister are unbelievable." Mrs. Dixon turned to Ava. "Oh, we're going to get it on film, right, dear? We just have to. I want to be able to replay the look on his face when he sees it." Not waiting for an answer, Mrs. Dixon made her way to the door. "I've got to go speak with Daisy about those flowers. She hasn't returned my call, and I need to make sure she's not falling down on the job." With a wave over her shoulder, Mrs. Dixon bounced out the door. "Tootles!"

"I hope I have a quarter of the energy she has when I'm her age."

Ava's husky voice penetrated our Dixon fog.

We turned back to Ava. "Right? I swear I double my runs every day just thinking of her. Then, by the time I'm done, I'm dragging my ass back home." Rocky shook her head. "I don't know how she does it."

"My guess? She doesn't use words like *ass* or abuse her friends," I responded dryly.

I jumped back as Rocky tried to pinch me once more.

Ava's laughter reminded me we weren't alone.

"I'm so sorry. Rocky usually demonstrates better manners. I can have her wait outside?" I jokingly apologized.

"I'm not one of your animals to sit and stay at your command." Rocky glared in offense at the comparison.

"You two are exactly like I imagined you would be."

Rocky and I stared at Ava.

"You imagined us? Why the hell would you do that?" Rocky's bugged eyes matched the disbelief in her words.

Ava shrugged. "In school, you two were always together. Laughing, talking, happy. I sort of just imagined you two would be funny and sweet." She looked between us, smiling. "And, clearly, I was right."

"Well, I'm glad we didn't disappoint you." This time it was my turn to shrug. "But I'm sorry, I don't remember you." And would you be this happy if you were the female voice I heard screaming from the bottom of the cliff? The woman who might have caused my accident?

Ava briefly touched my arm. "No apologies necessary. I was a grade younger, and my family left my first year of high school, so I didn't get to foster a ton of friendships before that."

"I'm sorry to hear that. Why did your family leave?" I didn't have to finagle a way to bring up our earlier years; she made it easy for me to ask.

Ava looked at her receptionist before turning to us. "I'm sorry. Where are my manners? Please follow me."

Rocky and I eyed each other but followed Ava into her office.

What was it about her family's relocation that required privacy?

Ava closed the door behind us and pointed to the chairs. "Please have a seat." She walked around her desk to her own chair.

I was afraid to speak in case she changed her mind about answering my questions. I needed the information she could provide me.

"Before we get onto my personal life, what can I do for you ladies? Someone's birthday?"

We shook our heads.

"Wedding?" She looked between our hands as we shook our heads again.

"Business event?"

More shaking.

I blew out a small breath to release some of the uneasiness inside me before telling Ava, "We're actually here for your personal life."

Ava's eyebrows shot up to her hairline. "What? Why?"

"I don't know how to explain this." I looked to Rocky for assistance.

Rocky sat forward. "We're not creepers. We're not sitting around imagining what you do in your spare time or anything like that."

I swung my head to Rocky, bugging my eyes. "Rocky!"

"Shit. That's not what I meant," Rocky pleaded with Ava. "I mean, we were sitting around thinking about you but not like a creeper kind of way."

I dropped my head and mumbled, "God, help me."

Ava's laughter had me looking up.

"I'm so glad you find this funny because I'm so embarrassed right now and totally afraid you're going to kick us out before I get any answers."

She waved off my apology. "I love this. You two are *so* real." She plopped her forearms onto her desk. "Ask away."

The hope inside me fluttered. "Why *did* you leave Feldspar ten years ago?"

"My dad was offered a better job out of town. Better pay, better benefits. The whole nine yards. So we moved. At the time, it sucked because I was on the cheer team, and I had all these big plans of how I was going to be a popular cheerleader in high school, fall in love with a football player, yadda, yadda, yadda. You know, teenage girl dreams."

Not quite what I was looking for. "There wasn't any other reason? Nothing related to your brother, Blake?"

Ava's cheerfulness slowly drained. "Blake? Do you know my

brother?"

I glanced at Rocky before answering. "No. I can't say I remember meeting him."

Ava looked at Rocky, who shook her head as well.

Ava stood, professionalism firmly in place. "Any questions you have regarding my brother, you'll have to contact him. I don't speak to the press or anyone regarding my brother's career or anything related to his fight journey." She opened her office door. "Now, if you'll excuse me."

I shot up out my chair, extending an arm toward Ava. "No! I mean, wait."

Ava's stony face didn't change.

I rushed on. "I'm not here about Blake's career. I mean, I'm sure he has a great career, and it's totally worth knowing about it. I just don't want to know about it."

She squinted.

"Wh—"

Rocky clamped her hand over my mouth. "What my friend is trying to say but is doing a poor job of is, we are not here about your brother's career even though I'm sure it's an amazing story. And I can promise you we're not after the latest juicy tidbit on Blake King." Rocky paused. "Although, since he was eyeing our friend the other day, we'll take any information you have pertaining to Blake's sexual history. You know, just so we can tell our girl it's either okay to dump him or *jump* him."

I yanked my head away from Rocky's hand. "You think *I'm* doing a terrible job. You don't tell the guy's sister you want his sexual resume."

Ava chuckled and we stopped bickering. After closing the door, she made her way back to her desk.

"I hate to break it to you girls, but my brother attracts a lot of women. It comes with the territory." Ava sounded genuinely sorry.

"I wouldn't say he was hitting on her. It was more like a gentleman helping a woman with *manly* things and then, bam!" Rocky slapped her hands together. "Emma didn't want his help or attention, but he went as far as to give her a week's free trial at the gym to get her attention."

As Ava retook her seat, she stated, "Oh, this is interesting. Blake doesn't pursue women. They just fall in his lap." She rubbed her hands together. "Is Emma going to the gym? I wanna be there for this."

"We're hoping to get her there tomorrow." And just as quickly, Rocky's joking was replaced with solemnity. "But only if he's a good guy. Emma doesn't need to be yanked around again."

"He's the best. Besides my father, he's the most honorable man I know." Ava responded just as seriously.

"Perfect. We'll be there tomorrow." The relief that swept across Rocky's face was immediate.

"What did your brother and Bruce Evans argue about at Coop's last week?" I blurted. I was not willing to miss my chance to get answers from her.

Rocky shot me a glare, but I ignored her and kept my focus on Ava. Her look wasn't any friendlier. She pursed her lips and steepled her fingers in front of her mouth.

"Yeah, I was there. Bruce stopped at my table and was making small talk before Blake showed up. Blake asked him to leave, but Bruce wasn't in a hurry. Brooke was at our table before long and asked Bruce to leave." Ava shrugged jerkily, trying to appear casual but failing. "Sorry to disappoint you ladies, but it really was nothing."

"Did either of you know Bruce before Coop's? Back in high school, maybe?" I pressed.

Ava leaned back in her seat, stalling. "Not really."

"What does not really mean?" Rocky asked, catching on that there was something to find.

"It means, like in any high school, I'd heard of him, but I'd never met the guy." Her smile was forced and definitely a lie.

"And your brother? Did he know Bruce?" Rocky fired back.

Ava looked between us as fury lit her eyes. "I can assure you, Blake had nothing to do with Bruce's attack. No matter what happened back in high school. Blake wouldn't wait ten years before exacting any type of revenge. He *wouldn't* exact revenge. It's not in his makeup."

This time I leaned forward. "I'm not saying Blake did, but what happened ten years ago that would make someone think Blake would want to revenge?"

"I'm truly sorry about what happened to Bruce. I am, but Bruce wasn't a nice guy back then and I'm guessing not now either. So in the ten years we've been gone, I'm sure Bruce has pissed someone else off you can point the finger at that *isn't* my brother. Or since you're stuck back in high school, I bet you can even find other people Bruce and Richard bullied as well." She pushed her chair back. "You know? It pisses me off Blake is the one who was tormented by them, hospitalized by them, and now he's being questioned when one of them has been attacked."

"Bruce and Richard put Blake in the hospital ten years ago? Why? What happened?" Nausea rolled through my stomach.

"You don't know?" Her surprise wasn't hard to miss as she glanced between us.

Both Rocky and I shook our heads.

"Blake missed his curfew the night of the Winter Formal, and he wasn't answering his cell. My parents were about to contact the school when our phone rang. It was the school principal letting us know they found Blake, who had been severely beaten and was being rushed to the hospital." Ava quieted for a moment. "He never admitted it was Bruce and Richard who beat him, but they were major thorns in his side throughout his school years. My parents complained to the school, but it didn't help. I believe it's the real reason my parents decided to move. The new job was just a bonus."

I leaned forward, desperate to learn more but not wanting to interrupt.

"After that, Blake changed. He started multiple martial arts training, learned the discipline behind them, and became a huge advocate for the underdog. Blake focused on self-betterment and gaining control of his entire being and how to teach others the same. It's one of the reasons he's helping out at the gym across town. He wants to make sure no one else goes through what he did."

Her mention of the Winter Formal backed my questions at lunch yesterday. She didn't outright link the events, but I didn't think the two weren't just coincidences.

"I'm sorry your brother went through any of that, but it sounds like Blake's turned his life around to help others in similar situations. It's very noble." I did my best to hide my frustration, but I needed *more*.

Rocky, sensing my dissatisfaction and realizing we weren't going to get any more out of her, stood. "Ava, we can't thank you enough for speaking with us, but I'm sure we've taken enough of your time."

We were making our way to the front office door, exchanging pleasantries when Dean's growl cut through our chatter.

"Bella, what a surprise to see you here."

"Yes, it *is* a surprise to see you here too." I narrowed my eyes at Rocky for support.

He tugged my arm, forcing my body to collide with his. He bent his head and looked me in the eyes. "What part of *stay out of it* don't you understand?"

"I understand." I might not obey, but I understood.

One strong eyebrow went up, calling me on my bullshit.

I attempted an innocent expression.

"You must be Dean Cannon?" Ava asked.

He looked over my head to Ava. "Yeah. And I'm taking it you already spoke to Bella and Rocky about Blake?"

"Yes, but somehow I don't think my answers are good enough for you." I could hear Ava's guard was back up.

Dean, still looking at Ava, replied, "Let me see Bella and Rocky out."

Ava nodded as Dean led us out the front door.

I swung back to Dean and tried to head him off. "Don't even start. I'm going to do whatever I can to help Leonard bring whoever did this to Bruce to justice. I can't not help him."

"You could just let the professionals do their jobs," he retorted.

"Dean..." My response was cut short as Dean's lips briefly met mine, lulling me into a Dean fog.

"I've got to get back to work. Dean, can I leave our girl with you, or do I need to make a blood pact promising to get her to work safely?" Rocky's voice broke me out of my trance.

The briefest twitch of his lips before looking back at me. "You two go on ahead." Another kiss and he was gone.

Meanwhile, my lips burned.

"Now, that's a man you should *definitely* jump," Rocky murmured.

CHAPTER TWELVE

Bella

AFTER AVA'S OFFICE, I DROPPED ROCKY OFF AT WORK AND HEADED toward Margie's coffee shop. All the while, thoughts bounced around in my head from Ava's comments about the night of the Winter Formal to Blake's attack and the Kings' departure from Feldspar shortly thereafter—none of it made sense together. Add in my accident, my parents' deaths and Emily's departure, and my brain was screaming at me to find the common denominator. Was it Bruce? Blake?

Everything brought me back to Leonard. The way he avoided answering my questions or giving me vague cryptic responses kept circulating through my brain. What was he not saying? What was he saying? I didn't understand.

All of my attempts to reach him today had gone unanswered. So, I did what any resourceful friend would do. I contacted the hospital to speak with him and was told he'd left about an hour ago. Part of me felt guilty about my lie of omission, but I wasn't responsible for the fact they didn't ask me if I was a practicing doctor at their facility. Or if my doctorate was medical or veterinary.

Because I wasn't some random person out looking for the latest news. We were supposedly the kind of friends who had each other's back.

So with my anger in check—sort of—I stepped onto the sidewalk in front of Margie's shop, breathing in the fresh smell of coffee. My body moved without my conscious thought toward the front door, knowing what it needed was inside. The richness of the aroma engulfed me when I opened the door.

"*Mulher!* I thought you forgot about me," Margie bellowed at me.

"Forget you? That's not possible." Even if her coffee wasn't to die for, Margie lived her life out loud. She made it impossible to forget her.

She pointed her finger at me. "Don't you sass me, or I'll give you the coffee I reserve for the pain in my ass customers."

My hand to my heart, I begged, "No! Please don't!" I stopped next to the countertop. "Wait, you have coffee reserved for moody customers?"

She snorted. "No, but now you got me thinking. I could make my own line—*Aroma de Bundo*. It'd be a hit." Her Portuguese nature out front and center.

"I don't know what it means, but just the name would get my attention."

Margie winked at me. "Aroma of Ass."

"Selling ass is one way to get customers. Although, I wouldn't suggest it as a long-term plan." Dean's rich voice strummed through me.

Barely managing to strangle the shiver wanting to escape me into submission, I looked to my left at Dean. "Seriously, how do you sneak up on people? You're six foot plus of muscle." I reached out and attempted to pinch his side with no luck. "And you got here fast. Did your conversation with Ava not go well?"

He looked at my hand and shook his head. "It went fine."

"Dean, if I sold your ass, I'd be set for life."

Margie wasn't wrong about that. Women would line up for blocks to get a piece of Dean, and I'd drive by with a flamethrower, frying their asses.

"Mmhmm. You got that right, sister," a female customer behind us agreed with Margie.

"It depends on what he's packing." Her friend looked Dean up and down. "It'd be a shame if all that wasn't true to the packaging."

A woman at a corner table piped in favor of Margie's early retirement plan. "Margie, if you got all his friends to participate, you'd retire in one night."

"His friends hot?" The customer behind me asked the woman in the corner.

"They'd burn the house down," Corner Table vouched.

"They packing too?" The package woman stared at Dean.

Dean stared at the woman and looked back at Margie. "Give me my usual."

The women fanned their faces and asked the woman at the corner table, "Do they all have voices like him too?"

"Mmhmm," was her answer.

"Bella, do you think Alex and Trent would be up for it?" Margie asked as she made Dean his coffee.

My stomach dropped. "Stop. I do not want to think of my brother and sex."

"You do know Alex has sex." Margie chuckled.

"You got any pictures of your brother?" Package woman asked me.

"Sorry, but I'm not pimping my brother out. More importantly, Alex and Trent are police detectives, so I don't think they'd be on board with selling their bodies for Margie's early retirement benefit." I pointed at Margie. "Stop trying to sell my brother and his friends for sex and make me two of my usuals."

"You a cop too?" The woman was relentless.

Dean looked at her. "I'm not available." He turned his attention to me. "Two?"

What? How was he not available? Who was he seeing? Did I know her? My stomach dropped at the thought of Dean with another woman.

I stepped forward to look at Margie's pastry display and give myself space from Dean. "Yup." I didn't want to tell him I was going to go see

Leonard. Dean, Alex, and Trent had made it clear they wanted me to stay out of whatever was going on.

"Who's the other one for?" Unhidden in his tone was the demand I answer.

"A friend." I studied the pastries and avoided looking back at Dean.

Dean grabbed my belt loop and pulled me back. Once my back was flush with his front, Dean wrapped his other arm around my waist and spoke in my ear. "Which friend?"

The shivers that ran through my body were unavoidable. Dean's heat warmed me everywhere as I breathed the word, "Leonard."

"Stubborn." Dean nipped my ear as his arm tightened around my waist.

"Sweet baby Jesus, please tell me the man delivers on all that promise," the package woman muttered.

This time I couldn't stop my response to the nip. My body heated and it took all my concentration to remain in place and not pull him down for a more thorough taste.

Unfortunately, I only dreamed about Dean's deliverance.

"Here you go." Margie placed our coffees on the counter and looked over at the woman. "To answer your question, I'd like to believe the Big Man wouldn't be so mean to give us all of that"—she waved her hand up and down Dean—"and not follow through."

"I hear you," the woman mumbled.

Dean released me and stepped forward to pay.

I took the space he gave me to regain control of my body.

"Uh-huh. I feel you sister and his arms weren't even around me." The woman devoured Dean with her eyes.

She had no idea. Sucking in another breath, I moved forward to pay as Dean handed me my coffees.

Dean lifted his cup to Margie. "Thanks." He grabbed my belt loop and said, "Let's go."

"Wait, I haven't paid for my coffee," I said to his back.

"I got it." He continued moving us toward the door.

My chest warmed at his generosity. "Thanks, Dean." And I yelled over my shoulder to Margie as Dean continued to tug me out the door. "Thanks, Margie!"

"*De nada!*" Margie bellowed.

"Good luck! Come back and tell us if he delivers," the persistent and stubborn package woman yelled as the door closed.

My face was twenty shades of red as I secretly wished I was able to fulfill that request.

Lucky for me, Dean was busy getting away from Margie's shop, so he didn't see my discomfort. It was then I realized Dean had walked us to his truck.

"Dean, I'm parked on the other side."

"That's good, but we'll take my truck to Leonard's," he answered. Opening the passenger door, he commanded, "Get in."

I looked at Dean. "We're not going to Leonard's."

We stared at each other, and then I remembered Dean could be stubborn too.

"And you think *I'm* stubborn," I mumbled as I attempted to get into this truck without the use of my hands. Dean set his coffee on the rim of the truck bed, picked me up and plopped me in the seat.

He closed the door behind me, grabbed his coffee again and walked around to the driver's side of the truck.

"Why are you going to Leonard's with me?" I asked him as soon as he was in his seat.

"Why not?"

"You don't normally visit Leonard. You don't normally speak to Leonard at all."

"Maybe I want to change that." Dean sipped his coffee as he maneuvered the truck down the street.

I snorted. "Yeah, right." After all the years of knowing Leonard and he wanted to befriend him now? I didn't think so.

"Did you get to talk to him last night?"

"Some." I sipped my coffee. Hopefully, today I'd get some straight answers out of Leonard. "What'd Ava tell you?" And are you willing to share it with me?

"Not much."

"Is that not much as in you got something to work with or...?" I prompted.

His lips kicked up in amusement. "I'm guessing she told me the same thing she told you."

Not about to give up, I nudged Dean, "Why don't you tell me what she told you, and then I can tell you if it's the same or not?"

"You went into the wrong line of work. You should have become a detective or a private investigator." Dean flat-out smiled.

My heart fluttered at his smile and compliment. "Thanks, so you won't mind answering my questions then."

He chuckled.

"That's what I thought, but I was thinking about it, and you have no reason not to talk to me about it."

Dean's thick eyebrow shot up. "What makes you think that?"

"Normally, you have client confidentiality to protect, but who in all of this is your client? Bruce? Ava? Leonard? Since none of them are your clients, then you don't have to worry about discussing anything confidential with me. Besides, I'm not going to tell anyone anything you tell me." I felt pretty smug I'd found a loophole.

"You're right. The people you listed are not my clients. However, I am a consultant with the Feldspar Police Department, so any information I receive on any police case, whether I'm contracted for it or not, is confidential. It wouldn't do me any good to spill secrets because of a" —Dean glanced at me before he continued—"loophole."

Dammit. Of course, I couldn't ask him to ruin his reputation because of my need to help Leonard. It didn't mean I had to like it though.

"You're such a spoilsport."

He chuckled as he parked in the visitor parking space at Leonard's apartment complex.

I watched Dean walk around the front of his truck to my side. Once he had my door opened, I asked, "How much are you not telling me?"

He stared at me.

Jumping down placed me squarely in his personal space. "That's what I thought." I tilted my head and asked, "But if I found anything out, I'm supposed to tell you?"

"Most things I cannot tell you. Again, confidentiality." He wrapped his hand around my neck.

"What about the other things?" I pushed.

Humor lit up his face. "The others would make you stop talking to people."

"Really? Like who?" My curiosity winning out.

He shook his head and gave the back of my neck a squeeze. "Let's go talk to Leonard."

I tried to grab his sides, but the coffees in my hands didn't allow any purchase on his shirt. Although, I did get his attention with my movement. "Um, I don't think that's a good idea."

"Why? That's why you're here."

"Yeah, but Dean? You make Leonard nervous. We're not going to get anything out of him with you standing there being all badass." Among other things.

"Badass?" His grinned like only a badass could—hot.

My eyebrows shot up. "Uh, yeah. You breathe, so badass."

He shook his head and released me. "Go on. I'll wait here."

"Thanks."

At the top of the stairs, I turned back to see him watching me. What did Dean know and would anything I learned from Leonard today help him connect the missing pieces? Would Dean tell me if he did?

Pushing Dean out of my mind, I awkwardly knocked on Leonard's door and heard him coming closer.

"Bella? What are you doing here?" Leonard's russet-colored hair was disheveled, his brown eyes were puffy, and his clothes were wrinkled. It looked like I'd woken him up.

Not waiting for an invite, I pushed past him into his apartment. It was small. A one-bedroom, one bath, and I wouldn't really call it a kitchen because it was one with the living room. To top it off, Leonard's furniture was just as drab as the outside. I ignored the smell because, honestly, it needed a good scouring with Pine-Sol and bleach.

Shoving the state of Leonard's apartment out of my mind, I turned to Leonard and held out one of the coffees. "I'm here for answers."

Poor Leonard looked confused, and I'm sure his sleep-deprived brain wasn't keeping up with me.

"Answers?" he asked as he took the offered coffee.

"Yeah, answers."

A quick shake of his head. "Bella, I'm not following. You're going to have to give me a little more to go on here."

Even though I wanted to tear into him, I couldn't forget why this was all happening. His brother was in the hospital after a brutal attack. I made my way to him and hugged him. Leonard automatically returned my hug, laying his head on top of mine.

I whispered, "I'm sorry about Bruce." Because even though I was mad, his brother was hurt, which meant Leonard was hurting too.

Leonard sighed. "Me too."

I stepped back and asked, "How's he doing? Any changes in his condition? How are you?"

"He's the same. The doctor finally told me to go home before he admitted me for exhaustion." Leonard walked over to the couch and pushed the blanket to the side. "Have a seat." He lifted his cup up to me. "Thanks for the coffee."

I sat on the couch and patted the spot next to me. "Sit with me. I didn't mean to wake you, but last night you weren't up to talking."

Leonard plopped down next to me, flinging his other arm over his eyes. "I got home a few hours ago. I was trying to get some shut-eye before I head back to the hospital."

Part of me felt bad for waking him up. I knew this wasn't easy for him.

"I'm sorry I woke you, but I promise I won't take a lot of your time. You haven't been acting like yourself, and I wanted to check on you." Leonard and I were pretty open with each other about our lives, so for Leonard to evade me during this tumultuous time was weird. More importantly, I didn't know how to be there for him if he wouldn't let me in.

Dropping his arm from his eyes, Leonard answered, "I'm just tired, Bella. I know most people don't care for Bruce. Heck, most of the time, I don't care for him, but he's my brother." Leonard's voice cracked. "Without him, I wouldn't have survived our home, and lately, he's been different. He was really trying to change, to be better."

"He's strong. Bruce will fight his way through this, and before you know it, you'll be wishing he was still laid up." I reached between us and held his hand.

"Yeah." It wasn't a very convincing response.

Squeezing his hand, I braced, knowing I was pushing him. "Are you ready to tell me what's going on? To let me help you?"

Leonard sat up and bit out, "Is that why you're here? To find out what happened to Bruce?" His tone harsher than it'd ever been with me all the years of our friendship.

"What? No! I mean, yes." Confusion and hurt battled inside me. "I'm only trying to help you. To repay you for everything you did for me back when my parents died." I sucked in a breath. "I thought we were friends, but you're acting like..." Everyone else back then who wanted the latest tidbit. That's not who I was and the fact he'd implied it rocked the foundation of our friendship.

He got up and began pacing his apartment. "Shit, I'm sorry Bella. I know you're not like that. It's just everyone assumes Bruce deserved what he got it, that it had to be his fault. What no one understands is he was *really* trying to clean himself up. He met someone who makes him want to be better." Leonard stopped his pacing. "I think he actually might love her." His tone carried his disbelief and astonishment.

I stood and did my best to understand where Leonard was coming from. "I get it. I really do. Love does crazy things to people. Does she know Bruce was hurt?" Because if what Leonard said was true and Bruce actually loved this woman, she deserved to know someone she cared about was hurt.

"I don't know. He never brought her around. He said he didn't want her to know about this part of him. The side where everyone thought he wasn't worth it. He said she believed in him and that she made him laugh."

Wow. Could it be true? Bruce turning a new leaf all because of the love of a good woman? To wanting something good in his life not tarnished by his past mistakes. Leonard was right—Bruce had years of his reputation to combat. He had a hard road in front of him to change the views of people.

I walked over to him and grabbed his hand. "I keep saying this, but I am sorry. That's a difficult situation to be in, but it does mean she's not local, so maybe she hasn't heard about it on the news. Can you get her number from his cell?"

"No, the police won't give me his phone."

"Of course they won't." I blew out a breath, thinking my next statement might put Leonard on edge again. "I spoke with Ava King today."

Leonard's hand spasmed around mine.

"She mentioned Bruce and Richard used to bully Blake back in high school and that the night of the Winter Formal they went too far. What happened that night that caused them to beat Blake so badly he ended up hospitalized and forced his family to relocate?" I held my breath, waiting for his response.

Leonard stared at me. "She told you that?" His question was open in speculation.

"Yes." In a way. "What happened at the Winter Formal?"

"I don't know." Leonard released my hand and began pacing again, agitation in his every movement.

"Nothing? Not a single thing? Does it have to do with Emily? I know they all hung out together, and she left Feldspar right after too."

Leonard's steps faltered as the color drained from his face. His next word was barely audible. "What?"

Leonard's fear confirmed I was getting close to answers. These people and events were connected. All I had to do was figure out how.

"What happened the night of the Winter Formal? Does it have anything to do with the incident at Coop's? With Bruce's attack?" My accident? My stomach flipped.

He shook his head, not in disagreement, but like he was trying to clear it. "Blake... He... Why did he come back? At least Emily stayed away, but Richard never could keep his big mouth shut. Why can't everyone just leave everything alone? It's been ten years since..."

He stopped his ramblings to look at me. Remembering I was there with him.

"What does that all mean? What are you hiding?" My frustration stamped my every word.

"Bella, I'm sorry about all of this." He shook his head, determination lining his face. "Everything will be the way it used to be soon. I promise you."

What did that mean?

"I don't want to rush you, but since I'm up, I should get back to Bruce." He marched past me to the door.

Shock held me in place. It wasn't like Leonard to not open up to me, to not work through our problems together. It was even less like him to rush me out.

"I don't understand," I mumbled, the shock still rooted in me.

"I'm sorry, Bella, but I gotta go. It's still a risky time for Bruce." Leonard's impatience wasn't difficult to miss as he stood next to the opened door waiting for me to leave.

He was lying. Not that Bruce wasn't out of the woods. No, my instincts were telling me Leonard didn't want me here.

Pain shot through me as our friendship crumbled around me. My feet subconsciously moved me to the exit while I processed this.

He grabbed my arm, stopping me before I stepped out. "Promise me something. Promise you'll stay out of this. That you'll let the po —me handle it."

There it was again, his distrust of the police.

"Bella, I'm going to fix this. I promise. I'll keep you safe. Everything will go back to how it was." His voice firm in his vow.

Even though his sincerity leaked out, it wasn't enough. "How? What's going on?" I could feel the indecision pouring from him.

He shook his head, let go of my arm, and stepped back into his apartment, and said, before he closed the door, "Stay safe."

CHAPTER THIRTEEN

Bella

Sitting in Dean's truck outside Leonard's apartment, I filled Dean in on my conversation with Leonard. "What do you think it all means?"

"I'm not sure." Dean stared out his window.

My irritation at being held at arm's length, again, came out in my harsh response. "Don't do that. Don't withhold information because of...whatever bullshit excuse you, Alex, and Trent fall back on."

He reached out and cupped my face, turning me to him. "I'm not, Bella. I honestly don't know what it all means, but I think you're right. Everything and everyone—then and now—are somehow connected, and your friend knows how."

I wanted to jump at his words. To believe after all these years he finally believed *some* of what I'd been saying about the accident. But I squashed it before I carelessly gobbled up misplaced faith. Instead I focused on Leonard. "He's never not talked to me. Why won't he now? What happened that night between everyone that he can't tell me?" I couldn't stop the tears that pooled in my eyes.

Dean kissed my forehead. "I'm sorry."

"I'm so done with people saying that. Stop saying sorry and just tell me." I growled, doing nothing to hide my frustration or anger.

"You're cute when you're mad." Dean had the nerve to chuckle.

I banged my fist on his thigh. "I'm not being cute. I'm serious, and I'm h..." Hurt that everyone I trusted didn't trust me.

"I'm sor..." He stopped when he saw the icy look on my face. "I'm not keeping anything from you. I don't know what it all means."

But he made it clear he wouldn't tell me everything either. I moved back to my side of the truck. "Please take me back to my SUV." I just wanted to go home. To get away.

I felt Dean staring at me, but I didn't look back.

"Do you have anywhere to be?" he asked.

"I just want to go home, Dean," I muttered, beyond hurt by everyone's supposed need to protect me. It's not that I minded their need to protect me. It was basked in their love. What I minded was the fact they ignored me in the entire equation.

"Yeah, but do you want to follow Leonard with me first?" Dean started his truck.

I swung my head to him. "Follow him? He's going to the hospital. I told you that."

"Wanna bet on it?" His smirk was branded in confidence.

"How do you know he's not going to the hospital?" I stared at him.

"Watch and learn." He pointed out his windshield.

I followed Dean's finger and saw Leonard rushing to get into his car. "Maybe the hospital called him with some news?"

Dean shook his head.

It was clear Dean had lots of practicing following people. He didn't tailgate Leonard. Dean kept so much distance between Leonard and us, I thought we'd lost him a few times. More importantly, it was clear Leonard wasn't going to the hospital. Nope, he went nowhere near the hospital.

"How did you know?" I looked over at Dean.

"Nothing solid, but he seemed short in his answers to you. He avoided answering them, and then he rushed you out." He glanced over at me before returning his attention to the road. "Mostly, it was you."

"Me?"

"You said it yourself. Leonard's never not talked to you, so why isn't he now?" He shrugged. "Add it all together, and I had a hunch he was up to something."

"So, a lot of your PI skills are similar to my vet skills—hunches?" I asked.

"Logical hunches that are based on evidence." He winked.

"Uh-huh."

"Am I out of the doghouse now?" He had a hopeful look on his face.

"Is that the only reason you brought me with you? To save face?" I tried to hide the pain his words brought me.

He sobered. "No. I brought you because you know Leonard better than anyone, and you're right. We don't tell you a lot, but that doesn't mean you can't know some." He reached out and squeezed my knee. "But you can't go off on your own, Bella. You're not a trained professional."

Hope fluttered in my chest. Dean was trusting me. Did this mean that Dean was finally believing me about the accident? That my brain injury wasn't playing *more* tricks on me.

"Thanks." I awkwardly grabbed the hand on my knee. I mean it was Dean's hand on my knee. Did I pat it like he was good boy? Dumb. Or did I keep my hand on his? So he could never, ever remove it?

He flipped his hand and squeezed mine, and butterflies took flight in my stomach for a whole other reason.

Dean Cannon was holding my hand!

"Do me a favor?" He interrupted my internal party.

I cleared my throat before asking, "What's that?"

"Make sure Margie knows she can't pimp us out."

I burst out laughing.

"I'm not being funny, Bella." Dean's rumble bounced inside the truck.

Which set my laughter off more.

He tried to remove his hand, but I held on, doing my best to gain control of my laughter. Wiping away the tears from the corner of my eyes, I replied, "I'll make sure Margie knows she can't sell you guys for her benefit."

He didn't answer.

"I'm sorry, Dean. It was mean to laugh at your request." I couldn't help the laughter that bubbled out of me, which I quickly swallowed when he glared at me. "Oh, come on! You know it's funny!"

"With Margie, you can never be too sure."

I sobered instantly. Dean was right. Margie could have been joking, but you couldn't be too sure. "I'll make sure she knows."

"Much appreciated."

I looked out the window at the scenery passing us by. "Leonard's heading to Granite Creek. What's he going there for?"

Dean hesitated. "We're about to find out."

I squeezed his hand and pushed for an answer. "Why do *you* think he's going to Granite Creek?"

"Emily Castor."

"Really?" I clutched his hand tighter.

He shrugged. "It's a guess, Bella, but with everyone involved, she's the only one who lives in Granite Creek. It's an easy enough leap."

"But why her? I would have thought he would have approached Blake. It was Blake Bruce argued with at Coop's. It was Blake Bruce beat up in high school. How does Emily fit in with all of that?" Did she play a part in my parents' death?

"Maybe it was a lovers' triangle. What if Bruce and Blake both liked Emily, but she only reciprocated with Blake? Bruce wasn't a great loser then or now."

"Yeah, but they were still arguing about it now? Really? Do guys hold onto that kind of thing this long? I mean, I can see a girl doing that, but a guy?" Even I could hear the disbelief in my voice. "Besides, Leonard stated Bruce met someone, so if that's true, then it wouldn't make sense for Bruce to confront Blake about Emily, again, after all these years."

Dean nodded. "Yeah, but I bet she's a part of whatever reason Bruce and Richard beat Blake the night of the Winter Formal. If it's not a lovers' triangle, then what is it?"

"No clue, but I'm pretty sure we can assume whatever happened the night of the Winter Formal, Emily, Richard, Bruce, and Blake are all a part of it," I concluded. "What about my accident? Leonard seemed..." I shrugged. "I don't know. He seemed concerned I remembered more."

"Yeah, I'm wondering about that too. Maybe whatever happened at the Winter Formal spilled over to your accident." Dean's voice lowered in contemplation.

Chills raked over me. "Do you think? I don't remember any of them." Except I remembered a woman's voice that night and two shadows. Could it be Emily? But who had been the other shadow? Bruce? Richard? Was that why Leonard seemed worried? Because Bruce was somehow involved? But how did it relate to Bruce's attack, and why now?

Dean squeezed my hand. "We'll find out soon enough."

His comment made it seem as if he was trying to find an answer. That he wasn't blowing my thoughts off about that night off like he usually did. Or circling everything back to my head injury.

But where did that leave me? With more questions.

I watched the neighborhoods pass us by as we slowed down. "Do you know where Emily lives in Granite Creek? I mean, if we get there, will you know it's her?"

"No, but I can find out. I just need an address," Dean admitted.

Dean stopped the truck at the corner where Leonard turned.

"Why aren't you turning?" I asked.

He nodded down the street. "Leonard stopped. I want to see which house he goes to before we drive by." Dean's concentration was absorbed by Leonard's actions.

I was glad Dean was driving. If it'd been me, I would have driven past Leonard as he got out of his car.

"Doesn't it look suspicious that we're just sitting here though?" I looked around but didn't see anyone.

"There's no one around, and Leonard is more focused on what he's doing than his surroundings." Dean's focus on Leonard didn't waver.

Sure enough, Leonard tunnel-visioned his way toward a house. Not even bothering to check his surroundings, which made me wonder how many times someone might have possibly been watching me. Goosebumps erupted over my arms as I thought back to the night I'd run and my subconscious alerted me to something. I shivered at the thought. What if someone really had been there and my subconscious was telling me to be careful? It was too easy for people to focus on themselves and not pay attention to their surroundings.

Dean drove forward a second later. "You okay?" His question letting me know while I thought he was preoccupied by Leonard he was still very much aware of me.

"Yeah." I promised myself I'd pay more attention to my surroundings. To not stay in my little Bella bubble.

He glanced at me. "You sure? You looked spooked."

Taking a deep breath, I admitted the truth, "I was just thinking of how easy it is for someone to watch someone else. We're always so focused on ourselves that we never really know when something bad is about to happen until it's too late."

"Something happen to you, Bella?" Dean turned at the next block.

I hesitated. I didn't know for sure, and I didn't want to make something out of nothing. "It's nothing."

He kissed my knuckles in reassurance. "Try me. I'll let you know if it's nothing."

"Do you remember the night you found me outside Alex's house?" I asked.

He nodded.

"Well, when I was leaving to jog, I heard...something. I don't know what it was, but it stopped me in my tracks. I didn't see anything and didn't hear anything after that. I thought it was just my mind playing tricks with me after the nightmare, so I brushed it off." I shrugged trying to downplay all of it. "But, after seeing what you just did, I'm wondering if there was someone there. After all, when we came back, my bulb wasn't working when I know—*know* it was working when I left." Okay, now I was scaring myself.

Dean didn't answer right away. "First thing first. When we drive by the house, memorize the number, but don't make it obvious you're looking. Then after we're out of the way, I'll address your concerns."

"I can do that." We drove by, and I did my best to behave like a regular person. I grabbed my cell and murmured, "Got it. I'll text it to you."

"Thanks, Bella. I'll dig into whoever he went to see once we get back to my office. Now, as for your observation. Always go with your gut. If your gut is telling you someone or something was off when you were leaving, believe it. Don't second guess yourself."

"That's not helping me." He only cemented my building fear.

He pulled my hand to his thigh. "I know, but it's true. I haven't received the tapes for your apartment complex yet. I'll give them another call today. Until then, take extra precautions coming and going anywhere. I know Alex drilled security into you—use it. Don't live in fear but be aware. Be safe."

It was the *be safe* that triggered my memory of Leonard's last comments to me. "You just reminded me. When I was leaving Leonard's apartment, he told me he was going to keep me safe, and then he told me to stay safe. If this is all related to Bruce, Blake, and Emily, then why am I in danger? Why would he say that to me? Is it because it's related to my accident?" I chilled at the realization that I might be involved in some unknown danger related to *Bruce*? Bruce of all people.

"Bella, I don't know, but I'm going to find out. I promise no harm will come to you." The adamant steel in his voice topped off the unyielding look on his face.

And while that left a warm and squishy feeling inside me I knew he couldn't guarantee that. My dad had been the most cautious driver I knew, and he'd still swerved and crashed. So while Dean might be an expert in uncovering truths and saving people from disastrous situations, there was no way he could stop someone from coming after me.

"Thanks, Dean. That means a lot." It did. I wasn't a client, and he didn't have to take time from his paying customers to help me. He could just hand it off to the police or my brother and be done with it. "Are you going to tell Alex and Trent everything that happened today?"

"Yeah. They might want you to come in for a statement later on down the road." Dean quickly glimpsed at me before turning his attention back to his driving.

"I know the drill." This was potentially related to Bruce's attack, an open police investigation, so of course Alex would make sure all his *t*'s were crossed, and *i*'s dotted.

"You don't sound happy about it."

I turned fully in my seat to look at him. "It's just—how do I fit into this? How does the night of the Winter Formal fit into this? The only thing of relevance for me that night was my accident and parents' death. Bruce, Blake, Emily, and Leonard were not a part of that night for me. I definitely wasn't involved in Blake or Bruce's attacks. So, why am I now even peripherally involved? I'm not happy about any of it, and I'm certainly not happy Alex has to be the one to find out. He's been through enough too without having to investigate our parents' deaths." I paused. "And, I can't help but wonder if my friendship with Leonard was all ruse for whatever happened that night. Is that why he's worried about my memories coming back?"

Dean pulled in behind his office and shut his truck off. "First off, don't jump to any conclusions. We don't know anything for certain, and I can't believe I'm going to say this, but don't write Leonard off yet. I've seen the way you two are together, and there's no way he's that good of an actor to pull off that many years of friendship with you. The man genuinely values you as a friend—it's clear as day. As for Alex— there's no one more qualified to get to the bottom of this than him. Besides, he has Trent and me to help him navigate through all of it, and you know he wouldn't hand this off to anybody else."

I stared into Dean's eyes and knew he was right. The right people were working this. The answers would be here soon enough. I had enough on my plate, and I didn't need to add more worry to it.

I took a deep breath and answered Dean, "I'll do my best not to jump to conclusions, and I'll be more patient with all of it." I unbuckled and put my hand on the door handle before continuing, "This is me being patient—let's get inside so I can find out who Leonard visited."

I didn't wait for his response and exited his truck with the sound of his laughter following me.

I walked into his office. "Hey, Lily. How ya doing?"

"Not bad, and you?" Lily's smile was more friendly than professional.

"Same."

"Lily, anything urgent I need to know about?" Dean propelled me forward with a hand on my lower back.

To distract myself from the feel of his hand on me, I chastised him. "Hi, Lily. It's nice to see you, Lily. How are you doing, Lily? Those are all appropriate greetings, not, 'What you got for me?'"

Lily giggled but answered Dean, "Nothing urgent."

Dean ignored me and raised his eyebrows at Lily, who sobered.

"Don't be a grouch to her." I elbowed him even though it didn't faze him.

Lily's giggles followed us into his office.

Dean's hand fell as he moved around his desk. "Have a seat while I get this going."

I'd never really been in his office before, so I didn't take a seat. Instead, I wandered around it, taking it fully in. This opportunity might never present itself to me again, so I was going to memorize every corner for my dreams later. "Thanks, but I'm going to snoop instead."

One corner of his mouth lifted at my nosiness.

He had several shelves around the room with various awards, books, and knickknacks throughout. Everything was masculine in sight. Dark wood colors, black accents, and nothing frilly or flowery in view.

"Who's your decorator?" Whoever it was without a doubt knew Dean was the no-nonsense type. It flowed with the appeal of his home as well.

"Some woman I hired." Dean's reply was distracted as he focused on his computer.

"Did she do your house too?"

"Uh-huh."

Not able to help myself, I walked around his desk to look at his computer. "Do you have a secret database full of people's information?"

"If I did and I told you, it wouldn't be secret anymore." His response was dry and filled with humor.

"Huh." I peered over his shoulder at the screen. "Does that mean what I think it means?"

Dean twirled his chair to me and pulled me between his legs before he answered, "Yeah. Leonard visited Emily."

"Now what? Do we go back and talk with Emily?" He rubbed circles into my waist with his thumbs as I stared down at him. I pushed how that felt to the side.

"*We* don't do anything. I'll let Alex and Trent know what we found out today, and *they* will do what they do." Dean's tone brooked no argument.

Putting my hands on his shoulders, I looked into his eyes. "Okay." It was challenging to focus with his hands on me.

He used his leverage on my waist to pull me closer. "That was too easy."

Dean had thick, lush eyelashes. Women paid good money for eyelashes like his. I wondered what product he used to maintain their health. Then I looked down at his full lips when they tipped up at the edges. The slight pink of them glistened when his tongue made a quick appearance.

"Fuck it," had barely left his lips when he pulled me down for an earth-shattering kiss.

Those pink bitable lips were firm but soft. My hands snaked up his neck into his silky hair, and I fisted it, holding him to me. Slicking my tongue across his sinful lips, I moaned. Heaven didn't do his taste justice.

Dean's arms banded around me as he dominated my mouth with his tongue—feasting on me.

I weakened with need, and I pressed myself fully against him. My breasts were heavy with desire, and my core was wet, ready for Dean. The sounds I made were indecipherable with hunger as I rubbed my body against him.

One hand slid down my back to grasp my ass as Dean deepened our kiss, but didn't stop until his fingers slid across the very private seam of my pants. I flowed, readying myself for more.

"Dean, I've got Mrs. Hanson on line one." Lily's voice interrupted us.

He reluctantly pulled back, and the heat in his eyes scorched me.

"I'll be with her in a minute," Dean growled—and I felt that every-where—at Lily.

I stared at him, thinking *tell Mrs. Hanson you'll call her back. We are not done.*

"Sure thing," Lily replied.

"As much as I don't want to stop, I have to take this call." The heat stamped on his features and pressed against my stomach made it impossible to disbelieve him.

Pulling myself together, I nodded because my voice was not yet operational.

"I don't like the idea of you walking by yourself. Be safe walking to Margie's shop from your car. Stay alert," he ordered.

My desire disappeared as I remembered there was possible danger lurking out there.

Even with the reminder of danger I still had to clear my throat before I answered Dean. "I will."

He stood. "Shit, I do not like this."

"I'll be fine. I'm just going home. I'll be fine."

I wasn't sure if I was reassuring him or me.

CHAPTER FOURTEEN

Dean

BELLA'S TASTE WAS A DRUG. IT'D SLIP IN UNANNOUNCED AND EACH time it reared up, my focus would splinter. It's as if the berry-flavored lip balm she wore refused to leave, grasping at my lips and tongue in its determination to stay with me. To torture me.

Now, sitting at my desk a day later, I could still hear the sounds Bella had made as we'd kissed. I blamed my lack of will on Bella. Her scent, her closeness, her curiosity—it all intrigued me. Top it off with her not keeping her distance—the case and me—I fell.

"Alex and Trent are here to see you." Lily's voice cut through my thoughts.

"Thanks, Lily. Send them back."

Alex and Trent strolled into my office and took a seat across from me.

"Hey, Dean. How's it going?" Trent asked.

"Not bad." A lie. Bella was driving me nuts. "And you guys?"

"Frustrated but same." Trent ran his hand over his almost bald head.

Alex rested his hands on the arm of the chair and muttered, "Same."

"I take it you guys haven't had a break in the case yet?"

"Nothing solid," Trent replied.

"I've sent the evidence from the night of Bella's accident to the lab but I haven't heard anything back yet. What about you?" I heard curiosity in Alex's voice. "Is that what you wanted to talk to me about yesterday?"

"Yeah, and thanks for calling me back." My words dripped in sarcasm.

"Sorry, I got caught up with something at the station." A one-finger salute accompanied Alex's apology.

"Well, while you two were sitting on your thumbs"—they flipped me off—"I found out some interesting information that might be of use to you two. The first part, Alex, you're not going to like."

He scrunched his eyes in trepidation. "What?"

"Bella *is* investigating Bruce's attack. I caught her leaving Ava King's office yesterday. She grilled Ava on Blake's history with Bruce and Richard, the night of the Winter Formal and last week's Coop's incident."

"Shit." Alex cursed. "I knew she wasn't going to leave this alone, but dammit if I didn't wish she would. Especially now knowing she might've been right all these years."

"It gets worse," I continued.

Alex braced. "How?"

"After she visited Ava, she went to see Leonard."

Alex bolted forward in his seat. "Shit!"

"Shit!" Trent echoed.

And they didn't even know the rest of it. "That's not the bad part."

Alex ran his hands through his hair. "Jesus, what could be worse?"

It was my turn to brace. Once Alex found out I'd taken her with me to follow Leonard, he'd lose his shit. Or more. "We followed Leonard after."

Trent's mouth opened and closed in shock while Alex stared at me in disbelief. I could see them processing my words.

Alex was finally able to speak. "You...both...followed Leonard? Together?"

"Yeah."

He leaned back—almost plopped back—in his chair. "Why don't you start at the fucking beginning?" He very much ordered me.

I'd expected his response. He never wanted Bella near any type of danger, especially after the accident. "After Ava's encounter, I found her at Margie's ordering coffee for Leonard. Instead of letting her go by herself, I tagged along to make sure she stayed safe." No need to tell him it wasn't the only reason I hung around her. "By the way, you two should be prepared for Margie to pull you both into helping her retire early."

"She wants us to help her retire early? How are we supposed to do that? Buy more coffee?" Trent's eyebrows shot down.

"No, she wants to pimp you both out." My cheeks creased from the wide-ass smile on my face.

Alex dropped his head. "Goddamn, Margie." His tone stated it all —belief, acceptance, and horror.

"She does know we are officers of the law?" Trent asked for confirmation.

"Yeah, Bella reminded her and the customers asking for your bios." I didn't even try to hide my laughter.

Alex's head shot up. "Customers were asking for our bios?"

"More like...measurements."

"Fucking Margie. I don't know whether to laugh or arrest her," Trent's deep voice held an edge of humor followed by disbelief.

"She might like handcuffs," I helped.

Alex shook his head. "Can we get back to Leonard? Now?"

Still smiling, I decided to give them a break. "Sure. I waited outside while Bella spoke with Leonard. By the time she came back and reported everything they discussed or didn't, I decided to wait and see where he went. I couldn't do that and take Bella back. I'd miss him if I did, and it's a good thing I didn't."

"What tipped you off that you needed to stick around?" Trent asked.

I leaned my forearms on my desk. "Leonard evaded a lot of Bella's questions which, according to her, is something he's never done. She stated he's pretty open with her but was tight-lipped with anything related to Bruce, Blake, the Winter Formal—essentially all of it. That alone adds weight to Richard's ramblings at Shackles. To top it off, he rushed her out of his apartment so he could get back to Bruce." I tamped down my anger and continued, "Something he's never done before either according to Bella, and he left her confused and wondering what the fuck was going on. By the way he came running out of his apartment, I knew he wasn't in a rush to see Bruce."

"She's right. Leonard falls short of the worship Bella shrine, but he's always been open, upfront, and careful with her," Alex said. "Where'd he go?"

"He went to see Emily Castor."

They asked in unison, "Emily Castor?"

I nodded. "The one and only."

"Well, I didn't see that coming," Alex murmured.

"Neither did I." Trent agreed.

"I don't think any of us did," I added. "Castor isn't going to like any of us pulling his daughter into this."

Trent nodded. "He's already riding our ass over Bruce's case. This is going to tip him over the edge." His voice spiked with irritation.

"Let me know if you want me to make an approach. Castor's rules do not bind me," I offered.

"We might take you up on that, but for now, let's hold off. We don't know what her involvement is or why Leonard went to see her. We might be better off if we come at her soft, showing solidarity to the uniform and her father." Trent's experience showing in his thoughtful but decisive response.

"Let me know if you change your mind."

They both gave me chin lifts in acknowledgment.

"But, breaking this down, Leonard unknowingly linked Bruce's attack to Blake, Emily, and the Winter Formal but isn't telling anyone what that connection is? Did he mention Richard? Shackles? They were thick as thieves," Alex surmised.

"Pretty much, and he got itchy when Bella told him she remembered more from the accident. Something about a woman and shadows. Bella said he couldn't understand why after ten years they couldn't leave everything alone." Uneasiness spread through me.

Alex's face suffused with surprise. "Bella remembers more of the accident?"

"I think she was going to tell you the other night, but then Bruce got attacked and your guys' plans got side railed. Talk about being side-tracked, Leonard mentioned Bruce had a new lady friend who made him want to change his stripes. I'm assuming she's not local since she hasn't visited him at the hospital."

"We haven't found any evidence of Bruce having a lady friend." Alex squinted in concentration. "I'll take another look and see what I can find. I'll also pull any files we have on Blake's attack back in high school and see if there is any connection to Bruce or Emily. Both Blake and Emily left Feldspar at the same time but supposedly for two different reasons."

"What about asking Castor about Emily's departure?" I asked.

Alex shook his head. "I don't think so. Back then, Castor swept a lot of Emily's indiscretions under the rug. I think I'll uncover more if he stays in the dark for now regarding his daughter." He paused. "She never got back to me when I left a message for her the other day. I think a visit is unavoidable now. It's the only way to get an accurate read on her and the situation before we possibly get our asses handed to us by Castor."

"He's always been overprotective of Emily after his wife died. I don't see him not getting upset," I added.

Trent rubbed a hand over his face. "Fuck, this just gets better and better."

"Yeah, I don't feel for either of you, but since you'll be handling the Castor family, do you want me to follow up on Blake? See if he'll give me anything to go on?" I volunteered.

"No, we hit him up yesterday. If you come at him today, he might feel cornered. Besides, I want to get my head wrapped around all of this a bit before we make any more moves." He sighed. "I also need to figure out to how to tell Bella she was right all these years. Fuck, that's going to kill."

I could see the wheels spinning in Alex's head.

"You do realize Bella isn't going to let this drop?" I asked him. "Even though Leonard upset her yesterday, she feels she owes him for being there for her all these years. For believing in her theories about that night when we didn't. Even if he peripherally had something to do with it. She's not going away."

Alex raked his hand over his face. "I know." He sighed. "I wish she would listen to me for once and stay out of trouble."

My blood heated as I remembered Leonard stating he would keep Bella safe. "Speaking of trouble, Leonard also mentioned he was going to do whatever he had to do to keep Bella safe. What I want to know is how does Bruce getting attacked translate to keeping Bella safe? But what worries me more is I think she might indeed be in danger." I relayed what Bella had mentioned about sensing something or someone outside her apartment the night of the anniversary. "So what does Bella have to do with Blake getting beat up back in high school and Bruce getting beat up now?"

Alex sat up. "I have no fucking clue, but I will. Bella will come to no harm." His brotherly protective instincts were front and center.

In that, we agreed.

No one would fucking touch Bella.

CHAPTER FIFTEEN

Bella

I FILLED ROCKY IN ON MY CONVERSATION WITH LEONARD AND HOW Dean and I had followed him to Emily's house yesterday on my way to the gym. I even mentioned how I think Dean might actually now believe me regarding the accident. She wasn't able to see how any of lined up either but vowed we'd ask Blake a few questions in between him kicking our ass into health.

Until we actually started exercising, and I realized Blake was into torture.

Running was a whole different ballgame than working out at a gym. Yeah, as a vet I lifted heavy animals occasionally, but it wasn't a consistent, repetitive motion as, say, boosting a hefty weight over my head or lunging across a room. What Blake had Rocky, Emma, Ava, and me doing as a part of our free trial was just plain cruel. I mean, was he trying to scare us away?

"So, your brother is hot. I won't debate that. Buuttt, what he's putting us through on our first day?" I stopped to catch my breath. "That's just plain mean."

Rocky paused in the middle of her rope snakes and narrowed her eyes at Ava. "What did you do to piss him off?"

Ava grunted through her kettlebell squat before replying, "Nothing! I told you he's serious about health."

Rocky dropped the ropes and bent at her waist. "Emma, this is all your fault."

Emma didn't stop her pedaling on the stationary bike but threw her hands up. "How is this my fault?"

Making it back to them after my last round of lunges *with* kettle-bells, I replied, "Well, for one, you didn't say one word when we got here. You could have at least batted your eyelashes at Blake when he asked if we wanted a full-body routine. Instead, you ducked your head and let Rocky answer." I chugged some water before continuing. "What did you think would happen? You ignored the guy, dented his ego, and now he's torturing us because of it."

"For the umpteenth time, Blake does not like me!" Emma yelled.

"I wouldn't say that." Blake's baritone sounded from behind Emma.

Emma blanched as her eyes widened. "Please tell me he's not behind me."

The smile Rocky aimed at Emma was evil in payback. "No can do." She dropped the mask of civility and aimed her next comment to Blake. "If that were true, you wouldn't be torturing her friends. I hate to break it to you, but this"—Rocky pointed to the ropes—"does not gain you favor."

Blake ignored Rocky, coming up beside Emma. "I'd like to think Emma would want a man who had her friends' best interest at heart."

Ava's gagging caused giggles to escape me.

"I'm going to be sick. My brother flirting. Save me." Ava bent over so she couldn't see Blake anymore.

"I don't flirt." His attention never diverted from Emma.

"Oh, he's good," Rocky murmured. "Emma, you gotta give him a spin."

Blake's smile was slow and wicked as poor Emma's face flamed a deep red.

"Rocky!" I chided.

She wasn't the least bit worried. "What?" Looking Blake up and down, Rocky turned back to me. "He's hot and is undoubtedly interested in Emma. I didn't say she had to jump him on the first date or even the second, but there's nothing wrong with her going out with him either."

I sighed. "Tact, Rocky, tact."

"I think I'm going to be sick."

We all turned to Ava, whose coloring now favored the milky white clouds in the sky.

I rushed forward. "What's wrong? You look a little pale. Sit down." I turned to Rocky, "Go get her some water."

Ava sat and looked up at me. "I don't know how but the mental image of Emma riding my brother flashed through my brain." She swallowed. "I can't get it out of my head. Make it go away." The horror the images conjured made her voice soft with dread.

Emma giggled, and Rocky followed her. Then me. Our laughter rang through the gym as Ava continued to look like she was going to hurl. Blake, on the other hand, stood with his head bent, smiling at his feet.

"It's not funny. Imagine Alex doing the dirty with Rocky." Ava begged me to understand.

My laughter died at her words. "Eew, that's gross."

Rocky winked at Ava. "I've imagined it."

"What?"

Rocky shrugged, not bothered by the fact she'd just admitted to imagining have sex with my brother. "Alex is hot. He's always been hot, so of course, I imagined it. Why do you think I always wanted to come over after school to study at your house? You had some serious eye candy at your house."

"I'm taking it by the turn of the conversation you ladies are finished with your workout?" Blake's tone brooked no argument.

"I sure am. I didn't sign up for this when I said I wanted to spy on you and Emma," Ava piped up.

Blake's dark eyebrow popped up at Ava's words.

"Me too. I'm out," Rocky agreed.

"I'd rather work out than continue that conversation." I pointedly gave Rocky a shut-up look.

Emma giggled again. "I'm out. I need to be able to stand tomorrow and right now I can barely sit. My legs are jelly."

"Jelly's good, but I'd rather have chocolate." Rocky looked at Blake, hopeful. "Do you have any chocolate here?"

"It's a gym, Rocky. Of course, he doesn't have chocolate here." I turned to Blake. "I'd apologize for my friend's behavior, but I don't think it'd matter."

"No—"

"He can have chocolate in the back," Rocky interrupted Blake. "I don't expect him to have it out on the main exercise floor. He doesn't strike me as that sadistic of a health nut. Although, that'd be a great exercise slash business plan. For every set you complete, you get a piece of chocolate. You should think about that. I know I'd join for that reward."

Sighing, I bent my head. "Only Rocky."

"Umm, I'm gonna agree with Rocky. Or a glass of wine. Can you imagine all the women who'd join knowing after each set they got to indulge in chocolate? Wine?" Ava piped in.

"How are we related?" Blake's face was a mask of horror.

"You ladies almost got it right," Emma joined in. "You need to add something spicy to blend in with the chocolate and wine. You need to indulge all of our savory senses."

Blake's heated stare zeroed in on Emma.

"Clearly, the visual senses are taken care of." Rocky waved at Blake.

Ava gagged and Rocky threw her hands up in the air. "It's not my fault both of your brothers are hot."

Pulling in a deep breath, I tried to maneuver our conversation to the primary purpose of my visit. "Please, enough about hot brothers." Well, at least in that way. "I like that Blake came back to help reinvigorate the gym and our community. It's great for our younger generation to have positive role models."

Blake tensed subtly.

Rocky plopped to the ground. "I'd agree with you, but after the torture he just put us through, I'm not sure teenagers are going to be willing to return for an encore performance."

"You do remember we have a *one-week* pass?" I smirked at Rocky. It was the least payback I could muster for her earlier Alex-sex comments.

"Shit, I forgot."

Blake chuckled. "Don't worry, Rocky. I'll save the best for last for you." Blake's brotherly smile grew as Rocky paled. "But, all joking aside, besides the MMA coaching, we've set up a youth center in the back where we rotate between the trainers and focus on different physical and mental activities for the teenagers. All of it's meant to engage not just their physical forms but their intelligence as well, with a mandated one-hour homework session, tutors included, before the fun begins." He sobered. "We're in the middle of negotiations to add onto the gym for a rec room and shelter. There are kids out there who don't have a positive home environment, or one at all, that could use a safe place to eat, shower, and just be out of the harsh outside environment."

"That's a really nice thing you're doing," Emma said gently. "Most people who come from a good home don't always think to offer those types of services to disadvantaged youths."

"A good home life can sometimes hide other not-so-positive elements." Blake's solemn response wasn't lost on Emma or the rest of us.

My heart ached, and any other time I wouldn't have approached the comment, but I needed answers, and he'd just given me a way in. "Kids can be mean, especially in high school. I'm glad you're giving them a safe place to hang out."

Blake's eyes cut to Ava.

Ava threw her hands up in surrender. "I didn't tell her anything she wouldn't have figured out on her own, and something tells me you two should talk."

"What did you say your name was?" Blake's demeanor didn't change but I had the feeling he was assessing me.

Since he wasn't the one who had checked us in, I wasn't quite sure how he would respond. "Isabella Hall."

"As in Detective Hall's younger sister?" he asked.

"The one and only." I tried for humor and fell short at Blake's continued unsmiling face. Changing tactics, I went for straightforward. "I take it you're not a fan of his?"

Please, dear Lord, tell me Alex never arrested him.

"I don't know him."

I pushed through the awkward silence. "So, I'm trying to help my friend, Leonard, figure out what happened to his brother, Bruce, who was recently beaten."

Blake remained unmoved.

"And he mentioned you and Bruce had a falling out last week at Coop's and back in high school."

Still nothing.

"Not that I think you have anything to do with what happened to Bruce, but I thought maybe you could tell me about it so I can help Leonard get some closure." And possibly learn how I fit into all of this.

"What makes you think the two are connected?" His tone was composed and even.

"Something Leonard said made me think there might be a connection."

"I'm sorry, but I can't help you." Blake turned to Ava. "Don't forget to stop by the store before heading home." He glanced at us as he made his way out. "Ladies, I hope today's workout was what you were looking for. If you have any other questions, please don't hesitate to reach out to a staff member."

Shit. This wasn't going as planned. "Wait! Sorry! Shit!" I needed him to stop and fill in some blanks. I continued speaking to his retreating back, "Look, I am genuinely sorry Bruce and Richard were major dicks to you. Truly I am, but Leonard also made it seem like I was somehow a part of Bruce's attack and whatever happened at the Winter Formal. Would you mind answering a few questions? Please."

I took Blake not moving as a sign to continue. "Why was the night of the Winter Formal different? I mean, what happened that night that pushed Bruce and Richard to be more than their usual jerky selves? Was Emily involved? Me? Did I do something?" Anything?

He looked over his shoulder at me. "You had nothing to do with it. Be careful of the friends you keep." Blake didn't wait for my response and left.

What did he mean? I looked at my friends. "I don't understand."

Ava stared after her brother. "I don't either."

"I didn't mean to upset your brother. I was hoping he'd be able to tell me something to help."

"It's not over yet. You just met him, and you're asking him to open old wounds. Give him some time." Rocky came over and gave me a side hug.

"Yeah, you're right." But the defeat was kicking in as my avenues for answers narrowed.

"I know what will make this better." Emma's soft voice broke into my melancholy. "Chocolate cream pie!"

We burst out laughing.

CHAPTER SIXTEEN

Bella

"WE'LL GET INTO THE FACT YOU WENT TO THE HOSPITAL AFTER THE gym without me later, but for now, what you're telling me is Nurse Booby wouldn't even let you near Bruce's doorway *and* Leonard didn't even come out to say hi?" Rocky held her beer halfway to her mouth.

Leave it to Rocky to zone in on that one tidbit. I swallowed my beer before I answered. "Yup, that's what I'm saying."

"What the fuck?" Rocky hissed.

I shook my head. "I don't know, but I do know I'm working my way past understanding to being annoyed."

"Fuck annoyed. I don't care if Leonard's brother is fighting for his life. You weren't asking him to go out and tie one on. *You* are *not* just anybody. *You're* Bella. *His* Bella. What the fuck?"

I got up to recycle my empty beer bottle and grab myself another. "Rocky..."

"Don't *Rocky* me. There's no reason, no excuse for Leonard's behavior."

I joined her back on the couch. "You're too hard on him. His brother *is* fighting for his life." I paused to remember the time when I had been in the hospital fighting for my own life. "I'm willing to give him some passes during this time. It's not easy."

Rocky shoulder-bumped me. "You're such a softy, but the two are not the same. More importantly, neither you nor Alex were ever that rude. All I'm saying, Bella, is you're not someone out to get the latest bit of gossip. You're returning the favor, in a way, that Leonard showed you back then. If anyone understands what he is going through, it would be you, and he *knows* it. So why isn't he taking you up on it?"

I took another gulp of my beer. "I don't know, but I'm not going to let Leonard avoid telling me much longer." I leaned into her and changed the subject. "What are you going to do about Kevin? The zoning maps I found at City Hall the other day didn't help clarify the zoning issue."

"Well, I'm going to make an official appointment to meet with the vice mayor in his very professional office." She wriggled her eyebrows. "I will also be taking my very professional attorney with me."

"I thought you said Mr. Quincy was visiting his granddaughter back east?" I asked.

Rocky nodded. "He is, but Mr. Lively is assisting me while Mr. Quincy is gone. I'm hoping after the meeting, Mr. Lively will tell Kevin to stick all this crap up his ass, and that will be enough of a deterrent for Kevin."

Rocky held her beer up for a salute.

I stared at it a second. "I hate to break it to you, Rocky, but I have a feeling Kevin isn't going to be easily deterred."

"I hear you, and after him RSVPing on *our* behalf to the mayor's birthday celebration, I might be getting a little bit annoyed with his determination." She drank more of her beer, yanking the bottle back to continue her tirade. "The thing is, he holds the cards right now with the zoning committee, so I have to play nice. For a while anyway." Another, this one long, and definitely annoyed pull from the bottle. "Meanwhile, I'm going to keep my nose in my work, and let me tell you, the DeVille is not a hardship."

Rocky came off confident, but when it came to the shop she'd inherited from her father, she worried about doing right by him. So with Kevin pulling this crap, the fear of losing her father's legacy gnawed on her confidence and kept her up at night.

"I still can't believe Kevin RSVP'd for the both of you for the mayor's birthday. It's like he lives in his own little world and plots us in it where he sees fit. It's just all a tad disconcerting." I took a swig from the bottle before I continued, "This DeVille—you really like this one." It wasn't a question, but it was.

"Yeah, she's a beauty. There's something about her I can't put my finger on. Or maybe it's because of what she means to the family." Rocky sighed. "The way her owner talked about her. I don't think he realizes, but she's more than a part of their father's history. She's a part of them all. It's a beautiful thing."

"Remember, you have to give her back when the job is done, so don't get too attached." Knowing Rocky, if she genuinely wanted the DeVille, she'd find a way to buy it out from the owner. Or be grumpy for weeks.

She took another swig of her beer and muttered, "Don't be such a party pooper."

I burst out laughing.

"Talk about downers, you'll never believe who reached out to me today wanting to know if I'd go to the mayor's birthday with him."

Swallowing my laughter, I thought about it. "Well, I can't say Kevin because he already RSVP'd for you." Shrugging, I asked, "Who else is creeping after you?"

Rocky lifted her empty beer bottle. "I don't think I brought enough beer, and we can't switch to liquor now."

"Wow, that bad, huh?"

Her face said it all but the "Carson" she muttered cemented it.

I almost spewed my beer. "Again? You're kidding me."

"I wish I was. Carson thinks he can be nice to me, and I'll forgive him and take him back." Rocky spoke over her shoulder as she went to the fridge.

"Wow. What is it with guys being completely oblivious?" I stared at Rocky as she sat next to me with another beer. "We have work tomorrow," I reminded her.

"One of the perks of owning your own business—you can make your own hours." A smug smile spread across Rocky's face.

I pointed my bottle at her. "Shut up and drink."

The mischievous smile she aimed at me had me bracing at what could possibly come out of her smart-mouth. "Enough about my horrible love life. What's up with Dean and you?"

Wasn't that the million-dollar question? "I have no idea." And I honestly didn't.

"All these years, he never once made a move, and now in the last few days, he's made some very delicious moves."

I gulped more beer as my brain puzzled through Dean.

"Besides everything going on around you, what's changed?" Rocky tilted her head to the side in curiosity.

I started to shake my head but stopped when the room moved with me too. "Nothing, and I can't believe what's going on is enough for him to want anything private with me. Besides, if he wanted to protect me, he wouldn't have to maneuver getting into my pants to do that." Although I wouldn't complain.

"Or maybe he's just using this latest fiasco as a way to finally get in your pants." Rocky's eyebrows shot up in hope.

"Um, Rocky? Dean doesn't need an excuse to get in any woman's pants. All he has to do is breathe." No joke. The man was sex on two legs.

"That explains it," Rocky solemnly responded.

"Explains what?"

"Why I've been orgasming every time I'm around Dean. He's breathing."

I shouldn't have been surprised by Rocky's comment—she was always saying something that made me shake my head—but I was, and because I was, I sucked in a surprised breath and choked on my own damn saliva.

Shit!

It burned my throat and hurt like a mother.

No matter the amount of coughing I did the pain didn't ease and I felt like any second I was going to see little bits of me that I didn't want to see spewing out of my mouth.

Rocky, casual as can be, leaned over, pounded on my back and continued as if I wasn't hacking a lung up. "Now that we know the reason you want Dean is because of his Breathing Orgasms we can move onto all the other stuff swirling around the attack."

I finally sucked in several calming breaths and shot Rocky a murderous glare as we leaned back on the couch.

"It's looking more and more like everything originates with the beat down Bruce and Richard gave Blake at the Winter Formal. But where does Emily fit into it? Leonard admitted Bruce never dated her, and Ava didn't mention Emily." I leaned my head back on my couch. "And I remembered more about the accident. Did I tell you about the woman I heard screaming in my dreams? She's with someone else at the top of the road."

"No! What'd she say? Can you see her? What about the other person? Do you recognize either of them?" Rocky fired questions at me.

"She yells, *'Oh my God! What are you doing?'* That's all I got. Nothing else."

"It's more than you had before, even if it still leaves you with more questions." Rocky chewed her bottom lip.

I scrunched my nose at Rocky. More questions. Great.

"I also didn't tell you but I think the guys are coming around to my views regarding that night. Dean's made some comments that have me thinking they or at least Dean might finally believe me."

Her eyebrows shot up to her hairline. "Whoa. That's huge."

"Yeah." And it was.

She bumped my shoulder. "Go get the box, and we'll go over it again."

The box was my collection of articles and reports related to the accident. Over the years, whenever I hit a particularly rough spot, Rocky or Leonard and I'd pull out the box and dissect the night all over again. Usually, I left with the same unanswered questions as well as the sense I was *not* responsible for my parents' death, no matter how much my subconscious tried to dump it on me.

I hoped tonight would be different and that I'd find something to close all the gaps in my memory.

Rocky met me at my kitchen table. "All right, let's put it all up on the wall in chronological order. Then we can inspect it."

Article after article went up on the wall, and when we pinned the last one, Rocky and I stepped back to admire our work.

Rocky scanned the articles. "Okay, so looking at them now after learning about Blake, Bruce, Richard, and Emily, does anything stand out to you?"

"No, but I don't have anything up there about them. I didn't know to look for them."

Rocky nudged me. "Go get your laptop. Let's put them up there now and see if anything dislodges in your memory."

Hope bubbled inside me. Maybe I was finally going to find some-thing to help me find out why my dad had swerved that night. Although I never imagined I'd find the answers through Bruce, Richard, Blake, or Emily. What could they possibly know?

After I returned with my laptop, Rocky and I sat at my kitchen table and scoured the internet for any information we could find. The same articles I'd discovered the other day popped up, setting my printer went to work. Article after article joined my already-crowded wall.

Rocky and I, with fresh beers in hand, examined our handiwork.

"Anything?" I asked Rocky because I sure didn't spot anything.

Rocky shot forward, wobbly but vertical, and pointed with her beer bottle to the taped articles. "What do you see?"

"Articles."

Rocky slowly walked closer to the wall. "Smartass."

I joined Rocky at the wall. "Nope. I got a smart brain. My ass is just cute."

Slightly waving back and forth, Rocky pointed to the wall again. "What if some of the tire marks and vehicle debris are from another vehicle involved in *your* accident and not from an earlier accident, like everyone is claiming? I mean, you're dreaming of hearing someone yelling so why not?"

"How are we supposed to figure that out?" I stared at the pictures trying to decipher if the broken car parts belonged to my parents' car.

"Ask your brother. He should be able to pull the official police report and check into it. And you mentioned it seems like Dean, Alex, and Trent were talking like your original thoughts about the accident weren't so far off anymore." She pointed at the wall again. "Besides, what does *Small Talk's* picture of Richard's accident look like?"

"Like a car accident." I squinted at the picture, hoping it would come into focus.

Rocky faced me. "Look closely. Where was Richard's accident?"

I leaned closer to the new article about Richard and saw what Rocky was trying to tell me. "Oh shit," I whispered.

"Oh, shit is right."

I clenched my hand around the bottle slipping through my fingers. "How is that possible?" I whispered.

"Do you think it's a message? To you? Alex? I mean, what are the chances someone would have a car crash in the same spot as you all these years later?"

I stared at the picture. "I don't think it's a coincidence, but I have no clue what it means."

Then I jumped along with my heart because there was a loud pop and crash right outside my door.

With my hand to my heart, I turned stiltedly to Rocky.

"What was that?" Rocky's eyes widened.

I shook my head warily. "I don't know."

Slowly, we moved toward my front door as if expecting something to jump out at us.

I peeked through my peephole and thought Dean would be proud I did, only to see darkness. With the flick of my left wrist, I turned the outside light on. Or I tried to. Nothing happened. A few more flicks and still darkness prevailed.

I turned to Rocky. "The light won't come on."

"I thought you said Dean replaced it?" Rocky asked.

"He did."

"So how won't it turn on?"

"Because the light is not coming on," I stated the obvious. "It's completely dark out there."

"Are you sure? Maybe the connection didn't click." She walked over and flipped the switch several times. "Anything?"

I peeked through peep and shook my head.

"Okay, let's not get our panties in a bunch."

I giggled.

"He probably didn't twist it all the way on. Let's check before we make any assumptions." Rocky pushed passed me and opened the front door before I protested.

Mr. Stewart stood at his open door, his light illuminating our joint entryway, again looking down at the broken glass.

"Miss Hall, what is the meaning of this?"

"I don't know, Mr. Stewart."

Mr. Stewart looked down at the glass and back at me. Right before my eyes, his face hardened. "Are you in some sort of trouble, Miss Hall?"

Great, if Mr. Stewart thought I was going to be more trouble, he would probably convene the apartment board to have me removed. I did not need to find a new home amid all the drama swirling around me.

"I'm sure it's nothing, Mr. Stewart. I'll sweep this"—I pointed to the broken glass—"up right away."

I yanked on Rocky's arm and closed the front door behind us.

We stood there, staring at each other when Rocky burst out laughing.

Between her laughter, she breathed, "Did you see the look on his face?" More giggles. "He looked like he wanted to kick some booty." Rocky fell to the ground, holding her midsection. "I would love to see that!" She lay in a ball, laughing on my floor.

I stared down at my friend. "I've never seen Mr. Stewart like that. I just hope he doesn't call management again."

Rocky turned to her back and attempted to control her laughter. "I have a feeling if he calls management, it will be because he wants tighter security. Not to have you removed."

"Are we talking about the same Mr. Stewart? The one who complained about me parking a quarter of an inch *on* the white line?" I asked as I gathered my broom and dustpan.

Rocky pulled herself together and pushed off the floor. "Yes, the one and only. Whatever his predilections are, the man was *not* happy you were in danger. And Mr. Stewart is a good guy. Just a *little* stringent in his ways."

"Yeah." I opened the door on a smile to Rocky.

"Do you have any idea what broke it? I don't see any rocks. Nothing stands out." Rocky twisted her head as she surveyed the ground.

I swept the last bits of glass into the dustpan. "No, and there's nothing here besides the lightbulb fragments."

We were securely back in my locked apartment when Rocky, with her hands on hips, stated, "The end of the bulb was still screwed in so whoever broke it had to be standing at your door. That's pretty bold."

"Uh, huh." I returned after depositing the cleaning supplies in the storage closet.

Rocky's face grew more serious. "Hear me out, Bella. You know I'm not the first person to go running to my brother for help." Rocky ignored my snort. "But I think you should call Alex and let him know about the broken lightbulb. Whatever is going on, the person who broke your light, again, is confident enough to do it *with* you *and* me *in* the apartment."

"I know you're right, but I don't wanna," I grumbled.

"Oh, stop your whining, you big baby." Rocky handed me my cell phone.

I deadpanned, "You mean you, right?"

"*La la la. I don't hear you.*"

I stared down at the phone. I knew the right thing to do was to call Alex, but once I did, he would go all big brother slash cop overprotective on me. He would insist I not stay in my apartment by myself, and he would do his best to get me to stay with him.

"You're stalling."

"More like delaying the call."

"Potato, po-tah-to."

"Hear me out. Alex, Trent, and Dean get together all the time when they're working on a case. I bet my favorite stethoscope they're together tonight."

"Okay, they do that all the time."

"Yes, they do, but today we're going to use it to our advantage.

We're going to search Alex's house and see if we can't find out anything about Bruce's case and anything new about my accident. I mean if Dean is starting to believe me then that means Alex must too since they work most things together. So I'm guessing Alex must know something we don't. Maybe whatever he's uncovered in his investigation can help us piece things together."

Rocky sat up. "Oh, I like this. We get to break into a cop's house, but how do we know they're not at Alex's house?"

"Umm...because it won't work if they are," I countered.

Rocky stared at me like I had grown a second head. "Ookkaaayyy. That doesn't help us but, whatever. Let's go break into a cop's house."

Okay, I had a key.

CHAPTER SEVENTEEN

Bella

Since Rocky and I had been drinking, we decided to limit our criminal activities to just the one and walked to Alex's house. On a good day, it'd take me fifteen minutes at a solid pace. Tonight, well, between our chatter, tripping, and giggles, we made it in thirty.

I should have known better than to try to get one past Alex, Trent, and Dean. All the years of failed attempts should have been proof enough tonight would not be an exception.

And, if I'd been paying attention all those years, I wouldn't be lying face-down on the floor barely inside Alex's front door with someone's knee in my back.

Rocky was in the same position as me but smooshed against the wall next to the closed door.

And my heart wouldn't be trying to beat its way out of my chest.

On top of that, I wouldn't be in fear of losing my arms, which were securely clutched behind me and forced up toward the ceiling.

Or in fear of peeing myself. Or puking.

Instead, I'd've pulled myself together and used all the years of Alex,

Trent, and Dean training me defensive maneuvers to get myself out of this predicament.

I didn't.

Because I was terrified out of my ever-loving mind and maybe just a *little* bit buzzed.

Then the pressure on my arms and back relaxed. "Bella?"

"Rocky?" The person holding Rocky spoke at the same time.

"Yes?"

The pressure on my arms completely relaxed, the knee on my back lifted, and I was up on my feet in two seconds flat, staring at Dean.

"What the fuck are you doing here?" Dean growled.

Eek! How did I answer that?

"You might want to turn the lights on now that they've blown any fucking decorum of stealth."

Blinking at the sudden light, I saw Trent standing next to Rocky.

"We didn't blow any stealth. We weren't being stealthy." I looked down at the gun hanging loosely from Trent's left hand. "Why do you have your gun drawn?"

Rocky glanced at Trent's hand and smacked his arm. "Did you have that against my back? What were you thinking? You could have hurt me!"

"You broke into a police officer's house. What did you expect?" Trent questioned Rocky's common sense.

"Not to be pinned against a wall held at gunpoint!"

He stared at her.

"What the fuck are you two doing here?" Dean's voice vibrated with anger.

Turning my attention back to Dean, I wasn't quite sure the best way to answer him. I didn't necessarily want to admit I was planning on snooping through Alex's house for clues on an active police case. They had all made it clear they wanted me to stay out of it.

I turned my head away from Dean, hoping for inspiration from something in Alex's house. It took my brain a second to register what I saw. Alex's home looked like someone had let loose a room full of kindergarteners, unsupervised. Alex's coffee table was flipped over, magazines tossed across the carpet, and the couch cushions laid at odd angles. The potted plants I'd given Alex for his birthday last year were broken, and the soil slung about. Anything hanging in Alex's house was either crooked or tossed several feet away from its original spot.

I pushed past Dean. "Oh my God! What happened?"

Dean grabbed my arm. "Bella, dammit! Answer me—what the fuck are you doing here?"

Rocky spoke before me, "Holy shit balls. Alex needs some tips in tidiness."

Trent actually growled.

I ignored them all and looked over my shoulder at Dean. "Do you think that matters right now?" I looked at the wrecked room. "I mean, look at that." I gestured at our thrashed surroundings to make my point.

Rocky, undeterred, continued as if I hadn't spoken. "No, really. I don't remember Alex being such a slob. I mean, I know he's hot and all but if he ever wants to get lucky, he's going to have to clean up a *little* bit. I mean, there's only so much a girl can ignore and then hot or not, we're steppin'." She looked up at Trent. "Please tell me you pick up a little more than this. It would be such a shame to know being hot meant guys thought they had free rein to be slobs." Not leaving Dean out, she asked, "What about you? Tell me you don't live in a pigsty." She shook her head. "Never mind, Bella already told me about your house." She glanced back up at Trent. "Well?"

"Rocky! Stop calling my brother hot! That's gross."

Her eyebrows shot up. "What? It's true even if he is your brother."

"Enough." Dean snapped, "Tell me what the fuck you two are doing here? At night."

Our mouths clamped shut with an audible snap.

Dean used his leverage and pulled me against him. "Uh, huh. Spill."

We were full frontal with his arms holding me. My brain was receiving all kinds of signals. All of them rioting to press closer, wrap my arms and legs around him and take a small nibble. Hell, who was I kidding? I wanted to devour him.

A slight shake ran through my body as Dean gently jostled me. "Bella?"

I mentally gave myself a shake and sucked in a breath. "We planned to visit Alex."

"Are you drunk?" Dean focused on me.

"No." I wasn't. Highly tipsy, yes. Drunk, no.

"We don't have time for this." Trent stepped toward us. "Bella, you're going to have to call Alex to ask him what's up with his house. When you don't reach him, you're going to call me to report what you found at Alex's house. Do you got all that?"

I stared at Trent. *When* I didn't reach him, not *if*. He *knew* I wouldn't get a hold of Alex.

Looking back, I surveyed the room once more. This wasn't Alex being a slob. Something he categorically wasn't. No, this was something else.

Poof! I wasn't tipsy anymore. Oh no, I was something else. Fear rushed through me. This couldn't be happening. I'd already lost my parents. I couldn't lose Alex too.

I pushed past everyone out the back door and threw up on Alex's planters. I bucked with each heave, expelling my dinner and beer. Dean pulled my hair back and rubbed small circles on my back. My body continued to revolt even though my stomach was empty, and the only thing left to expel was air.

Dean held a water bottle in front of my face. "Bella, swirl this, spit and then take a small sip."

I didn't argue with him and did as I was told.

"Better?" he asked.

I stood back up and looked at Dean. "No." Alex was gone.

"Hey. Don't go there." The gentleness of his tone paired with his soft expression dented my resolve to pull myself together.

"Dean..." It was a plea and a question.

He pulled me close. "We don't know what happened, but we're going to fucking find out. Until then, I need you to do what we say. Can you do that for me?"

I nodded because I was incapable of speech.

A small smile graced Dean's not-too-happy mouth. "That's my girl. Trent and I are going to disappear. When we leave you, you need to call Alex first, then Trent, then me. After all that, I need you just to wait until we get here. Do you got that?"

"Yes." I whispered.

Rocky's delayed response indicated her cottoning onto the situation. "Alex isn't a slob, is he?"

I WAS STANDING in Alex's front yard, giving my statement to Detective Donny Markson about how I'd found Alex's home a mess. Rocky was a few feet away, giving her account to Trent. It wasn't like I was new to police work—I'd been through something similar ten years ago when my parents died. Question after question. Did I remember anything? Why had my dad swerved? Had I seen an animal? Lights? Had my parents been fighting? And so on.

And this time, I had the same answers. No, I didn't know anything. No, Alex hadn't answered when I'd called. Ditto to how I had no clue where he could be. He was always either working, home, or at Coop's, and no, I didn't know if he was dating anyone. No, I didn't see anyone when I got here.

I was doing all I could not to panic. It was a repeat of ten years ago, and I desperately prayed Alex didn't come to the same ending as our parents. Was he missing because he was investigating Bruce's attack? Or was it because he believed me and was now investigating our parents' death?

It didn't help Leonard's words were playing havoc on me. Did he not trust *every* single person employed with Feldspar PD, or were there only a few? And who exactly did he not trust? Could I trust Donny, or were his questions based on ulterior motives?

Goosebumps covered my whole body, and I wasn't sure if it is from the cold night air or the fact that I was questioning Alex's coworkers.

I jumped when the sheriff placed his hand on my shoulder and scolded myself for letting my wayward thoughts get the better of me.

"I'm sorry, Bella. I didn't mean to scare you."

I shook my head, hoping it would help clear it. "It's okay. I'm a little on edge."

Donny gave me a sad smile.

"Bella, I wanted to let you know we're doing everything in our power in our search for Alex. We'll find him, don't you worry."

Sheriff Castor's reassurance did very little assure me. There wasn't any way I wasn't going to worry.

"Thank you, Sheriff."

He squeezed my shoulder, reminding me he hadn't let go and stepped in front of me. "I know you've answered Detective Markson's questions, but I hope you don't mind answering a few of mine."

After my parents' deaths, Sheriff Castor had visited me regularly, either to check to see if I remembered anything else about the accident or to just check in on my recovery. However, during my stay at GCH, the sheriff's visits had subsided until finally ceasing altogether. Not once during that time had I ever questioned the sheriff's motive for being there.

The combination of tonight's events launching my fears into overdrive and the possibility that I might genuinely lose Alex hampered my ability to determine if Sheriff Castor was genuine in his concern. So, I tried not to let the fact Sheriff Castor referred to Donny as *Detective Markson* and Alex as *Alex* not bother me. For now, I had to push it all aside and do whatever I could to find my brother.

Looking between Donny and the Sheriff, I replied, "Whatever it takes to find Alex."

"Do you know what Alex was working on before he left?"

Shouldn't you know what he's working on? "I'm assuming it was the Bruce Evans case."

His hand was still on my shoulder, and I really wanted to take a step back so he had to drop it.

"Why do you assume that?"

"Because I saw him at the hospital when I visited Leonard there the night Bruce was brought in."

"Ah, yes. You and Leonard are very close."

He stared at me, expecting an answer even though he hadn't asked a question.

Donny spoke up. "Did Leonard mention anything to you about Bruce's case?"

What could I tell them? Did the sheriff know Emily might be involved? "No." I wasn't technically lying. Leonard hadn't told me anything about the case. He'd just mentioned Bruce getting kicked out of Coop's.

Donny nodded.

"Bella, can you think of anything Alex could have been working on outside of work? Anything he didn't have official authorization to dig into?" Sheriff Castor squeezed my shoulder again.

"No."

"I know you want to protect your brother, but if you know anything he could be doing that isn't on the books, now isn't the time to withhold information." His eyes narrowed in a silent reminder that he was the authority here.

"Alex didn't talk to me about his cases." Even when I pestered him for a friend—say, Leonard, for example—he never gave up the goods. Not even if it possibly was about our parents.

Sheriff Castor opened his mouth to speak again when Dean slid his arm around my waist and pulled me into his side, effectively dislodging the Sheriff's hand.

Thank you, Dean.

My body trembled being pressed against Dean and my female parts quivered in delight. And hopeful expectation. Who knew Dean was the cure for the chills?

Donny looked between Dean and me and lowered his head to inspect the sidewalk, trying to hide his smile.

"It's late, and Bella's had a hard night. I'm going to take her home now. If you have any other questions for Bella, I'll bring her by the station tomorrow."

Sheriff Castor's face closed off, and anger touched his eyes. "Unfortunate as this all is, I'm not done questioning Bella."

Dean tensed beside me. Placing my hand on his stomach, I spoke before the situation deteriorated further. "Sheriff Castor, thank you for personally looking into this situation. However, I honestly don't know anything about—anything. Alex didn't share his work with me. He wasn't dating anyone that I know of. I don't know anything. If I did, I would tell you. Believe me, I wish I did. I wish I knew where Alex was. I wish…" I swallowed the tears clogging my throat. "I wish I knew."

"We're done. I'm taking Bella home now." Dean tightened his embrace.

"Hold up, Dean. I need a word with you all." Trent and Rocky walked over to us.

Once at our small huddle, Rocky held onto my hand.

Trent addressed Sheriff Castor. "Sir, with the recent events"—a nod toward Alex's house—"I'm going to have patrol do frequent drive-bys by Bella's."

Any warmth I had fled.

"Detective Cooper, I don't see the relevance or the need for spending the taxpayers' money."

"Bella has experienced some minor vandalism at her apartment that may or may not be related to tonight's incident. I'd like to keep an eye on her until we can determine the relevance." Trent didn't back down.

"Vandalism that was justified by teenage pranks. Not targeted at Bella," Sheriff Castor countered.

Rocky squeezed my hand, reminding me I was indeed a target. Clearing my throat, I broke into their debate. "Um, excuse me." Four sets of angry male eyes turned to me. "Tonight before Rocky and I came over here, while Rocky and I were"—I didn't want to admit we were reviewing my parents' case or Bruce's in front of Donny or the sheriff—"talking, we heard a crash outside my front door. We went outside to check out what caused the sound, and we found my front porch light busted." *Again.*

Dean's arm spasmed around me. "What the fuck?" he growled. "Why didn't you tell me?"

"Well, I was going to but then…" I looked over at Alex's house.

Rocky leaned against me, giving me her strength.

"I think we can say Bella is a target, and the drive-bys are relevant and necessary," Trent told the sheriff.

"If this is a matter regarding the budget, Sheriff, I'm pretty sure several of the guys are willing to keep an eye on Bella off the books.

Anything for Alex." The smile Donny aimed at me was a little too friendly. "And you, too, Bella."

Dean's already-tense body solidified next to me.

"Thanks, Donny." I ignored Donny's subtle overture.

"As soon as I return to the station, I'll reach out to the local federal bureau office regarding Alex's disappearance. That should help with any budget concerns you may have." Trent pushed the point with the sheriff.

"I can't authorize my men working off the books on an active case." It seemed Sheriff Castor didn't like his authority questioned. "However, since this is one of our own, I'll allow the rules to be bent slightly. I have a buddy who works with the local FBI, so I'll handle contacting them. You stay focused on picking through any clues you can find in Alex's house."

"Thank you, Sheriff." I knew the drive-bys wouldn't stop anyone if they wanted to get to me, but I hoped it would be a deterrent. And I wanted to believe with the FBI assistance that Trent and Dean would find Alex—soon.

"Now, I'm getting Bella out of this cold air. I'll bring her by the station tomorrow for any follow-up questions you may have." Dean was already turning us toward his truck, and since Rocky still held my hand, she came with us.

Trent stopped our progression. "Hold up. I'll take Rocky home and Dean, I need a word with you."

Rocky and I hugged.

"I love you, Bella," she whispered in my ear.

"Love you too, Rocky."

Dean tugged me away from Rocky and toward his truck as Trent led her toward his vehicle.

Dean grabbed a sweater from his back seat and wrapped it around me. He looked down at me and said, "Get the truck started, heat going, and I'll be back in a minute."

My body knew to listen to Dean. Who was I kidding? I was tired, cold, and scared. Someone had ransacked my brothers' house. He wasn't answering his phone. No one knew where he was, and I didn't know if I could trust the police department to find him.

Dean

"How's she doing?" Trent jerked his chin in the direction of my truck.

"She's scared. Rocky?"

"Same." Trent's gaze grew severe. "You're not going to like what I have to say, but I'm going to say it anyway."

I braced.

"This whole situation is more dangerous than we originally thought. Whoever this is, is willing to search a police officer's house and, more than likely, kidnap him as well. That tells me this has less to do with Bruce being a dick and getting an ass whoopin' and more to do with him and Alex looking into Alex's parents' accident. That's leaving a huge ass target on Bella and we both already knew Bella was going to interject herself when it came to Leonard."

I nodded again because everything he said was true.

"I didn't tell get the chance to tell you, but I spoke with the original officer on Bella's case and it seems like she may have been right all these years. He said that the skid marks were fresh and not from the earlier accident. On top of that, he said some of the vehicular debris wasn't congruent with the Hall's vehicles or the earlier accident. However, he was unable to document all this because he was advised against doing so. He wouldn't tell me who, but he did tell me to tread carefully."

"What the fuck?" The sour in my gut threatened to roll.

"Yeah, man. This is dark. And after tonight, there's no way in hell Bella is going to keep away." Trent's focus sharpened on me. "She needs a distraction big enough."

I went rigid as I stared at Trent. I knew where he was going with this, and I couldn't fucking believe he would.

I was already shaking my head when Trent continued, "There's only one distraction that will prevent Bella from meddling and keep her safe at the same time."

Fucking hell, I didn't want to hear this.

"You," he finished.

I bent my head, squeezing my neck, trying to ease the tension.

"It's been a few years of circling each other—it's time to put an end to it. Think of it this way, while keeping your eye on Bella, you'll be able to keep her safe and out of danger. You'll get firsthand knowledge of anything she'll attempt, therefore thwarting any action she may undertake."

I looked back up at Trent. "And what happens when this all ends and I walk away? What happens to Bella then?"

"Then you're a fucking fool," Trent muttered.

"Careful."

Trent stepped closer and bit out, "Fuck careful. We have one person dead, three if you count the parental Halls. One brutally attacked and on the verge of death and one of our close friends is missing. We have no fucking clue if *he's* been brutally attacked and on the verge death or if he's already dead." He sucked in a breath. "I love Bella like she's my sister, and that's one of the many reasons I'm even having this conversation with you. We can't afford any distractions, and we can't have Bella trying to find Alex on her own. It's not fucking safe."

I glanced back at Bella. She was huddled in my sweater, head against the side window, watching us. I didn't want to admit it, but Trent was right on all counts. Just with Leonard in the picture, she had been a small nuisance during the investigation. Now with Alex missing, she'd *be* the investigation. Any hope of saving Alex would be deterred by us having to manage Bella.

But Bella was in my truck, waiting for me.

I would make sure no harm came to Bella, and I would find Alex.

I just had to find a way that didn't involve Bella's heart.

Or my bed.

Turning back to Trent. "I'll keep her safe."

"What does that mean?" Trent didn't let it go.

"It means I'll do what it takes." Absolutely anything and everything.

He studied me for a minute before jerking his chin up.

"I'll drop Rocky off at her mom's house for the night. Later after I drop Dusty off at school, I'll swing by your office."

"Sounds good," I said as I turned toward my truck.

I opened the door when Bella spoke. "That looked pretty serious.

Everything okay?" She stopped because we both knew nothing was okay. "I mean, there's not more bad news?"

I glanced at Bella. More bad news? That depended on her definition of bad.

"Just more of the same."

I felt her eyes on me as we drove away from Alex's, but she didn't ask anything else.

I wasn't sure if that was good or bad.

CHAPTER EIGHTEEN

Bella

I HAD A MASSIVE HEADACHE. BY THE TIME DEAN AND I MADE IT TO my apartment, all I wanted was some aspirin and Alex home safe. Instead, my darkened entryway served as another reminder of what was at stake.

We stepped inside and the articles Rocky and I had pinned on the wall solidified the fact I did not want to be home alone tonight.

Making my way to the kitchen to grab the aspirin, I watched Dean scan the articles. "Dean?"

He turned to me. "Yeah?"

"I..." I swallowed to moisten my suddenly dry mouth. "If you don't mind, I was hoping I could stay with you tonight." I rushed before he could deny me. "I promise I won't get in your way, and it'll only be for tonight. It's just ..." Taking a deep breath, I admitted, "I'm scared, and I don't want to be alone tonight."

He made it to me, cupped my face as his face softened and his eyes warmed. "Absolutely, Bella."

"Thanks." My shoulders dropped as some of the tension left me.

"A lot's happened to you tonight. How are you doing?"

I wanted to admit I was scared out of my ever-loving mind. I was worried Alex wasn't alive, and if he was, someone might be doing horrible things to him. Or that I might be the last Hall alive, and maybe not for long, if the broken lights were a serious threat.

"I'm...okay. I'll be better once Alex gets back." An understatement.

Dean scanned my face. "We'll get him back, Bella. I promise."

Staring into his eyes, I believed Dean would do whatever it'd take to get Alex back to me.

"Go pack." He bent and kissed my forehead.

I pulled myself together and headed to gather my supplies.

Dean

I scanned the articles Bella had pinned on her wall, thinking Alex and Bella were like hound dogs with a scent when it came to the night of her parents' death. They had similar if not the same articles with the same notes in the margins and timelines. It may have taken Alex several long years to get to the same conclusion as Bella, but it was getting harder and harder to doubt that the accident that claimed their parents' lives wasn't an accident.

And the way she'd lined them up made it impossible to miss the obvious. Richard's accident mirrored hers. I pulled it down from her wall and placed it side-by-side next to the report regarding her parents' accident.

"Do you see it too?"

I turned to look at her. "When did you figure this out? Did you tell anyone?"

"Tonight, right before Rocky and I headed over to Alex's. We printed out the articles"—she pointed to the articles—"about Bruce, Blake, Emily, and Richard tonight. She's the only one who knows." She tilted her head. Her gorgeous silky hair fell to the side. "Do you think it's relevant?"

Fuck yeah, I did. "It's one hell of a coincidence."

She straightened her head. "We thought so too." She was staring at the clipping as if it would magically provide her with answers.

"I don't think I need to tell you this, but I'm going to say it anyway.

You need to be extra careful. Anywhere you go, you need to let me or Trent know, when you get there and when you're leaving." I put my hand up. "I know you're a big girl and can take care of yourself." I softened my voice but pushed, "But, Bella, Alex *is* trained, and *he's* missing. I don't want to take any chances with you."

"You're right." Tears gathered in her eyes before she pulled herself together again.

"You ready?" I nodded to the bag in her hand.

"Yeah." Her smile was a sad attempt at gratitude but it worked because it was Bella. "Thanks again, Dean."

"Any time." I pinned the article back on her wall.

For Bella, any*fucking*time.

Bella

My sleep was fitful and no matter how hard I tried to blank my mind, I couldn't. Instead, I spent my time staring at Dean's ceiling, replaying the last several hours and coming up with absolutely nothing. Instead of beating myself up more, I pulled one of Dean's flannel shirt over my PJs and headed down to make coffee.

Standing next to Dean's coffee pot, I forced all thoughts of Alex's possible torture out of my mind and onto what I needed to do to rescue Alex.

"Couldn't sleep?"

Jumping, I turned to see Dean in a navy thermal with some seriously comfy-looking flannel bottoms leaning against his kitchen island, arms crossed across his massive chest. From his bare feet to his sleep-mussed hair, he was yummy.

"Bella?"

My eyes shot up to his. "What?"

"You couldn't sleep?" The slightest curve of his lips.

Ah, yes, he had asked me that. "I slept a little." I tilted my head to the coffee. "I hope you don't mind, but since I couldn't sleep, I made some coffee. It's almost done. Do you want some?"

"Yeah, I'll take some."

He made it to me and reached behind me to grab the coffee cups.

But the only thing I saw was Dean's chest inches away from me. And the only thing I could think was, yes, he *did* smell better than coffee.

"You okay, Bella? You keep spacing out."

That depended on what he was referring to. My brother being kidnapped—no. Dean standing so close to me—hell yes.

Looking up into his piercing blue eyes, I answered, "I'm tired. Worried. And..." I bit my lip not quite sure how to ask him. "At your office, we...kissed..."

He pulled me into his arms. "As for our kiss? We'll explore that after we get Alex back."

Did he mean explore it as in continue where we left off or explore all the reasons why he thought we could never be?

"And we will get Alex back. I promise."

"I don't think I can handle it if we don't." I decided to ignore any possibilities between our future for the moment and focused on what's important—Alex.

"Hey, don't go there."

"I can't help it. You said it last night—Alex *is* a cop, and he *is* trained, but he was still taken. You saw his house; it was thrashed." I bit my lip to stop the tremble.

"Those are the same qualities that will save him. Trust in the fact your brother knows what he is doing. Trust your brother has every incentive to get back to you. Trust your brother." He pulled me closer to him. "Trust me to do what it takes to bring Alex back to you."

Laying my hands on his chest, I looked up into his eyes—to the man I trusted almost as much as Alex. Even if Dean wasn't going to be someone I spent the remaining years of my life with, I knew in my very soul he was someone I could trust to help me get Alex back. To run every avenue available to him in his search for Alex. That didn't mean it was natural to trust him with my fear, or I'd step aside while worked his ass off finding my brother.

"I know you'll do everything you can to find him. I mean it's pretty evident that Alex's disappearance was intentional. What if my brain wasn't messing with me but was only giving me bits and pieces of the truth and whoever took Alex is freaking out that I'm figuring it out and turning to my brother. My brother who is a police detective?" I took a deep breath and decided to give Dean more. "It's just after my parents died, Alex is all I have. He wasn't a dad, but he wasn't just my brother either. He's so much more." I shook my head, trying to clear it. "Without him, I wouldn't be whole."

"I get it. There's no fucking way I'm letting that happen to you again."

Seeing the resolution in his face, I knew he believed he would do just that.

"Do you think the FBI presence will scare the person into releasing Alex?" Unasked—would it cause more harm to come to Alex?

Dean scanned my face. "I don't think so. They were bold enough to kidnap a police officer. I think the FBI will be a nuisance for whoever has Alex, but not necessarily put the fear of God in them."

"That was my thought too." Because if they weren't worried about the local police searching for them, then having the FBI in the hunt wouldn't matter either. "So what does Alex have or know that this person is willing to face the wrath of the local police force, the federal bureau of investigation, and a serious badass private investigator?"

Dean's face remained blank, but his eyes held knowledge.

"What aren't you telling me?" My frustration seeped through.

He shook his head.

I pushed against Dean's chest as he tightened his grip on me.

"I only have assumptions at this point. Nothing concrete." He tried to appease me.

I fisted my hand on his chest and repeated, "What are your assumptions?"

He engulfed my fist in his. "Pretty much the same as yours. Bruce, Richard, Leonard, Blake, Emily, the Winter Formal, and your parents' death are intertwined. Nothing solid to connect the dots." He squeezed me. "Whatever it is and with Alex gone, I have to assume they might think you know something too."

"I know. I don't know what happened with any of them. I can't even remember what happened to cause the accident. I wish I knew something about any of it." I blew out a breath.

"You ready to tell me what you do remember? Maybe I can see something you can't."

Petting his chest with my free hand, I nodded, safe in his embrace. "You know most of it, but the night you found me running?" At his nod, I continued, "I woke up because I heard a woman screaming. In all the dreams I've had of that night, I've never heard anyone but... me." I took a deep breath. "I was in the car still at the bottom of the cliff. There were lights and she screamed, *'Oh my God! What are you doing?'* Then I woke up."

"Did you recognize the voice? Was it a young voice? Far away or close? Anything stick out to you about the voice?" He drew small circles on my back.

"No, she was far away. By the lights." I scrunched my eyes trying to remember. I pulled on the vague memory and grabbed Dean's biceps. "She was being pulled away by someone. Their silhouettes highlighted by the lights."

The slightest tension filled Dean's chest under my hands. "What?"

"The lights—you mentioned at the time you saw the looks on your parents' faces right before everything went to shit." At my nodded, he continued, "According to the report you guys went over the edge to the right. If your dad was trying to avoid a car coming right at you then he would have swerved to the left. Unless he was clipped from behind. Hence the lights highlighting their faces for you to see."

All the oxygen left me as I stared at Dean.

He didn't seem to notice my inability to breathe. "It also corroborates the fact you stated your mom yelled *'Watch out!'* right before impact. She was looking over her shoulder at you and must have seen the other vehicle getting too close."

Little black dots filled my vision.

Dean gave me a gentle shake and commanded, "Bella, breathe."

I sucked in a breath and focused on breathing while I let the connections Dean made penetrate my brain. "I was right all this time."

"Yes, you were. We're sorry we didn't take what you were saying more seriously. We're sorry we pushed it off as your brain injury. We're sorry we didn't believe you."

"Does that mean Alex believes me too? Trent?" I was still numb from this discovery.

"Yeah. We were connecting things after Richard's commentaries at

Shackles. We didn't and still don't have anything conclusive. Right now, it's just suppositions so I don't want you to get your hopes up."

"What did Richard say?" The article I read in *Small Talk* didn't mention anything about him mouthing off.

"Something about it's been ten years and Castor can't do anything. Not much but when you add it to everything else it seems like more."

"Do you think Richard was one of the people I saw that night?" Maybe that's why he thought he got away with it.

Dean shrugged. "I don't know. Were they the same height? Thin? Anything odd about their shapes?"

Hope lit up inside me. "No, she was shorter than the other person. Kind of like you and me. She was at his shoulders."

"What makes you think she was the shorter one being pulled away?" Dean asked.

I shrugged. "I don't know. It seems right. Besides, do you think a young guy could be hauled away by a woman? I don't want to step on stereotypes, but I know I would struggle to wrestle a guy away—and she was struggling—so it just seems right. The guy was stockier than her, and he didn't seem to notice she was struggling. He just pulled her away."

He squeezed me again. "We don't want to jump to conclusions. Maybe the taller person was helping her get away, and he had nothing to do with the accident or vice versa. We need to keep our minds open to all the possibilities, so we don't miss anything."

Relief and gratitude vied for dominance in my smile because without Dean's assistance I wasn't sure I'd be able to solve the mystery of ten years ago or find Alex now. "That's why people pay you the big bucks." My face slackened at the thought of Dean's fees. "I can't afford your rates. We'll have to come up with a payment plan or..."

My breath caught at the look on his face.

"You think I'd make you pay me? To help find Alex or to help you figure out what happened to your parents?"

I'd hurt him. I hadn't meant to. My only thought was he was losing hours to help Alex and me reminding me we weren't just anybody. We were family. I felt like such a bitch. "I'm so sorry, Dean. Of course, you wouldn't accept payment. I wasn't thinking. I was..." I stared down at his chest. "I wasn't thinking. I know we're family and"—I shook my head—"I'm sorry."

"Bella." Another squeeze to get my attention. "Stay with me."

Stay with Dean? My body melted, answering for me, knowing by the time we found Alex, I would be beyond saving. I'd never recuperate from the loss of my heart.

"You know I'd never accept payment from you, but it would make me feel more comfortable if you stayed with me. My house has better security than your apartment building. We can also pool our knowledge in solving all these mysteries and get Alex home." Dean bent to get eye level. "Plus, it'll make me feel better knowing you're safe throughout all of this." Quietly, he added, "I can't lose anyone else that I love."

I froze. *Dean loved me?* My heart kicked in hope.

"Bella, stay with me." Dean gently pleaded with me.

More of my weight relaxed into his embrace. "Okay. I'll stay with you while Alex is missing." Any more time and I'd never leave, and after Dean's earlier confession, I'd handle a little suffering while staying with him if it meant easing some of the hurt I'd caused.

The tension in Dean's body faded as he started rubbing my back again. Controlling the pleasure filling me from his touch by sheer will, I patted his chest—my hands were *on* his chest—and stated, "But I wouldn't feel right not helping out somehow." I raised my hand before he objected. "I know we're family, but I need to do more."

Bracing his hand on my upper back and fisting my hair in his other, Dean growled, "We'll find a way to work it out."

Oh, boy. I would *love* to work it out. I snaked my hands up his neck into his hair at the same time I raised up on my toes to get closer to his sinful mouth.

Dean didn't make me work that hard. His head descended and our mouths fused. Our kiss was slow, smooth, and detailed. We licked and sipped at each other, and I savored his taste. The feel of him in my hands and pressed against my body.

The length of his erection pulsed against my stomach, letting me know it too wanted attention. I whimpered at the thought of obliging and shamelessly rubbed against Dean.

Slowly, Dean pulled back and looked down at me. "Consider that part of the repayment."

Woohoo! A plan I wholeheartedly agreed with. "Okay." And can we continue with more?

Dean rubbed my lower lip with his thumb before he stepped back and released me. "Until then, we have work to do."

I'd be good with multitasking, but one look at Dean told me he wasn't.

"You're right." Forcing my lust back into its box, I saw the sunlight peeking through the slits in the shutters, reminding me I'd barely slept. Coffee was categorically necessary. "Let me grab some coffee, and then I'll call the clinic to let them know I won't be in for a few days. After that, I'll be good to go in thirty."

Dean stepped to my back and slid his cup next to mine. "Fill me up too."

How about you fill me instead?

Controlling my rioting hormones was problematic on a typical day, but with Dean so close, I was failing to maintain my grip.

Dean, it seemed, didn't have the same problem. He wrapped an arm around my waist. He bent down and murmured in my ear, "We'll find him."

The million-dollar question was, would Alex be alive when we did.

CHAPTER NINETEEN

Bella

"What do you mean Castor won't let you question Emily? According to Alex's notes, she's possibly the last person to see him." Dean's low and disagreeable growl vibrated through his truck.

My stomach clenched. Why would Sheriff Castor prevent Trent from following up on a lead?

Dean shoved his keys in the ignition and bit out, "Well, I don't have to fucking follow his rules, so I'm heading to Emily's now." The muscle in his jaw ticked as he listened to Trent. "There is no way I'm not approaching Emily. I don't give a fuck what Castor says. It's a viable lead, and if the fucking FBI were here, they'd be following it and telling Castor to shove it." Dean's mood deteriorated the more he listened. "I hear you, brother, but you're just going to have to deal. There's no fucking way I'm leaving any stone unturned or waiting to turn the fucking stone just because Castor wants to protect his daughter. You feel me?"

What happened to Castor telling me he was going to do everything he could to find Alex? My parents would have done everything to protect me, but they'd also taught me to step forward when a wrong was being done. They would have expected and been proud of me for helping the police. It didn't make sense with Castor's history of civic duty to hinder the investigation in this manner.

He jabbed the off button on his phone and threw it on the dash. "Fuck!"

"It doesn't make sense. Why doesn't the sheriff want Trent to contact Emily?" I asked what I thought was a really relevant question. "And does Trent have any news regarding Alex?"

Dean shoved his hand through his hair in frustration and dropped it on a growl. "According to Trent, Castor already spoke with Emily and he stated there isn't anything to follow-up on and if there are to be any further questions for his daughter they are to go through Castor and Castor only. To top it off, Castor's buddy with the feds states they're closing a major case right now and won't make it out for another couple of days." He shook his head. "And, no he doesn't have anything new regarding Alex."

I stared at Dean in disbelief before determination kicked in. "Then it's up to us. We have to find Alex on our own. We can't get Trent in trouble. He has to think about Dusty, so we have to do this."

His eyes roamed my face as the anger drained out of him. "I don't want you to get hurt."

"Me neither." I agreed with him as I pointed out the windshield. "Let's go see Emily."

"You undeniably went into the wrong profession." He shook his head once and started up the truck.

Let's hope whatever Dean saw in me made it so we found Alex.

EMILY'S HOUSE was small and neat. Her deep green grass was freshly cut with flower hedges lining the front of her home. It was your usual basic yard design that was well maintained. Her vibrant but straight-forward yard complemented the sea blue trim against the white house. All in all, Emily Castor's house was quaint.

Even the doorbell chime was whimsical.

"Be yourself, Bella. That's all it'll take." Dean eased some of my tension with a hand on my back.

"Hello?"

Emily looked like her picture on the Granite Creek Hospital website. She was short, maybe no more than five-five, thin but toned as evident by the muscles showcased by her tank top and shorts. Her hair was pulled high into a ponytail and her face makeup-free. Her warm light blue eyes assessed us warily but friendly—the complete opposite of her father.

"Hi. Emily Castor?" I sounded anxious even to me.

"Yes. How may I help you?" She glanced over her shoulder.

"I'm Isabella Hall, and this is Dean Cannon. I was hoping I could ask you a few questions."

Recognition shown in her eyes, quickly followed by panic she tried to hide.

Emily shook her head. "I'm kind of busy right now."

"I'm sincerely sorry to bother you, Emily. I promise we'll only take a few minutes of your time. It's important." No way was I giving up.

I could see Emily's struggle play out on her face before she finally stepped back to let us in. "Okay, just a few minutes."

Her front room was small, orderly, but comfortable. Soft colors accented the room, floral-covered pillows, and the scent of fresh flowers mingled with baked bread permeated the air. Emily clearly set up home here in her small house.

"You have a beautiful home."

She looked around her room, taking it in before she replied, "Thank you."

We stood there staring at each other and I wasn't sure how to proceed.

"Thank you for taking the time to speak with us. I promise we'll make this quick." *As soon as you give us all the information we're seeking, we'll be out of your hair and on our way to finding Alex.*

Emily smiled stiffly at me.

Dean continued where I left off. "I'm not sure if you've kept up with the news in Feldspar, but Bruce Evans was recently attacked and is in critical condition at Feldspar County Hospital."

"Yes, I did hear that." Uneasiness crossed Emily's face.

Dean continued, "And Richard Coleman was murdered almost two weeks ago."

Emily's face paled. "I thought it was ruled an accident?"

I hadn't pieced Richard's death as a part of all the mess flying around me even after Dean's comments last night.

"Officially." Dean's calm and professional demeanor highlighted Emily's emotional response to a subject she insisted she knew nothing of. "He had a lot to say the night before at Shackles when your dad arrived to oversee the officers on site."

"I'm sorry. I don't understand what this has to do with me." Emily clenched her hands together.

I wanted to call her a liar but knew it was a surefire way to be shown out the door.

"Richard mentioned there wasn't much your dad could do after ten years. That he was untouchable." Dean did his best to bait Emily.

"I still don't know what that has to do with me." Emily's unshed tears called bullshit on her denial.

As much as I wanted answers, I didn't see Dean's line of questioning giving us the answers we needed. At least not at this moment. So, I tried a different route. "When I visited Leonard at the hospital waiting for Bruce to get out of surgery, he mentioned you." Emily's fingers were bone-white from her death grip on them. "Since Leonard is my friend." Maybe. "I want to help him however I can. So here I am." Technically, helping Leonard *was* helping myself.

"Leonard's your friend?" Emily gasped in shock.

Hmm. I wanted to know why that was a surprise to her.

"Yes. We've been friends for about ten years." If Emily lost any more color, I was afraid she'd pass out. "And in those ten years, I can't remember Leonard ever mentioning you. Until recently when he mentioned he was glad you stayed away."

Emily braced a delicate hand on the back of the chair as she looked back at the hallway.

"Are you okay?"

Emily passing out wasn't going to get me the answers I needed.

"Yes. Yes, I'm fine," she lied.

My friendship with Leonard bothered Emily.

I decided to push for answers. "Leonard thinks you might know what the link is between why Bruce and Richard beat Blake up at the Winter Formal and why Bruce was recently attacked. Since Leonard is holding vigilant at Bruce's bedside, I was hoping you wouldn't mind talking to me." Aiming for sincerity wasn't difficult. "Anything you can tell me would be helpful." Anything that moved me closer to finding out who attacked Bruce, what caused my accident, and brought Alex home.

The oven timer buzzed before Emily responded.

"Excuse me. I need to get that."

Not waiting for a reply from us, she headed back to the kitchen.

Dean and I stood by the door, waiting.

I glanced at Dean. "I keep getting whiffs of Alex's cologne. Alex was here. I know it."

"Yeah." Dean snaked an arm around my shoulder, drawing me into his body.

"Shouldn't we be doing something? Like snooping?" I'd never interrogated someone before, so I didn't know if we were just supposed to wait.

Dean nodded. "Go the restroom."

"I don't need to use the restroom." I wanted to snoop.

Dean chuckled. "I know." He paused. "But Emily doesn't."

"Don't laugh! It's not like I do this for a living."

Still chuckling, he squeezed my shoulder. "Let's go."

I'd taken two steps toward the hallway when I noticed Dean was following me. "Why are you coming?"

"Because I know what I'm doing."

"Hmph." What else could I say? He was right, but I wasn't going to tell him.

The bathroom was the first room to our right. It was small, like the rest of Emily's house with soft grays and peach tones. It was no-frill with the usual bathroom accouterments and not much of anything else. Since I didn't need to use the bathroom, I flushed the toilet then turned the faucet on, letting the water run for a few seconds.

I shut the faucet and stepped back out, making my way to the kitchen, which was small, comfy, and organized like the rest of her house. But it wasn't the look of her kitchen that caught my eye. No, it was the two roasted cornish hen sitting on Emily's stove, the home-made loaf of bread on her countertop, and the potato salad Emily was in the middle of placing next to the bread.

"Wow. That looks and smells delicious."

She jumped before giving me a small smile. "Thanks."

Eying the array of food on her countertop, I commented, "I'm sorry. I must be interrupting your preparations for your dinner guest. I promise I'll only take a few more minutes of your time." Hopefully, in that time, Emily would give me something to go on.

Emily stopped her movements and looked over the small spread of food in her kitchen. "What exactly do you want to know, Miss Hall?" she asked.

"Bella is fine." Choosing to ignore the food, I pursued information relating to Alex. "As I mentioned earlier, Leonard thinks you might know something about the incidents surrounding Blake, Richard, and Bruce. Any little thing could help figure out what happened."

We stared at each other for the longest time; I assumed Emily wasn't going to answer.

"I don't know this Blake guy, but from what I remember, Richard and Bruce were good friends. Always did everything together." She paused in thought. "They were thick as thieves looking for the next rush." Her eyes cleared. "Most of the time, they were harmless."

Chills broke out on me. "Most of the time?" Was she referring to what they had done to Blake the night of the Winter Formal?

Emily gathered containers, breaking our connection. "I haven't spoken or seen either Richard or Bruce in ten years, Miss Hall. I'm not sure what I can tell you that would be of help."

"Why did you leave Feldspar?"

A stillness overcame Emily as her movements arrested.

I held my breath, waiting, hoping.

"My father, he..." A quick shake of her head as she continued to look at the counter. "My aunt was having health issues and required assistance. I stayed because I like it here. I like what I do." She turned fully to face me. "I help people through a difficult time in their lives. I'm a rape counselor at Granite Creek Hospital."

It wasn't a secret I'd been a patient at Granite Creek Hospital, but Emily hadn't been around when I was. It could just be a coincidence, or was Emily insinuating something else? Or was I just looking for more, hoping for more?

"That's a very noble profession."

"Yes, it is." Her words were quiet but resolute in their meaning.

My mind raced. "It seems both you and your father are dedicated servants to the community."

No response.

I carried on, "My brother, Alex, is as well. He's a detective who serves under your father." The slightest twitch of Emily's face made me hedge my next comment. "Oh! That's right; you already know that. He mentioned he was going to visit you the other day."

Emily's grip on the countertop whitened.

"And since you might have been the last person to see Alex before he went missing, I was hoping you'd tell me what time Alex left or if he said he was going somewhere else from here? What did he discuss with you? Maybe it can lead us to his next stop." I pushed for more information.

The color left Emily's face. "He..." She cleared her throat. "He's missing?"

"Yes, so anything you can tell me would be beneficial even if you don't think it's important." *Please give me something to find Alex.*

"He left my house around six last night." She hesitated. "He asked similar questions to yours. When was the last time I spoke with Bruce? Richard? Did I know Blake King? Did I know anything about why they beat him up at the Winter Formal? Did I know anything about your..."

I held my breath, waiting for her to finish. What about me did Alex want to know? Was it about the accident? And she just confirmed Alex had indeed been here yesterday. I knew I smelled his cologne, but

I needed to know where he'd gone from here. More importantly, I needed to know what he wanted to know.

"About my. . . ? Accident?" I pressured Emily.

Emily lost all her color and swayed back into the counter. "I'm sorry, Miss Hall, but I don't have any more time." She stepped past me on her way out of the kitchen.

I began panicking. I couldn't lose her now. "I'm sorry for keeping you, but I have one more question. Did Alex tell you where he was going from here?"

Emily's steps faltered, but she quickly picked up her pace. "I'm sorry, but I don't know anything."

She was slipping through my fingers. "Anything you remember might help."

Emily stopped at the front door. "I'm sorry, but I honestly don't know anything."

Dean was relaxing on the couch, looking as if he'd been waiting patiently for our return rather than snooping through Emily's home. He stood at the sight of us.

I bugged my eyes at him in frustration before I turned back to Emily, gambling my brother's life on my next words. "Well, what do you remember about Bruce? The Winter Formal? Because whatever is going on, Leonard believes you know something. Otherwise, he wouldn't have visited you the other day."

So stop fucking hiding and tell me.

"Leonard told you he came to see me?" Emily raised a shaky hand to her throat.

Shit, I didn't know which route to take. Tell Emily we'd followed Leonard to her house or lie. If she spoke with Leonard again, he would know I was here and asking questions.

Her whimsical doorbell sounded, saving me from replying.

"Excuse me." Emily opened the door, and outside stood Sheriff Castor.

Shit.

"Dad, what are you doing here?"

Great question.

Ignoring his daughter's question, Sheriff Castor addressed Dean and me. "Dean and Isabella, I didn't realize you were friends of Emily's." He leveled his stare on Emily as if expecting a response to his non-question.

Emily lifted her chin. "They were just leaving." She stared at her father, daring him to contradict her.

"Please don't leave on my account," Sheriff Castor replied.

"We *were* just leaving, but before we do, have you heard anything about Alex?" I stepped forward and asked the sheriff.

Between one breath and the next, the sheriff transformed from dutiful father to elected official. "Isabella, we're looking into all leads. As soon as we learn the whereabouts of your brother, we'll be in touch."

"Is there an official investigation into the whereabouts of Detective Hall?" Emily asked.

"Of course. I take the disappearance of any of my officers serious-ly," Sheriff Castor's solemn response was so patly official my teeth ached from the utter bullshit.

"Who is handling the investigation?" Emily's question raised the hair on my arms. Did her question have to do with Leonard's distrust of the police force? Did this mean Alex's disappearance wouldn't be hotly pursued by his brethren?

The sheriff stepped next to Emily, embracing her around the shoul-ders. "Emily, dear, please don't worry. My police officers are well trained to handle these types of things, but I am lending my years of experience to all involved."

Dean pulled me along as he exited. "Emily, we appreciate you taking the time to speak with us. Thank you for your time." A nod to the sheriff. "Sheriff."

Sheriff Castor merely watched us leave, but Emily wrapped her arms around herself and stared at the ground.

Inside Dean's truck, I looked back at the father and daughter, who hadn't moved from their position in her opened doorway. "Something is not right with them."

"Yeah." He pulled away from the curb.

I faced the front. "Emily knows more than she's saying."

"Yeah, and so does he."

Nausea rolled through me. I pressed a hand against my stomach. "I got that too, which means Emily is definitely involved because for a man who has devoted his life to helping people all of a sudden begin to hinder an investigation—even if minor—makes you wonder why. What would make a man like him do that?" My throat closed as the answer came to me. "To protect his daughter."

Dean cruised another block around Emily's home.

"Yeah."

"Why are we driving circles around Emily's neighborhood?"

He glanced at me before resuming his perusal of the neighborhood. "I'm looking for Alex's truck."

I hit the window button and gulped in the fresh air as everything hit me. "Do you think we'll find it? The sheriff would know to get rid of it."

"We cover all our bases, Bella."

And, hopefully by doing that we'd get closer to finding Alex.

CHAPTER TWENTY

Bella

ON OUR WAY BACK TO FELDSPAR, DEAN CALLED AND ASKED TRENT to meet us at Coop's so we could fill him in on our revelations. He said it'd be best if we weren't around other police officers.

Fear continued to slowly creep in because if the sheriff was covering for his daughter, the likelihood I'd find Alex alive significantly reduced. My frustration was at an all-time high, and I wanted to hit something.

Dean didn't miss my irritation. "Beating yourself up, trying to force it all together is only going to slow you down."

"It's right there. At my fingertips and I can't grasp it. What the heck am I missing?" I banged my fists on my knees.

He parked in front of Coop's and reached across to give me a gentle massage. "Let's get something to eat while we let our brains take us in the right direction. The more we force it, the more it will elude us."

"I don't think I can eat."

"Trust me, going without food will make it worse. If you want to help, eat. You need all your faculties working."

"Hmm." I didn't want to agree with him, but he knew using Alex as guilt would get me to do anything.

Coop's was packed as usual. We were enveloped in the chatter, pool balls colliding, and rock music blaring when we stepped in. Ignoring it all, Dean held my hand as he led us to the bar.

"I'm sorry to hear about Alex. Have you heard anything else? Trent tell you anything?" Brooke greeted us. "And I'm a little surprised to see you both in here."

I plopped down on the barstool before I replied, "No, but Trent's meeting us here, so I'm hoping he has something." Anything. "And, Dean says if we take our mind off of everything our brains will lead us in the right direction."

A knowing smile graced Brooke's face. "Trent tells me the same thing." She shrugged. "Not that I'd admit my brother is right, but it works most of the time."

"Well, I'm willing to give anything a try if it helps bring Alex home sooner. Even if it means agreeing with Dean."

Dean shook his head once, a small smile played on his face.

Brooke leaned on the bar. "How are you doing, Bella? Anything I can do for you?"

"I'm okay. Just focusing on finding Alex. I've texted him a few times and left him a few voice messages, but nothing."

She reached across the bar and squeezed my hand. "I know it's hard, but you know Trent and Dean are doing everything they can to find Alex. Besides, you know Alex is right now kicking someone's ass getting out of whatever predicament he's in."

Laughter bubbled out of me. "I can so totally see Alex, hands tied behind his back, kicking someone's ass while giving them his 'I am the authority' look."

Brooke and I giggled.

"If you girls are done gabbing, we'd like the club, fries, and two beers," Dean teasingly interrupted us. "And whatever Trent normally eats."

Brooke wiped a tear from her eye. "Coming right up." She bent over, grabbed two cold ones, and placed them in front of us before walking away to get our food.

"Feel better?" Dean rubbed circles on my lower back.

The more he rubbed, the more heat spread through me. My laughter slowly died, replaced by sexual longing.

"Mmm-hmm." I was undeniably feeling *something*.

I chugged my beer hoping to cool myself.

"You okay?" Dean's hand slid up to my neck, giving me a gentle squeeze.

Nope. No help.

I leaned forward, hoping to dislodge Dean's hand, and replied, "Yeah."

No luck in dislodgment. He continued to rub my neck, and I continued to fight the involuntary tremors his touch elicited.

"You sure you're okay? You're shivering." Dean's voice next to my ear shot straight between my legs. Everything was lighting up, raring to go.

Turning my head put Dean and me less than an inch apart. I focused on the small grooves on his unarguably sensual lips as I unconsciously licked my own. I knew for a fact Dean tasted better than the beer.

Not caring, I closed the gap between us and pressed my lips to his. The slightest movement to feel him. I sighed in pleasure.

Dean didn't waste the opportunity. His hand around my neck brought me closer as he took advantage of my mouth.

Yup, Dean definitely tasted better than beer.

"Two clubs with loaded fries." Brooke's barely restrained laughter stopped us from escalating our kiss. "And one steak sandwich."

Pulling back, I shot Brooke a thanks-a lot look.

"FYI, making out at the bar is not appropriate." Clearly Brooke wasn't bothered by my death glare.

"Not to mention you'd be cited for public indecency," Trent added as he sat next to us. "Thanks for the food, Brooke."

"Anytime, big brother." Brooke reached down below the bar and grabbed a bottled water for Trent. "How are you doing? Any news on Alex?"

"No." Trent twisted the cap off his water and downed it.

We waited for him to elaborate, and when he didn't, Brooke said, "Don't rush in spilling everything out. We can't keep up."

Her sarcasm wasn't missed.

Trent raised his eyebrows as he continued to chew, and like all little sisters, Brooke stuck her tongue out at him as she walked away. "Holler if you need anything else."

I swallowed my bite before I offered information, "Well, Dean and I had an interesting visit with Emily today. One where her dad showed up."

Trent lowered his sandwich at my words. "Shit. What'd he say?"

"Nothing, but his demeanor spoke volumes. The man controls his grown daughter, and she's afraid of him. She turned into herself when he made it clear he wasn't happy with her. It wasn't overt, but it was clear." Dean threw his napkin on his empty plate.

Trent took another bite and leaned back in his stool and mulled over the information Dean gave him.

"He's covering for her. There's no other explanation." No longer hungry, I dropped the remainder of my sandwich back on my plate and looked at Trent.

Trent looked over my head at Dean. "That makes things so much fucking harder."

"Which means Emily had some part in Bruce's attack, and her dad doesn't want it known. But she told us that she hadn't seen Bruce or Richard in ten years." The food in my stomach threatened to come back up as frustration seeped further into my pores.

"She also said she doesn't know who Blake is." Dean reached over and squeezed my neck.

Trent leaned his forearms on the bar top. "So if Emily hasn't seen Richard or Bruce in ten years and she doesn't know who Blake is, then why is Castor covering for her? And how would that make her involved in Richard's death, Bruce's attack, and Alex's disappearance?"

I leaned into Dean's touch. "Emily was a little wild back then, and the rumor through the grapevine was the sheriff covered many things up for her. Maybe it's a habit? Or maybe it's what a father does? Either way, Emily confirmed Alex was at her house asking about Richard, Bruce, Blake, and the Winter Formal." I took a deep breath. "Hear me out, guys. I think Bruce's attack is related to the beatdown he and Richard gave Blake at the Winter Formal. I also think that beatdown is related to Emily. She says she doesn't know Blake, but what if Blake saw or heard something that night that Bruce, Richard, and Emily didn't want him to talk about? Maybe Bruce and Richard took care of it without telling Emily. Since she says she hasn't seen Richard or Bruce in ten years, it has to go back to the Winter Formal and whatever happened there."

"That's what I'm thinking, but she could be lying too." Dean began massaging my shoulder.

"We need to talk to that aunt. Confirm if the reason Emily truly left town all those years ago is valid and see if she'll give us any other information," Trent said.

"She also mentioned that Alex was asking her about me. She didn't say what exactly but guys—the Winter Formal was the same night of the accident. What if it's related to everything else? What if she knows something about the accident?" About why my parents had died.

Dean and Trent gave each other a look.

I glanced between them. "What? What aren't you guys telling me?"

"I can't divulge information on an active case, Bella." Trent parroted words he and Alex had used over the years.

"No fucking way. You don't get to pull that shit on me now," I cursed. Anger, frustration, and fear poured out of me.

Dean looked at Trent. "She's right. She deserves to know. She's finding more answers than we are and she's been right all these years."

Trent did a double take at Dean's comment.

"Yeah, man, she knows we know."

Trent leaned into me. "First off, I'm sorry we didn't take you more seriously all these years, but I'm sure it's needless to say, Bella, whatever I tell you can't go any further than us." He waited for my agreement before he continued, "When Alex and I searched Bruce's cabin after he was attacked, we found a box full of articles and pictures going back ten years to the night of the Winter Formal. Articles and pictures regarding Emily, her dad, Bruce, Richard, Blake, and his sister—you, Alex, and the accident."

"What? Why?" My food threatened to come back up.

"I don't know, but we were digging into it. That's why Alex went to visit Emily. I spoke with Leonard, but he says he doesn't know anything. Same with Blake—nothing," Trent concluded.

Dean tugged me closer to him. "Bella, Bruce's content was almost a carbon copy of yours."

I felt sick. None of it made sense. "What? Why? Shit, does this mean it's truly all related?" All of it trying to come out at the same time.

"Smile, guys. You're drawing attention." Brooke smiled as she piled our empty plates on top of each other.

Trent laughed at his sister as he casually eyed the mirror filled with liquor bottles behind her. "Whose interested in us?"

"Outside, across the street." She winked at him, playing along.

"Wow, you're good. I'm impressed." I leaned fully against Dean's side and smiled at Brooke.

She laughed. "Practice."

Dean tensed next to me, smiled at Brooke, but spoke to Trent, "Do you see him?"

"Oh yeah. When did you peg him, Brooke?" Trent sipped his water.

She rolled up a napkin and threw it at him, "Just a few minutes ago."

He caught it before it made contact.

"I can't see past all the liquor bottles, who's out there?" I smiled, hoping I was as natural as they are.

Dean leaned down and whispered in my ear, "Castor."

Tilting my head up within an inch of Dean's, I did my best not to let the fear show. "I'm officially scared. And this is beyond creepy."

A flash went off in front of us, knocking my fear to the background.

"What the hell, Brooke?" Trent barked at her.

She smiled hugely. "They look super cute together, so I got a picture." She looked at her phone as if inspecting the picture. "Besides, I got the sheriff in the picture." She looked back up at us, still smiling. "I just sent texted it to the three of you."

"I want to be you when I grow up." My admiration for Brooke skyrocketed.

She laughed. "I don't have a hot guy in my bed. I want to be you, but with a different hot guy. No offense Dean." She winked.

All humor left Trent's face. "Stop. I do not want to hear my sister talk about hot guys and her bed."

Brooke's smile disappeared. "Why? Do you know how many women I've heard sit at this bar talk about their exploits with you to their girlfriends? Or the women who fantasize about wanting those exploits with you?" She shuddered. "Never mind. I get it."

Trent's eyebrows shot up. "You're shittin' me."

"I wish."

Trent bent his head to the bar. "Fuck me."

"That's what got you in this position in the first place," Dean joked.

Trent lifted his head and flipped Dean off.

Brooke wiped her hands in the air. "My work is done, and he's gone." She headed back down to the other side of the bar.

"What does it mean he was here?" I asked.

Dean shrugged and rubbed my arm. "Probably just observing our behaviors. If we're chillin', then we don't have a clue, but if we're actively working the case, then he knows he's got trouble."

Heat slowly built from his touch, stoking the fire inside me.

Dean tugged me closer. "Bella, I won't let anything happen to you." He'd mistaken my shivers for fear and not sexual hunger.

Unable to speak, I nodded and leaned forward to gain distance. To corral my body.

"He's not going to let this go. He'll be on my ass even more now," Trent commented.

"Good thing you have me then. I don't report to him." Dean absently rubbed my lower back.

My breasts grew heavier with each stroke. My body readied itself to forget the drama and release all the stress surrounding me.

"It goes without saying, but whatever you get has to be admissible." Trent turned fully to face Dean. "I want to make sure we nail whoever did this, and I don't want a fucking technicality getting in the way."

Dean's pinky slid across the top of my jeans, and my pussy swelled and moistened from the tease.

"No one will get off. I'll make damn sure." Dean's growl vibrated through me, intensify the need infiltrating me.

Oh, I don't know. I think anymore contact with Dean, and I'd *get* off on this barstool in a crowded barroom.

Standing, I put some room between the guys and me.

"You okay, Bella? You look flush." Dean stood, obliterating the space I'd gained.

My head bobbed—yes and no. "Yes. No. I need some air." *I need you inside me.*

"Okay, let's get you out of here. Trent, I'll catch you tomorrow." Dean pulled some money out of his wallet and threw it on the bar.

"Sounds like a plan." Trent stood up and placed a kiss on my forehead. "We'll get Alex back home and safe."

"Thanks, Trent." Just like Dean, I knew Trent was going to do whatever he could to find Alex and bring him back to me.

Dean hollered at Brooke, "Catch you later."

"See you two later," Brooke yelled at our backs.

CHAPTER TWENTY-ONE

Bella

THE WALK BACK TO DEAN'S TRUCK WAS TORTUROUS. HIS HAND ON my lower back felt like a branding iron. Tremors raked through me, and I consciously fought not to bolt out of his reach.

"Bella, you're still shivering."

Not for the reason you think.

I reached behind me and moved his hand away, allowing myself a deep breath of relief. To have it die a quick death as Dean tugged me into his body, rubbing my arms in an attempt to warm me up. The problem being I was already heated, and his proximity only served to crank my temperature to boiling.

At Dean's truck, he turned me to him, pulling me in close. He cupped my face and vowed, "Bella, I promise you I'll do everything in my power to make this right."

With his touch and his focus on me, the only thought running through my mind was *bend down. Close the gap. Kiss me.*

My mouth parted on its own volition, readying for the possibility.

Dean registered my internal needing and quickly mirrored my

want. His gorgeous lashes lowered as he stared at my mouth. My body responded immediately to the desire pouring from him.

Leaning the barest inch forward, I licked my lips in hopes of a small taste. Dean's grip tightened, and a rumble rose from his chest as his head started its descent.

"Good evening. May I be of assistance?"

We froze a bare breath apart, staring into each other's eyes, and the only thought that ran through my brain was I wanted to kick the ever-loving crap out of Kevin. Seriously, the man had the worst timing ever.

Dean looked over his shoulder as he rumbled, "No."

"Are you sure? It seems you two are having a very intense conversation. A third party may be the solution to your quandary." Kevin didn't take the hint.

Dean slowly turned fully toward Kevin. "There will never, ever be a third fucking party involved with Bella. And we do not need your fucking help."

Wow. Dean's proclamation left no room for interpretation, and my heart did a little happy dance in my chest. But the look on Kevin's face as he involuntarily took a step back had me thinking Kevin and I were not riding the same wave.

Regaining his composure, Kevin smoothed his tie. "I see. Then it would do you well to remember you are standing on public property in public view and to curtail your activities in a manner befitting proper etiquette." He leaned to the side to get a better view of me. "Miss Hall, please remind Miss Sterling the zoning meeting is at four pm sharp tomorrow afternoon."

"I'm..." I cleared my throat in an attempt to dislodge the need coursing through me. "I'm sorry you're going to have to notify Rocky of the meeting yourself." Although I'd make sure to warn her, I thought it best to keep things official, especially in regards to Kevin.

Kevin looked between us. "You are correct. This will allow Miss Sterling the benefit of spending time with me outside the conference room." Tipping his head to us, Kevin stated, "Good evening."

Crap! As if Rocky needed Kevin's pursuit intensified in any manner. Somehow, I needed to help Rocky figure out how to get the zoning issue resolved without giving Kevin any possible ammunition. And for the life of me, I couldn't understand how a man as intelligent as Kevin could be so clueless with women.

Reaching behind me, Dean opened the truck door. "Hop in."

It was no wonder Kevin had stepped away with the look on Dean's face. It pissed me off because we had been about to get to the good part, and Kevin had ruined it.

Sitting in Dean's truck didn't improve my mood. Every part of me touched by Dean felt seared from his touch. Of course, it didn't stop there. It was like an itch, starting at a central location working its way outward until every part of your body needed to be scratched.

And boy did I have an itch.

"You're still shivering." He leaned over and cranked up the heater. "Reach behind the seat and grab my jacket."

Great. Now the vents ensured that my every breath was infused with Dean. I could even taste him in the air. I needed an escape. I unbuckled and turned in my seat to grab his jacket from the back.

I caught myself before I face-planted into the back seat at a sharp turn. "Aah!" I yanked the jacket and pulled myself upright. I twisted back into my seat, tugging the seatbelt back on.

"What the heck, Dean?" I snapped at him.

And then I saw his white-knuckled grip on the steering wheel.

I looked out the back window. "Did we almost hit something?" My gaze flew over the road looking for anything. "I don't see anything." I twisted back to him. "Dean?"

"Don't ever unbuckle again." His jaw jetted out with the force of his clench.

"Seriously?"

He glowered at me.

I turned away from him before I caused an accident by punching him in the jaw. I stared out my window thinking what a big fat jerk. Here I was suffocating from desire, and he was acting like an overprotective Neanderthal. Out of the corner of my eye, I saw Dean moving. No, he was adjusting... *Oh!*

Was it just simple male biology response to a female's ass in your face? Or was Dean still feeling the effects from our earlier encounter? Every shift Dean made rippled the air in the cabin of the truck fanning his scent in my direction. And Dean's jacket? No help there. The smell on his coat was a thousand times stronger. I was either going to pass out from lack of oxygen or hyperventilate.

"You okay?"

A different kind of ripple went through my body at his voice.

"Uh, huh."

I leaned my forehead against the side window, seeking relief from his scent and hoped the coldness alleviated the heat in my body.

"You sure? You seem wound pretty tight."

I couldn't win. Dean's voice amplified the sexual awareness coursing through me. My breasts ached, and my every breath acted as sandpaper between the lace in my bra and my nipples. Goosebumps vied for space on my body, and that had nothing to do with being cold. Shifting even closer to the window proved to be the wrong move. The seam in my jeans brushed my sensitive clit, forcing me to suppress my groan. My eyes closed on their own volition, and I dropped my head against the window, praying for mercy.

"Bella?" I flinched at the brief contact of Dean's hand on my arm. It seared me. Opening my eyes, I searched and found the button for the window. The first whiff of fresh air was heaven. I gulped down the myriad of scents rushing in, praying the ever-lasting diabolical scent of Dean enveloping me magically dissolved.

"Dammit." Dean's curse followed the truck's merging with the side of the road.

Dammit didn't cover it. Somehow my control vanished, and I was a second away from jumping Dean. Screw the consequences—or maybe that's exactly what I needed. After twenty-six years of never having experienced an orgasm that wasn't brought on by my own hand, perhaps it was time I changed that. Maybe if I had sex, my infatuation with Dean could be something I brushed under the rug, and I could finally move on with my life.

Not waiting for Dean to park fully, I jumped out of the truck and headed toward the trees—away from him.

"Dammit, Bella."

While pulling in deep breaths of evergreens, I pinched my shirt away from my body with one hand while my other hand smoothed my pants down and away from my pulsating clit. Before I luxuriated in the minuscule relief it brought me, Dean swung me around and seized my arms.

"Jesus, Bella." He scanned my face, worry overtaking his anger. "You're flush." The back of his hand touched my forehead and cheek. "You're burning up. I'm taking you to the hospital."

I tried to shake my head, but I was overloaded. "Give..." I cleared my throat. "Give me a minute."

And let go of me. Give me space to breathe past you.

"You don't look good. I think you need to get checked out." He pulled me closer to him.

It wasn't a conscious decision. His hands were on me and his body was only a breath away from me. My body chose for me. Taking his face in my hands, I pulled him down to me as I lifted up on my tiptoes.

The instant our lips touched, we froze, staring into each other's eyes.

Electricity shot through me, blanking out any thoughts but more. More contact. More taste. More sensations. More Dean.

No hesitation. I pressed closer and slid my tongue past his full lips. Groaning at his exquisite taste, I stepped fully into his body.

Dean's arms became a vise around my body as he attempted to merge our bodies. Then he devoured me. Nibbles, licks, sucking. There wasn't any transition between one or the other. It was consuming, and I *loved* it.

My hands didn't know whether to keep his head pressed to mine, or to glide over the silk of his hair, or to explore the sinewy muscles on his shoulders or upper back. It was a competition to touch and taste *every* part of Dean.

With Dean's thigh pressed between my legs and his right hand on my ass, guiding me up and down, the friction on my clit was incredible. But it wasn't enough. I needed more.

And he delivered. He lifted the bottom of my shirt and shivers trailed his left hand up to my breast. Breaking the ziplock of his mouth and panted. Our breaths mingling.

I begged, "Please."

He stared at me as he lowered the cup of my bra, and finally touched the skin of my breast.

"Mmm..." Pushing my breast into his hand, I asked for more. For something. Anything.

Maintaining eye contact, he slowly lowered his head as he flicked his tongue out, lapping at my nipple. My breast. Sucking. Nibbling. Molding.

My shivers were uncontrollable, and the moans escaping unavoidable.

Unashamedly, I rode his thigh, desperately seeking release as his other hand snaked to the front of my jeans. In a lightning-quick move, the button on my jeans freed and my zipper unzipped, and his hand was finally where I needed it to be. His finger dived in me, pumping in and out.

"Yes!"

My head rolled back at all the sensations. Dean at my breast. Dean *in* me. Incomprehensible sounds escaped me as I reached for the elusive orgasm.

Grabbing onto his head, I held him to my breast as I rocked against his hand.

Then, Dean caught my nipple between his teeth as his fingers curled in me, and his thumb pressed against my clit.

I screamed as the orgasm tore through me. My womb continued to contract as I shuddered with the onslaught of the orgasm coursing through me.

Slowly, gently, Dean massaged his fingers in me, being careful not to touch my oversensitive clit as he continued to suckle my breast. Almost as if he didn't want to stop. And, I didn't want him to stop either.

When the lights hit us, Dean turned his back to the road, detaching from me while straightening my clothes lightning quick.

It was a rude reminder we were on the side of the road for anyone and everyone to see. This wasn't something special between us but an interlude to get me past the moment.

"You okay?"

I looked up into his eyes and prayed my heart hadn't taken things the wrong way. I prayed Dean's full participation meant he was finally going to take us where my heart wanted us to be.

No, the blank look in his eyes, on his face, meant my heart had flown the coop too early. Too early? No, searching his expressionless face, I knew it should never have even tiptoed to the door of the cage.

Pulling away from his hold, I answered, "Yeah." Not even close.

Moving toward his truck, I did my best to ignore how my bra felt cold against my breast or the fact my soaked panties rubbed against my sensitized clit or the fact my treacherous body screamed at me to go back and jump him. To finish what we started because one Dean orgasm was never, *ever* going to be enough.

Dean

This was precisely what I was afraid would happen if I took protecting Bella on. My body decided, against my brain's better judgment, all the opportunities I'd ignored over the years were now open for entanglement.

Fuck me. Bella's taste in my mouth, on my tongue. I was never going to be able to get rid of it.

Squeezing the steering wheel tighter in hopes of refocusing on anything besides Bella's taste only exacerbated the situation because Bella's scent drifted up to me. Quickly looking at my fingers to make sure that, yup, they were still attached to my hand *on* the steering wheel. It didn't matter though, because they could still feel how wet Bella had been. The way her pussy had clenched around them in an attempt to devour them. She was so damn tight and wet.

Fuck! With each tug of her breast in my mouth, her juices had drenched my hand. If it weren't for the fucking headlights reminding me I had her bent over on the side of the road, I would have fucked her right then and there.

Those fucking headlights had saved us both because no matter what my body wanted, I had a job to do—protect Bella and bring Alex home.

Too bad my cock didn't agree.

CHAPTER TWENTY-TWO

Bella

M Y LIBIDO HAD IN NO WAY COOLED IN THE SHORT DRIVE TO DEAN'S house. The orgasm Dean had given me on the side of the road was only a starter in the feast I salivated to devour, but he made it clear he didn't want to participate.

I rushed upstairs and readied myself for bed. All the while I did my best to ignore the thoughts spinning through my brain and the need coursing through my body. I forced myself to shut down for the night. After all I'd learned that day, I shouldn't have been surprised my sleep wouldn't go undisturbed; or that the nightmare wouldn't haunt me with such intensity. Instead, I allowed the promise of Dean's comfort and security to lull me into relaxing my guard.

The only reason the scream didn't escape my mouth was through years of practice containing it. Initially, when I was unable to control it, I'd wake Alex. The pain on his face as he witnessed me relive the night of our parents' death and to know he couldn't help me, all while he kept his own pain under wraps. No, I never let them out again.

Tonight was different, more intense and I knew I wouldn't be able to shake it off.

I exited the bed and dressed in my running gear, intent on pounding the tension out on the jogging trail.

Instead, I ran into trouble at Dean's security panel. It had more buttons than his TV remote and pressing what I thought were the obvious buttons to disarm it didn't work. The alarm blared through the house, waking even the dead.

A hand shot in front of me, pushing buttons and cutting the alarm off, and leaving behind a deafening ringing in my ears.

However, my brain wasn't functioning under its normal parameters. Alex's tortured face intertwined with the night of the accident, *and* Dean's NASA-level of security fought for my attention. Therefore, seeing an unknown hand in front of me set off my fight mode.

I utilized every trick Alex ever taught me to get away, but let's face it, against Dean, there really wasn't a struggle. He pinned me against the wall with his body, lifted my arms above my head, spread my legs with his legs, pressing them wide-open.

"What the fuck, Bella?" Dean clipped out.

I gasped for air while doing my best to slow my breathing and calm my erratic heart.

This one was a command. "Talk to me."

"You scared me." Understatement.

"Yeah, I got that. Why are you in your running clothes, staring at my alarm panel at three-thirty in the morning?"

"So I could go for a run?" It came out a question.

"Yeah, I can see that. Why?"

"To chase the images away. To make it all stop!" I yelled in his face.

Dean stilled against me. "Why didn't you come to me? I could have helped you."

The way I needed Dean to help me, to make it all go away, wasn't in a way he was willing to help me with. Our roadside tryst evidence enough. Frustration, anger, and fear fought for dominance in me. "Really? I need to clear my mind. How are you going to help me with that? You've made it clear we're not..."

Dean's eyes roamed my face before he pressed into me, sandwiching me between him and the wall. His eyelids dropped as his head descended. "It's not all or nothing, Bella, and I can think of a few ways to get your mind to stop thinking."

Yes!

Lifting up on my toes, I didn't make him work for it.

Our mouths locked onto each other, desperate. It's as if our earlier prelude only served to amplify the electricity between our bodies, making us frantic in our movements.

Dean took full advantage of the position and shoved his hands down the back of my yoga pants, grabbing my ass and shifting my core against the substantial length of his shaft.

I whimpered and my body undulated against his. I sucked his tongue into my mouth, mimicking what I hoped Dean would do with his cock inside of me.

The growl that erupted from Dean left me soaked.

I hooked my leg around his and opened myself up to get closer. The hand at my ass moved forward, and his fingers slid through my juices, spreading me for his taking.

The thud of my head hitting the wall didn't register as Dean put two fingers inside me. He released my arms, moved his hand from inside me, and I screamed, "No!"

His head shot up, and the feral look on his face made my knees buckle. Dean moved lightning quick, yanked my pants down to my shoes, taking my pants and shoes off in seriously hot man move, and dropped to his knees in front of me. Our eye contact scorched me as he slowly opened my folds and took one long slow lick. My hands shot out as I held his head.

Dean pushed his shoulders between my legs, grabbed my butt, and feasted on me. Each stroke and nip ratcheted me closer to explosion.

"Fuck, Bella. Your taste... I can't fucking get enough."

"Please." I stared down at Dean and begged.

Not breaking our eye contact, Dean leaned forward again and flattened his tongue against my clit. The vibration of his growl sent tremors through my body, and I continued to drench him with my pleasure. After a single lick, Dean inserted his tongue in me, drinking from the source and then went on to methodically tongue-fuck me.

Uncontrollable sounds escaped me, my head thrashed back and forth, and my hands clenched and unclenched in his hair. "Deaaannn."

"No, you fucking don't. Not without me." Dean stood up and yanked his pajama bottoms down.

He fitted the tip of his penis to my opening but didn't enter me.

"Dean," I begged.

"Yes?" The one word held so much withheld passion.

I bit down on his lower lip, released it and demanded. "Yes."

Dean slammed in me.

Once again, my head hit the wall as I luxuriated in the feel of Dean finally inside me. But he didn't move.

With extreme effort, I righted my head to stare at Dean. "Move."

"Did I hurt you?" His words were strained.

Hurt me? If he didn't start moving, I was liable to hurt him. "Move."

"Bella, did I hurt you?" he insisted.

Nipping his full bottom lip, I ordered, "Fuck me, Dean."

Dean didn't wait for another command. He pounded me into the wall, each stroke of his thick cock pushing me closer to release.

I ran my hand down Dean's six-pack and glided it to his backside where I got my first feel of Dean's ass. Smooth, firm, and bunching with each stroke.

Divine.

I molded Dean's ass as he continued to move in me, commanding him to pick up the pace.

"Come, Bella," Dean demanded.

I nipped and licked the taste of Dean from his lips. I wanted to prolong my orgasm. To savor the feel of Dean in me.

"Fuck." Dean didn't want to wait. He moved his hand down until his thumb hit my clit. He pushed at the same time his pounding turned feverish.

Dean's name bellowed in the house as my release left me.

A few more strokes and Dean stilled, filling me.

Leaning forward, I nipped his shoulder and then kissed it. I pulled back and asked, "Can we do that again?"

Dean burst out laughing.

I loved watching Dean laugh but feeling him laugh while inside me had me mesmerized. I didn't want him ever to leave.

He quieted and asked, "What's that look for?"

"I like you in me," I admitted.

Tenderness engulfed Dean's face. "I like being in you too, but we need to clean up."

Slowly Dean pulled out, and a small moan escaped me.

He bent down, picked up my undies and pants and handed them to me, right before giving me a small shove. "Go clean up."

Not bothering to call him on his bossiness, I just did as I was ordered, hoping a round two was coming up.

Standing in his bathroom, I looked at my reflection in the mirror thinking I looked like a woman who had thoroughly been fucked. Messy hair, swollen lips, face flushed, and the tingles continued to travel through me. I didn't want to jump to any conclusion that we were starting something long-term, but my heart wasn't keeping up with my brain. I'd just had wall sex with Dean Cannon, and I consciously was jumping in heart-first, and the rest of me just had to catch up.

When I stepped out of the bathroom, I found Dean standing in his kitchen, staring out the window. Making my way to him, I sidled up to his side and wrapped my arm around his back. "Are you okay?"

He lifted his arm around me. "Yeah. Just thinking about everything. Are you okay? Did I hurt you?"

"No, you didn't hurt me." The heat in my cheeks was inevitable.

He squeezed me once. "Bella, we didn't use any protection."

"I'm on the pill, so you don't have to worry about ..." I trailed off.

"If you were, we'd deal, and just so you know, I'm clean. I never went ungloved until you, but I can get tested if it makes you feel better." He tucked me around to his front and held me in his arms.

I melted further into him. "I trust you, Dean. You don't have to get tested, and I'm clean too." Oh boy, how do I tell him I had been a virgin until the wall?

"I know." He smiled as if he already knew my secret.

"You do?" I tilted my head to the side.

"Yeah."

Staring at his bare chest, I wondered if my performance had led to that knowledge. I mean, it wasn't like I advertised my sexual history, but I didn't think it was something Dean was keeping track of.

Dean jiggled me a bit to get my attention. "You were fucking amazing, so get those thoughts out of your head. But this was your first time, and I didn't want it to go this way. I wanted it to be special for you, not up against a wall like a caveman."

"Um ... how did you know it was my... first time?" I dared a peek at his eyes before resuming my perusal of his chest.

"I *am* a private investigator, Bella."

My eyes shot up. "Oh." He'd been paying attention to my dating.

His grin told me he thought I was being cute.

I'd been in love with Dean for years, so I always knew our time together would be wonderful. I didn't want him to think it had been anything other than what it was—perfect. "Dean, it was special. It didn't matter if it was against the wall, on the stairs, or in your truck. As long as it was you, it was special."

Dean locked solid against me. "Shit, Bella, you kill me." He tightened his arm around me as he squished me to him and shoved his face in my neck.

I decided to jump fully in, but subconsciously I held my breath, thinking he'd push me away. His reaction, the fierceness of his hold, obliterated my worries. I ran my hands over his shoulder and held him to me. Unable to stop myself, I kissed his bare shoulders, his neck, anywhere I could reach. Letting him know I loved him with my touch.

With my inexperience, I wasn't sure if a quick recovery was normal, but nestled against my stomach was a very thick, erect penis. My kisses turned to nips and licks followed by sucking. Dean's masculine scent invaded me, causing my breasts to swell with desire. I smoothed my hands across the solid wall of Dean's back and sexual current raced through my body igniting me once more.

I felt the instant my need became Dean's. He ground his fully erect cock against me and licked my neck. Shivers shot through me.

As one, we moved toward each other, our lips meeting causing us to freeze for the barest second.

My brain stuttered at the contact I'd been fantasizing about my entire life. It was as if I couldn't believe this was real. It was everything I dreamed of, and oh, so much more. His lips were full and firm. I swept my tongue across the seam and I got another in-depth taste of Dean. Luscious.

That was all the invitation Dean needed.

Our tongues dueled as I pressed myself into him in my attempt to merge myself with him. His left arm was a band across my back, locking me to him as his right hand tilted my head for better access.

I shoved my hands through Dean's hair and held him to me at the same time he thrust his leg between mine. The pressure of his muscular leg against my sensitive clit was almost as good as Dean's tongue in my mouth. But I wanted, *needed* more. Hooking my right leg around his thigh, I pressed my wet core further against his thigh.

I moaned into his mouth and Dean obeyed my command. His left hand trailed down my back, over my butt, and his fingers skimmed my folds through my pants.

He pulled away from my mouth and growled, "Fuck, you're wet again."

Yes, I was and *don't stop*. Yanking his head back down, I demanded another kiss as I pressed further into him.

Dean agreed. He locked me to him as his fingers continued to torture me with their slow back and forth against my core, avoiding the place I needed his touch the most. Sounds of frustration and need escaped me even as I sucked Dean's tongue into my mouth.

That did it.

Dean lifted me up and onto his countertop and, in one swift move, jacked my legs over his shoulders as he pulled my pants and thong down and finally—*finally!*—gave me the kiss I'd been wanting, needing. My head flew back and hit the cupboard behind me at the first contact of his lips and I clenched my hands in his hair to hold him to me. I dug my heels into his back as I savored his tongue inside of me.

He didn't let up. He licked, sucked, and fucked me with his tongue.

It was exquisite.

Then he added his fingers. One. Then another.

In and out. Alternating with his tongue.

"That's it, Bella. Coat me in your juices." Dean's voice vibrated against my clit.

Like honey, I flowed onto Dean's tongue.

"Dean," I begged, but for what I didn't know.

Dean did. He curled his finger in and sucked my clit.

I threw my hands out, seeking purchase on the countertop. In the fog of pleasure, I barely heard the crash, but I didn't care.

Dean shot up and commanded, "Together."

I automatically wrapped my legs around his lower back and met him thrust for thrust. The kiss he gave me was more than enough of a response. It was all tongues, nips, and sucks. Almost as good as the one he'd given me more intimately a few minutes ago.

Our rhythm was just as frantic as earlier. Our bodies were desperately making up for the years we'd neglected each other.

"Fuck, Bella. You're beautiful." His words drowned in his pleasure.

My nails scored his back as our control slipped, and Dean's powerful thrusts increased pounding me into his countertop. He captured my rear for better leverage and then he *moved*. Each stroke sending waves of undeniable pleasure through me.

"Dean. Please," I begged him. My orgasm was so close.

Dean tilted my ass and glided one hand forward up and under my sports bra. He cupped my breast and the sensation of his roughened hand against my sensitive flesh consumed me. He massaged and molded my breast in rhythm with his thrusts. I pushed my breast further into his hand and breathed against his lips, "Please."

Dean obliged my request and held my aching nipple between his fingers. "Now, Bella."

A twirl and yank of my nipple with one mighty stroke, and my orgasm staggered through me.

It was beyond heaven.

"Fuck, Bella." Dean stilled in me as his orgasm tore through him.

My hold on Dean was loose. All my energy spent from the back-to-back orgasms, but all I could think was I wanted to have sex with Dean forever. To have the option of having him in my bed, in the kitchen, against the wall—wherever.

Pulling back slightly, he spoke against my mouth. "Fuck me, Bella."

"Okay." Yes, please.

Rubbing his thumb across my bottom lip, he stated almost as if he were speaking to himself, "Fuck me." Inching back, he looked me in the eye.

Oh. I could go for that. Hell yeah, I could go for that. Again. And again.

He withdrew from me and helped me off the countertop. "I'll clean this mess up. You go on up to bed. I'll be there in a minute."

That's when I realized the crash I'd heard earlier was us knocking over the coffeemaker. The coffee was spread all over the counter and had dripped onto the floor. Luckily, we hadn't broken the pot.

"I can help you."

He stopped mid-wipe. "I only have so much control. Do me a favor and go get ready for bed."

Trying not to smile, I nodded before hopping off the counter and hightailing up the stairs, thinking this time we'd have sex *in* his bed.

CHAPTER TWENTY-THREE

Dean

WAKING UP WITH BELLA AT MY SIDE WAS INDESCRIBABLE. SURE, THE morning sex was an added bonus, but that wasn't it. It was having her in my arms, her legs tangled with mine, and her scent in my every breath—pure bliss.

Crossing the no-sex line with Bella weighed on me, on my ability to keep her safe. And with Bella's life on the line I knew it was a bad idea, but I couldn't resist.

Walking into the police station with Bella at my side raised the hairs on the back of my neck. Would Castor be here? How much has he impeded the investigation? Would he want to interrogate Bella?

"Oh, good morning, Isabella. Dean," Ms. Folgers happily chirped.

"Good morning, Ms. Folgers." Bella's smile seemed undimmable since our intimate interaction.

"Mornin'," I replied.

Ms. Folgers smiled. "Trent's waiting for you upstairs." She reached across the counter and touched Bella's hand. "I'm sorry to hear about this nonsense with Alex, but I know these boys will have him home lickety-split."

The faith she had in us. "We're working on it."

"Of course you are." Ms. Folgers nodded toward the stairs. "Go on up."

Leaving Ms. Folgers to the ringing phones, we made our way toward the bullpen. Trent looked up from the papers on his desk before he aimed his eyes toward Sheriff Castor's office.

Giving a few of the guys brief *hellos* or chin lifts in acknowledgments, Bella and I stood next to Trent's desk, and studiously ignored the empty one where Alex should be. "What's going on?" And what's up with the look and Castor?

"A lot of bullshit," was Trent's terse response.

"Isn't that your job? Handling a ton of crap?" Bella asked him.

"Normally, but I don't usually have Castor riding my ass to arrest people without any of evidence of wrongdoing." Trent stood.

I leaned against his desk. "What? Who does he want you to bring in? And why?"

The tension in Trent's voice matched the set of his body. "Blake, because he's the only person who is mildly a person of interest in Bruce's case. But, for some reason, Castor is ignoring we have no fucking evidence to suggest Blake has anything to do with Bruce's attack." Trent sucked in a breath. "And in regards to Alex's disappearance because I have no fucking clue why Castor would think Blake is involved. We have no fucking reason to believe Blake would want to kidnap Alex." Waving his hand to the mess of papers on his desk, Trent continued, "So, I'm sitting here banging my head trying to find some fucking needle of reason to bring Blake in."

Bella's gasp ricocheted through the room. "What?" She shook her head. "I don't get it."

Trent's comments surprised me. "That makes no sense. What purpose does hauling Blake in have? Sure, he may know something about high school, but he's not talking. So what does Castor know that's making him push for Blake?"

"According to Castor, Blake is in possession of valuable information that can lead to us locating Alex, and with Blake withholding this information, he is hindering our investigation." Trent looked over my shoulder.

I turned my head and saw Castor bearing down on us.

"Hello Sheriff." Bella attempted to soothe the rage on Castor's face with a cheerful greeting.

Castor didn't bother with pleasantries. "Isabella, now is not a good time for a visit. My officers have responsibilities that require their full attention."

Bella squared her shoulders and met Castor's angry stare with her own. "Well then I guess it's a good thing I'm here to get information on my brother's case then. What steps has the Feldspar Police Station taken in finding my missing brother—one of your detectives?"

Silence descended through the room as the officers looked at Castor, waiting for his response.

Castor surveyed the room, realizing his initial mistake. He pulled on his civil servant persona and attempted to placate Bella. "I apologize, Isabella. As I'm sure you know, it is quite distressing to have one of my own missing." He nodded to Trent. "That's what I came out here to discuss with Detective Cooper." Glaring at Trent, Castor demanded, "Why don't I see Mr. King in the interrogation room?"

Trent stepped up to Sheriff Castor before he responded. "Because I don't have any reason to bring him in."

Castor pulled himself up to his full height. "You were given a direct order by your superior, Detective Cooper. Are you disobeying that order?"

The muscle in Trent's jaw jumped in effort to hold back his retort.

"Detective Cooper?" Sheriff Castor pushed.

"No." Trent ground out through his clenched teeth.

"I expect to see Mr. King in my interrogation room in one hour." Sheriff Castor turned to leave while he continued to ignore me.

"Excuse me, Sheriff."

Castor stopped but only turned his head toward me. "I'm swamped, Mr. Cannon." He turned back around and kept going.

Not deterred, I raised my voice to be heard over the noise in the bullpen. "I'm curious when we should expect the FBI to arrive. It's been two days since Alex's abduction and the FBI still isn't here."

Castor stopped again and turned his angry eyes to me.

Quiet enveloped the room once more. Everyone looked and waited for Sheriff Castor to respond.

Castor looked around the room before smoothing out his expression to one of concern. "As I'm sure you're aware, the FBI is a very busy organization handling a multitude of serious assignments. They've assured me Detective Hall's abduction is a priority to them. Unfortunately, they're wrapping up another sensitive matter at the moment and will be here as soon they as can."

The weight of disbelief in the room pressed in.

"They'll be here as soon as they can? Isn't kidnapping a federal jurisdiction? And a fellow law enforcement officer?" I shook my head once. "When exactly is *soon?*"

Castor eyed the room once more. "I don't like it any more than you do, so I reached out to my buddy in the FBI again and asked him if he could use his weight to get the local agents here sooner. I'm waiting to hear back from him." He addressed the room at large. "Until then, we show the FBI we're taking this seriously. We follow all possible leads." The look he gave Trent was undeniably hostile. "We do our due diligence to bring our brother back. Get back to it."

Not waiting for another second, Sheriff Castor marched back to his office. The door slamming closed reverberated throughout.

"Do you believe him? Has the FBI been contacted?" I crossed my arms.

Trent shook his head once. "No clue. He's made it clear the FBI liaison is to be him and him only." He sighed. "Guess, I'm heading out to get Blake."

"I'll—" Trent's phone ringing cut me off. I knew it was Trudy just from the look on his face.

"Dusty okay?" Trent's opening remark made it clear he didn't want to speak to his ex-wife.

He listened before cutting Trudy off. "I'm at work and in the middle of a case." He listened again. "Yeah, Alex, so if Dusty is fine, then we don't have anything to discuss. I gotta get back to work." More silence. "Look, when I come by later to pick Dusty up, you can talk to me then. Yeah?"

She must have responded in the affirmative because he hung up.

"Everything okay?" Bella asked.

"Yeah." Trent grabbed his keys off his desk. "I gotta go before Castor decides I'm taking too fucking long, and I'm benched from the investigation."

BLAKE DIDN'T BEHAVE like someone who was on the wrong side of the law. He didn't fidget, trip over his words, or ask for an attorney. He was calm, watchful, but he was mindful of his answers. It could be his mixed martial arts training kicking into gear, helping him to remain unnerved in a somewhat tense situation. Whatever it was and no matter his training, I could see with my trained eye behind the two-way mirror, Blake was hiding something.

So far, Trent hadn't pushed Blake for any real answers. Just basic background information on employment, living history, and so forth. And that's when it happened. Sheriff Castor walked in on Trent's interview, and Blake's ease dissolved. In its place was now an alertness, as if Blake were sizing his opponent.

Interesting.

Sheriff Castor took a seat next to Trent and stared at Blake. "Don't mind me, Detective Cooper. Please continue."

Trent released his clenched jaw before he turned back to Blake. "Blake, this is Sheriff Castor."

"I know who he is." Blake's eyes never left Castor.

Hmm. Was that because of the beat down in high school, or was there something else?

Trent turned back to Sheriff Castor, scanning for any signs of recognition before turning back to Blake.

"Then, you know his daughter, Emily—"

Castor cut Trent off. "What does my daughter have to do with this?"

Bella squeezed my hand at the sheriff's interruption. His constant protection of his daughter was interfering with finding the answers we needed.

Trent continued to watch Blake. "At the moment, I'm establishing timeline and relationships." He paused. "As I was saying, tell me about your relationship with Emily."

"Emily never had any relations with this man." Castor pushed his chair back and barked at Trent.

Bella's hand twitched around mine before she whispered, "Why does he keep interrupting?"

"A father's love knows no boundaries," I whispered back.

Trent went rigid as his head cut to Castor. "I'd prefer Blake answer the questions."

Castor's furious glare tipped them into a silent battle of dominance. But Trent was a seasoned detective and wasn't backing down. Several tense moments passed before Castor averted his gaze.

A short and shallow breath was the only sign Trent showed of regaining his composure. "What was your relationship with Emily Castor?"

"Sheriff Castor is correct. Emily and I never had any relations." Blake calmly answered.

Trent waited for more, but Blake didn't bite.

"How do you know Emily?" Trent continued.

"I'd see her around school," Blake said.

"Ever talk to her? Hang out? Mutual friends?"

"No." Firm. Blake did not leave room for interpretation.

"What about Richard Coleman, Bruce Evans, and Leonard Evans?"

"What about them?"

Trent leaned his forearms on the table and asked, "Were they buds? Did you hang out with them?"

"Fuck no."

"That's pretty adamant. Why is that?" Trent pushed.

Bella's voice was whisper-soft. "Because they were major jerks to him."

Blake glanced at Sheriff Castor before responding, "You have to know they were dicks back in high school, and from what I've heard around town, they haven't changed."

"Being a dick doesn't negate having friends. What about them cut them off your friend list?"

Blake stared at Trent. "Besides the fact they're dicks? I didn't realize I needed any more reasons besides that."

"It had nothing to do with the fact they picked on you back then?"

Not missing a beat, Blake fired back. "That would be one of the parts of them being dicks."

"Or a major part," Bella added.

"Were they that way toward you all of high school? Or just Winter Formal?"

Castor fully pushed his chair back and stood. "This line of questioning is getting us nowhere, Detective Cooper." He moved to the side of the table and sent another belligerent look at Trent. "We're here regarding Detective Hall, not a trip down memory lane."

Trent stood and made his way to the door. He opened it and asked, "May I have a word in private, Sheriff Castor?"

It seemed Castor was impatient to get to the meat of the interview, and Trent's method wasn't fast enough. But, as a sheriff, he should understand sometimes the fastest way to an answer was to go around it. More importantly, he should absolutely know not to interrupt or degrade a fellow officer during an interview.

"No."

Trent froze.

Bella sucked a breath in. "This isn't going well."

"Uh-huh." That was an understatement.

Closing the door, Trent returned to his chair before addressing Castor. "Then I'm going to have to ask you to withhold any further comments until the end of my questioning."

I had to give it to Trent. I don't think I'd have been so civil—boss or not.

Blake leaned forward.

Castor looked back at Blake and then at Trent before giving a nod.

Trent sat back down. "How long did the mistreatment continue?" He continued as if a major verbal ego battle hadn't just occurred.

"All of high school." Blake looked up at Castor and back at Trent.

"Not after?"

He shook his head.

"Why is that?"

Blake scanned Trent's face. "Why are you asking me questions you have the answers to?"

"Humor me."

"My family left Feldspar in the middle of my senior year."

"Why did your family leave in the middle of your senior year? Why not let you finish the school year out?" Trent asked.

"My father accepted a better employment opportunity elsewhere. An opportunity he couldn't pass up, so we left."

"It had nothing to do with the fact you were hospitalized the night of the Winter Formal after being brutally beaten?"

Castor leaned against the table, drawing Blake's eyes to the sheriff's hip and badge and back to Trent.

"My hospitalization may have pushed my father into accepting the offer sooner than later." Lines formed around the edges of Blake's eyes.

"Why didn't you file a report against Richard and Bruce?" Trent asked. "They were of age at the time of the attack and could have been tried as adults."

"What exactly do you want from me, Detective Cooper?"

"For now, I'd like you to answer my questions," Trent replied. "What happened at the Winter Formal that sent Richard and Bruce on you?"

Blake crossed his arms.

"I've been more than patient, Detective Cooper, with your line of questioning, but I've had enough." Castor didn't let Blake answer Trent. "Where were you two nights ago?"

"Why won't the sheriff let Trent do his job? He keeps cutting Trent off and preventing him from getting any answers." Bella leaned into me.

I squeezed her hand once. "Emily."

"At the gym." Blake stared at Trent before looking up at Sheriff Castor.

"Can anyone corroborate this?" Castor demanded.

"Yes. The members who were there can confirm I was there."

"I'll need the name and contact information for these members." Castor shoved the pad of paper and pen toward Blake.

"Why?" Blake inquired.

"We're investigating the abduction of one of my men." Castor looked ready to strangle Blake.

One of Blake's eyebrows went up. "And this relates to me how?"

"You are a person of interest. We're doing our due diligence by researching all possible leads," Castor bit out.

Both eyebrows shot up. "Person of interest? For a police officer's abduction? Me?"

"That is what I said." Castor's arrogance blanketed his statement.

Blake remained calm as he asked, "How am I a person of interest?"

"Someone identified you as a potential suspect. We're taking all leads seriously." Castor stood.

"So you're saying I can say that Tom, Dick, and Harry at the gas station were the last ones to see your detective and they'll automatically become persons of interest? It's as easy as that?" Blake's disbelief was evident in his questions.

Castor's patience evaporated as he bit out between clenched teeth, "No, it's not that easy. Now, if you're done stalling, names and contact information."

"And if I refuse?" Blake called Castor on his bluff.

"You're more than welcome to spend the night in a cell rethinking your decision." Castor pulled out his handcuffs.

Blake eyed the handcuffs and Castor. "For not giving you an alibi because *someone* named me as a person of interest in your detective's abduction?"

"Yes."

Blake looked at Trent. "I want to make a phone call."

"That didn't go well," Bella muttered.

Trent slammed the pad of paper on his desk. "What the fuck was up with Castor?"

"I'm not quite sure, but I will say it makes me take another look at Blake."

"What makes you say that?" Trent ground out.

I shrugged. "Why not give up the contact information? Why choose to spend the night in a cell?" It'd be easy enough to clear his name if what he said was true so why not give that information? Unless he had something to hide.

Trent closed his eyes and blew out a breath. "Fuck." He shook his head. "Honestly? I think he did it to piss Castor off. I don't think he has anything to do with Alex's disappearance."

"I agree with you, Trent. I think he knows what happened the night at the Winter Formal, but not who has Alex," Bella agreed.

"It's plausible. It was clear Blake didn't care for Castor even though he didn't physically give anything away. Did you notice his smooth evasive answers to your questions?" I queried.

"Yeah, I noticed that, but it could just be his MMA training," Trent countered.

"Maybe, but he knows more than he's letting on," I agreed.

Trent sighed. "Yeah. Now I gotta hit the gym and see if I can't shake anything out of anyone."

"I can go back with Rocky and see if anyone will tell us anything. We still have our one-week promotion so no one will think twice about us there," Bella offered, her body ready to take put her words into action.

Trent leaned down and kissed Bella's cheek. "No. I have to do it for the case. We'll get Alex home soon."

Bella's smile was faint.

"Let me know if you need anything." I gave Trent a nod.

"Will do."

CHAPTER TWENTY-FOUR

Bella

AFTER THE POLICE STATION, DEAN AND I SPENT THE REST OF THE afternoon at his office where he caught up on work.

I spent more time snooping through his office and hanging with Lily. She didn't mind the company since she said Dean wasn't big on conversation.

Lily wasn't someone I'd usually interact with, but the last few hours made me realize I should change that. She was funny and sweet, and as soon as we found Alex, I'd invite her to a night out at Coop's with the girls.

Since Dean's work was taking longer than he'd expected, he had Lily grab us dinner from Harper's. As usual, it was delicious, but after the day we'd had, I wanted to do something besides eat. I wanted to be out looking for Alex. Interrogating someone, anyone on what they knew about Alex's whereabouts, Bruce's attack, the Winter Formal —anything!

I knew Dean wouldn't let me out of his sight, so I closed myself in his conference room and called Leonard. His time for avoiding me was over.

"Leonard?" I was surprised he answered the phone after all the times he'd pushed me to voicemail in the last few days.

"Yeah."

My back straightened at his short response. "Yeah? That's all you have to say?"

"I'm kind of busy right now, Bella."

Too fucking bad. "Busy with what? What's got you so preoccupied that you can't answer a simple text from your good friend?"

"Sorry, I've been busy trying to nail the bastard who attacked Bruce that I didn't jump when you beckoned," he snapped at me.

The hurt he inflicted ignited my anger. "What the fuck? Maybe if you leaned on your *friends,* you wouldn't have to do *anything* by yourself. And *maybe* if you didn't keep everything to yourself, Alex wouldn't be missing. Did you ever stop to think that *maybe* your way of doing things isn't the right way?"

"What?"

I was so beyond calm to care about Leonard's surprise that I continued my rant, "You know what's going on. You *know* why Bruce and Richard beat Blake up in high school. You *know* that Emily is somehow involved with whatever happened that night at the Winter Formal. You *know* all of it is related somehow to my accident, to my parents' death, and you still won't say a *fucking* thing. Now, Alex is missing, and you still sit on your *fucking* high horse and have the nerve to snap at me."

I was breathing hard from yelling and hadn't noticed Dean standing in the doorway.

Leonard's mumblings came through the line. "Fuck. Shit. Fuck. Shit."

"That's not telling me something I don't already know. What happened at the Winter Formal that people are dying, beaten, and disappearing over?"

He ignored me. "When did Alex go missing? What day?"

"Why should I answer your questions when you won't even answer one of mine?" I bit out.

"Dammit, Bella! When did Alex go missing?"

"The day after you visited Emily Castor. The last person to see him was Emily. How is the sheriff's daughter involved in all of this?" If he couldn't help me save Alex, then he wasn't the friend I thought he was.

"Fuck. Shit. Fuck."

I lowered my voice and asked again, "What is going on, Leonard? What do you know?"

"Alex was supposed to be safe. He's a fucking detective, for fucks sake. None of this is supposed to be happening. You were never supposed to know about that night," Leonard rambled. "Stay with Dean. He'll keep you safe."

"I wouldn't need Dean or *anyone* to keep me safe if you would just tell me what the *fuck* is going on," I repeated for the umpteenth time. "And what. In. The. Fuck. Am. I not supposed to know?"

"I'm fucking working on it, Bella. You have to trust me to make it right." Leonard disconnected before I could respond.

"Argh!"

I raised my arm to throw the phone, but Dean caught my hand.

"I'm taking it Leonard didn't tell you anything?" Dean held my hand, and my phone squished between our palms.

"You'd be right. He said to stay with you. That you'd keep me safe, and he was working on fixing everything. Why won't he tell me what he knows? He also said I'm not supposed to know what about that night. He knows Alex is missing, and he still won't tell me anything." I pounded his chest once.

Leonard, of all people, knew what Alex meant to me. Why would he withhold information that would bring Alex home?

"You're not going to like this, but you need to be prepared for the fact that Leonard may be involved in whatever transpired at the Winter Formal and is covering his tracks." Dean wrapped his other arm around me.

I plopped my head on his chest. "I was afraid you were going to say that. That means all these years, he's been pulling the wool over my eyes." Lifting my head back up, I asked, "But what do I know that I don't remember?"

"The only thing connecting you to the Winter Formal, besides attending it, is your accident. We need to know who the woman was you heard yelling. We need to know why someone waited ten years to kill Richard, attack Bruce, and what part Emily has any of this."

I plopped my head back on his chest and mumbled, "Yeah." I popped my head back up as I remembered my conversation with Rocky and Dean. "Wait. If our theory is right and there was another car present that possibly clipped my parents' car from behind, then wouldn't there be evidence from it? I know everyone kept telling me it was from the earlier accident but what if it wasn't? What if it was truly from the other car involved in mine?"

He tensed for a second. "Shit, I forgot to tell you. The guys and I discussed that, and Alex sent the evidence to the lab. We haven't heard back yet."

"I keep forgetting you guys believe me now. It messes with me when I'm hypothesizing about that night and you're like *'we're on it.'*" I squeezed the sides of his shirt.

Dean gave me a gentle squeeze. "Let's get going so tomorrow we can pay Leonard a visit and see if *I* can't get anything out of him."

"Okay, but I need to stop by my apartment for more clothes." I still didn't lift my head. Tears were close to the surface, and I needed another quick breath of Dean's scent to calm me down.

"All right. Let's go." Dean stepped back and released me.

THE DRIVE to my apartment was short, and it did nothing to alleviate the pain, anger, and fear swirling inside me.

Dean and I made our way to my darkened entryway. A reminder someone, maybe the same someone who had taken Alex, had been outside my door. So close to me the same night Alex went missing. Had they tried for me first?

"Hey, you doing okay?" Dean tugged on my hand.

I shook my head. "Not really."

"We'll get him back, Bella. I promise."

Nodding once, I opened my door, turned on the light, then stopped in my tracks.

Dean bumped into me, wrapping his arms around me as he closed the door behind him.

He quickly sidestepped me as we studied the mess. "Don't move from this spot."

Shit. Someone *had* been in my apartment.

As I waited for Dean to finish his walk through, I took in my front room. It seemed the majority of the damage was centralized around my makeshift command central.

Then I saw the hunting knife sticking out of the wall on my accident timeline. It was stuck to the article of my parents' accident with a note—*Tread lightly.*

Chills raced up my spine.

"Did you touch it?" Dean's heat hit my back.

I shook my head. "They were in my apartment," I whispered.

Dean gently moved me. "Let's get you outside. We need to call Trent."

TRENT AND DONNY showed about the same time, both upset with the continued wrong doings surrounding us Halls.

"You know it's a treat to see you, Bella, but twice in one week? First, Alex's house and now your apartment?"

I wasn't sure if Donny was actually asking me a question but luckily he kept going before I could come up with anything.

"Have you been to your apartment since Alex's disappearance?" he asked.

Trent watched me.

"No. I went home with Dean and haven't been back since." I wrapped my arms around myself as I stood next to Dean's truck.

"I know you and Rocky were inebriated a few nights ago, but did you notice anyone? Does anything seem out of the ordinary? Different cars?" Trent eyes stopped on the bushes, garbage cans and other bulkier landscaping materials around the complex.

I shook my head once. "No, but I wasn't looking."

Donny glanced around the parking lot. "Why don't you have your truck here? Is there something wrong with it?"

"It's at the clinic. I've been chauffeured around." Then it hit me. "Why? Do you think someone is going to mess with it to hurt me?"

"Let's not jump to conclusions, Bella." Donny held his hand up. "We didn't see it and wanted to make sure there wasn't something else going on."

Trent pointed to the pool noodles sticking out of the bushes. "Besides the *artful* decorations around the complex, have there been any other unexplained events?"

"Besides my lightbulb finding its repeated demise? Not that I know of." I looked toward Mr. Stewart, who was speaking to another uniformed officer and Dean near our front doors. "But Mr. Stewart would be the best person to ask."

Luckily, Mr. Stewart hadn't called the management police and seemed to be genuinely upset someone was out to hurt me. Of course, he'd expressed his displeasure in the most polite and civil manner.

Lights swung past our small huddle as a car approached.

Trent stepped closer. "Bella, the papers you have in your apartment..." He scanned my face. "Does Alex know about the most recent addition to your articles?"

I held Trent's stare. "No, I never had the opportunity to discuss it with him. I put them up the night he disappeared." And, then he was gone with no chance to ask him anything.

"Who knows about your personal investigation of these events?" Donny's question made it clear he had his cop hat on.

"Alex, Rocky, and Leonard know about my accident. I assumed you"—I glanced at Trent before continuing—"and Dean knew too. As for the articles about Richard, Blake, Bruce, Emily, and the others— just Rocky and Dean."

Donny leaned in a little. "You need to be careful, Bella. You need to let us handle the investigating. It's not safe."

Leonard's words from the hospital the night he'd found Bruce popped back in my head. Was Donny telling me to leave it alone because he was involved, or did he genuinely care about my safety?

Dean's heat engulfed me as he wrapped his arm around my waist and pulled me to him. "She's safe." His tone brooked no argument.

Donny looked back at my apartment and back to me. "I'd say her apartment says differently."

"Where are the officers who were supposed to be doing the drive-bys?" Trent spoke up before things heated between Dean and Donny.

Donny shrugged. "I'm looking into that next."

"I think people know more than they're saying." Dean looked past Donny.

Sheriff Castor stepped up to our group. "Isabella, you seem to be centered around quite a bit of activity lately." The greeting wasn't what I expected from him.

Not quite sure how to respond, I went with the obvious. "It seems that way."

"Yesterday evening, you stated you were not aware of any investigations your brother might be partaking in."

Goosebumps made their appearance on me at the sheriff's words. "That's also true."

His unwavering stare sent chills down my spine. "However, by the appearance of both your dwellings, you two are doing the same off the book's investigations—into your parents' death."

I stiffened. "I didn't realize there was a law against wanting to know what happened to my parents." And what did Alex have? Was he looking into my theories?

"Isabella, your parents' accident, while unfortunate, was ruled an accident and closed ten years ago, and as such, you and your brother have no cause that warrants any further investigation. And it seems your untrained interference in a closed case is creating an unnecessary ruckus and a waste of public resources for matters of importance."

Donny and Trent froze, their expressions full of contempt.

"How do you explain the note then? If Alex's disappearance had nothing to do with ten years ago, then why leave the note? Why break-in to my home, and why kidnap Alex?" I fired back.

"It's a classic bait and switch tactic. While we're forced to reopen a closed case and initiate another investigation into said closed case, the true investigation is not occurring. The criminal is given a reprieve, time to further the muddy the waters, and takes away precious time and resources for the true investigation." The sheriff patted my shoulder. "I know it's difficult, but you should leave this to the professionals and allow us to do our jobs."

Trent and Donny looked like they wanted to throw their notepads at him, Dean vibrated with his restrained frustration and I plain just wanted to kick the sheriff in the shins.

The depth of my anger emphasized my insincerity. "Thank you, Sheriff, for your words of wisdom." I ignored his glow of triumph. "With your insight and guidance, I'm sure your detectives must have found something useful in my apartment? Fingerprints?"

Another damn pat on my shoulder. "I haven't had a chance to speak to the officers inside. As soon as we know something, we'll let you know."

Beyond frustrated, I pushed the sheriff. "No offense to the police force, but it seems like you don't know anything. That's all I've ever heard from you. When *will* you know anything?"

"Miss Hall, the Feldspar Police Department is doing everything within our authority to resolve all our cases." The sheriff's face hardened in his anger.

Donny interjected before an argument erupted between the Sheriff and me. "Sheriff Castor, if you have a minute, I'd like to run some things past you."

"Of course, Detective Markson." Just as quickly, the public figure was back in place.

I watched them walk away and the urge to shake the Sheriff and demand he tell me everything he knew about Alex's disappearance almost overwhelmed me.

"Dean, you ever get the footage from Windham Terrace? See anything?" Trent's gravelly voice pulled me from my thoughts.

"I didn't notice anything, but I'm taking another, more detailed look later. There has to be some answers in them."

"With everything going on I'm going to need that footage too.

Make sure to send it to me as soon as you're done with it." Trent let Dean know.

"Will do."

I looked at Dean and asked, "Do you think it's the same person? I mean, who broke into my apartment and Alex's?" Chills raced up and down my spine. "The person involved in whatever happened ten years ago?"

Dean glanced over at Trent and back at me. "I can't say for sure, but I think it's related. Any chance we can take a look at the official police case on her parents' accident that Alex pulled? Also, do you mind checking in with the lab on the evidence Alex gave them relating this? Bella's remembering a woman at the scene and I think it might be a good idea to determine if all the evidence from that night is actually from that night."

"Yeah. I'll pull it from his desk when I get back to the office. I think we need to take another look at all of it." Trent said.

"What am I missing?" I asked them.

"Don't beat yourself up. We'll figure it out," Dean reassured me.

"Looks like they're wrapping up." Trent looked back at my apartment.

"Go grab an overnight bag." Dean gave my waist a squeeze.

The desire to give him lip on his directive flickered through me, but I'd be lying if I said I wanted to stay in my apartment.

That would be a big fat no.

CHAPTER TWENTY-FIVE

Bella

I'D SHOWERED AND CHANGED INTO MY PJs AND WAS SITTING IN THE huge ass swivel chair in Dean's bedroom, staring at his bed, wondering if he'd join me there or if he thought we were going to go back to the old sleeping arrangements.

"What are you thinking?" Dean's baritone reached me.

I swiveled to face him. "About you."

Leaning against the door jamb, he wore the same thing he had yesterday evening. The memory had me warming.

"Really? And what's that?" He ran his hand through his hair.

"Are you going to sleep with me? I mean in the same bed?" My stomach flipped.

He walked over to me and sprawled across his bed. "Hell yes."

"You are the most handsome man I've ever seen." My belly warmed at his firm response. I got up and walked over and kneeled in front of Dean.

"That's my line. Except you're the most beautiful woman I've ever seen." He slid his fingers through my hair, letting it drop down my front.

Bracing my hands on the bed in front of me, I changed the subject, "What's our next step tomorrow?"

One perfectly sculpted eyebrow shot up.

Ignoring him was hard, but I continued, "You know you're not going to leave me behind, so spill."

"Our first stop is my office. I'm going to review the footage from your apartment and see if I can't spot anything. Then we're going over to the police station and check-in with Trent." Dean graced me with a smile.

"While we're digging into things tomorrow is there any way to find out if Emily has any skeletons in her closet? I mean something Emily said to me—besides everything else she's said—has been bothering me. Most people don't speak to me about my stay at Granite Creek. They avoid the topic or tiptoe around it, but no one ever says those words, Granite Creek, around or to me. Emily..." Staring into Dean's eyes, I begged him to see what I saw. "It's almost like she wanted me to know something about Granite Creek."

"I knew you caught that. Emily has a sealed record."

"She does?" I gasped.

He nodded. "Not surprising. You know Emily was a little wild after her mother left, and with her dad as the sheriff, he covered for her a lot. I have a request in for the files, but with Castor effectively blocking our every move in regards to his daughter I don't think her records will be released to me. I'm going to check in with Trent tomorrow on them."

"Do you think she was there ten years ago?"

"I'd say it's a good guess."

"Do you think her stay at Granite Creek Hospital has something to do with whatever happened at the Winter Formal, and is the real reason why she left Feldspar?"

He ran his fingers through my hair again and tugged me closer. "I think Emily's sealed files will tell us or either lead us to the answers."

"Do you think whoever has Alex will actually harm him? Do you think Alex being a police officer will stop them?" I whispered.

"I think whoever did this is desperate, but Alex isn't stupid. I wouldn't be surprised when we show up to spring him free if he hasn't already tied and gagged his captor." He squeezed my neck.

A laugh burst out of me. I could totally see Alex doing that while cursing the jackass for putting him through the hassle.

I swam in Dean's ocean blue eyes. This man had held my heart, my soul, my everything since before I consciously knew what love was.

Love shone in his eyes.

He swept his thumb across my cheek before tenderly kissing me. He was reverent in his touch, his affection. Not rushing, not devouring, but savoring my taste.

I ran my hands through his hair, down his broad shoulders to his arms, where I simply held his biceps—enjoying their firmness and softness while I licked at Dean's kissable mouth. His minty freshness poured into me, but it was the taste of Dean that melted my heart and made my soul sigh.

Dean peppered my mouth with kisses, trailing his way to my ear. A nip and suckle on my lips to ease the sensual hurt made my breasts swell.

Squeezing his biceps, I tilted my head back, asking for more.

Obliging, Dean licked and sucked a line down to my shoulder. He sank his teeth into my shoulder for a quick second before releasing me to lick his mark. He lifted me onto the bed under him where he settled intimately between the v of my legs. I immediately wrapped myself around him, holding him to me.

I melted under him as my soul sighed at the full-body contact. Everywhere we touched I zinged in awareness, lighting up with need, but I didn't want to rush. Every single part of me tried to memorize each touch, taste, and sound for eternity.

The friction between us as I rubbed the back of his leg sent mini lightning bolts traveling through me. Closer and closer but never quite reaching my core.

Dean seemed as unhurried as I was. Each swipe of his hand, each stroke of his tongue, was leisurely as if savoring the finest brandy. The sips on my neck drew him lower, each stroke of his hand bringing him higher up my rib cage. Hand and mouth meeting at my breast.

The connection of his hand under my top and his strong mouth over it resulted in my back arching. Dean's unyielding suction on my breast shot through me. A moan escaped me at the first tug.

My body heated, readying itself for Dean. Juices flowed from me as my breasts swelled, craving more of his attention. Not hesitating, Dean switched his focus to my neglected breast at the same time he twisted my already-distended nipple. The friction of my top against my sensitized nipple and his incessant touch had me squirming. My legs scissored against my control and I blatantly rubbed my core against his solid rod. The whole time holding him hostage to my breast.

Indescribable sounds escaped me as pleasure short-circuited my brain.

Undulating, I skimmed his back, traced the top of his shorts. Following the edge between our bodies, I slid my fingertips inside his shorts and grazed the head of his penis. Precum coated my fingertips. Dean didn't move away from my breast as he watched me suck one finger at a time, taking his taste into my mouth.

Dean's reprimanding bite on my nipple emboldened me to continue my pursuit of Dean's goods. I pushed his shorts lower, exposing more of his cock, I lifted my hips, demanding Dean allow me to flip him.

Kneeling above Dean and seeing him in his naked glory, I couldn't wait anymore. After shoving his shorts down, I bent over and licked him from his balls to the tip of his penis, stopping to suck only the head. Swirling my tongue around the tip, I licked the seam and enveloped him in one swallow.

"Fuck!" Dean bucked as he fisted my hair.

Not yet.

The taste of his cock was exquisite. Solid, firm, smooth, wide, and mouthwatering. I gorged on him. I pumped with each lick, sucked, and swallowed and savored every drop of precum I squeezed out of him. Continuing to worship him, I reached lower with my free hand and tugged his testicles.

I ignored the pain in my scalp from Dean's hand in my hair. I wasn't giving my treat up for a little pain.

With a solid pop of release of his cock, I looked up at Dean, who watched me.

"Bella, your mouth..."

Not waiting for Dean to finish, I kept eye contact as I pumped him once. Twice. On the third, I drew his balls into my mouth, rolling them with my tongue.

"Fuck. Fuck. Fuck." Dean's head fell back as his back arched.

Precum coated my hand with each pump, and my mouth watered for another taste. Moving back up, I swallowed his cock to the root.

"Mmm." He was fucking delicious.

My panties were drenched. I needed some release—Dean's leg didn't provide enough pressure against my clit. Releasing my hold on Dean's cock, I sat up on my knees and slid my hand into my shorts and underwear and my other hand up under my top.

Dean lay motionless, intently watching me.

Cupping my breast and pulling my nipple with one hand, I used my other hand to slide my fingers through the moisture pooled between my pussy. My head fell back. "Ahh."

"You're so fucking beautiful." Dean was up and in front of me, tearing my clothes off.

Tracing my arm, his hand met mine and together our hands glided back along my pussy. Dean pressed my finger, our fingers deeper, and on our forward motion, he curled us inside in me.

"Show me, Bella. I want to fucking see you come." He watched me.

In and out, he pumped. I was so wet, our hands were soaked, but I couldn't, wouldn't stop.

Dean upped the pleasure, urging me to my release and reached behind me to my anus. At his intimate touch, my pussy convulsed. With his second pass, I waved toward my peak. The third, my body screamed for release.

It was too much and not enough.

"Dean," I begged.

He understood. "Now, Bella."

He curled our fingers inside me and hit my g-spot. Stars exploded behind my eyes.

Dean didn't wait. He flipped me onto my back, and with one hip swing forward, he was inside me.

Another orgasm swept through me as he filled me with his girth.

Wrapping my legs around Dean's waist, I met his rhythm, wanting to return the pleasure.

The feel of him sliding in and out of me—better than anything I ever dreamed. Each pass, each rub, each stretch of muscles built another crescendo in me. Reaching between us, I twirled his testicles in my hand, wanting Dean to release with me. The second I touched him, Dean's pounding increased.

Letting go, I reached behind me to the headboard, pushing against it to gain traction in our lovemaking. Bucking with Dean, I planted my feet on the bed, digging in and opened my legs wide, wanting him deeper.

Grasping my knees, Dean pushed my legs up as he leaned forward, continuing his punishing rhythm. Fully exposed in this position, I slid my hand down to where we met and felt Dean moving in me. Our juices coated my fingers, and I raised it to my mouth for a taste.

Dean lost it.

He flipped me, shoved me up on my knees, wrapped his hand around my hair, yanking my head back, and fucked me.

The power behind Dean's fucking was incredible. My breasts swayed, juices flowed down my legs, and incomprehensible noises escaped me.

I fucking loved it.

I was coming again.

"Dean," I pleaded.

He reached forward and pressed his finger against my clit.

"Deeaaan..." I yelled as my release hit me.

At the same time, Dean moaned his release into my ear as he stilled above me.

We lay panting, trying to gain our breaths. Slowly, Dean slid out of me, making me gasp.

With a little shuffle, Dean left me in the bed and returned with a warm washcloth. Gently wiping me, he asked, "Did I hurt you?"

With extreme effort I forced my eyelids open and answered him, "No."

He stared at me. Tossing the towel to the side, he climbed back into the bed with me.

"You're beautiful, Bella, but when you fucking let go, words don't even come close to your beauty."

I melted into him.

We were tangled in each other and I waited until I felt Dean relax under me. To hear his soft rhythmic breaths of sleep before I whispered my truth to him.

"I love you, Dean."

CHAPTER TWENTY-SIX

Dean

"Is this what your job is like every day?" Bella didn't hide her curiosity.

"With the occasional field trips, yeah." Lifting my eyes from the endless footage from Wyndham Terrace, I saw Bella reclined in the chair with her feet up on the edge of my desk.

She scrunched her nose. "If this weren't a serious matter or my brother, I'd say your job is really, *really* boring."

I chuckled. "It can be, but most of the time I'm out in the field." I pointed to the laptop in her hand and asked, "Did you find anything?"

She shook her head. "Nothing related to what we want, but I now know that Bobby, Ms. Folgers' grandson, has been spending the night with the new kindergarten teacher. Or the fact that my seventy-four-year-old neighbor, Mr. Simmons, gets his morning paper in his bikini briefs every morning, and he's *not* having the same issues that most elderly men have." She rubbed her eyes with the palm of her hands. "And I think I'm going blind because of that last fact."

My body vibrated from my suppressed laughter. "That explains the flowers Ms. Folgers said Bobby gave her the other day." I winked at

Bella when I got her attention. "And I told you if you knew half of what I did, you wouldn't speak to people."

"Fine, you're right, but seriously. I didn't need to know that about Mr. Simmons. I'll never look at him the same again," Bella grumbled. "What about you? Find anything?"

"Not yet, but I've got two more hours left to review from before we arrived at your apartment yesterday."

"Two sets of eyes are better than one." Bella dropped her laptop on my desk and strolled around to watch over my shoulder.

I raised my eyebrows.

She smacked my shoulder. "Yeah, I know you're trained for this, but the tapes I'm watching are boring. Besides, those two hours more than likely will have whoever broke into my apartment on them. I want to see it too."

I pulled Bella into my lap and we watched the last of the footage together. Luckily for us, the managers at Wyndham Terrace had decided after the latest pranks they weren't going to take any more chances and added extra security cameras throughout the complex. Thank fuck they had because the extra ones were the ones that caught him.

He was smart. He knew to use the shadows to hide the bulk of his frame. The large bushes around the complex provided plenty of cover. Not to mention he was dressed in everyday attire as if he were taking a stroll around the neighborhood. Even his demeanor insinuated he wasn't doing anything out of the ordinary.

The fucker capitalized on everything at his disposal and blended in with his environment—just another citizen with a no threat to see here kind of attitude. The dick.

However, all of this presented a huge problem. The man was a professional stretcher of truth and accustomed to hard questions in an intense situation. No matter which way we came at him, he'd have a plausible explanation for all of his actions. Except—how could he explain away the video of him purposely busting Bella's lightbulb? And it was absolutely on purpose. We couldn't pin the knife on him without his prints on it, but he was the only person going into Bella's apartment unauthorized.

Even knowing who was messing with Bella's apartment didn't align any of the damn dots in the case. Yeah, it tightened them up, but what the fuck were we missing? All the same players were on the board, the same events, the same timeline. Everything was the fucking same.

"He must really love his daughter." Bella looked down at me.

My gut soured at that knowledge because he'd already proven the lengths he would go to protect his daughter.

I picked up my phone and called Trent.

"Trent? Got some time to discuss Sheriff Castor?"

"You're fucking kidding me." Exasperation underscored Trent's next words. "It's making more sense but not enough. Castor's behavior has been off lately. He's been pushing back on procedure, requiring a step-by-step blow of Bruce and Alex's investigation from *everyone*, and the amount of time he spends on his cell phone behind closed doors puts a teenager to shame. It's no secret he always covered for Emily back in the day, but now? And a police detective?"

"What wouldn't you do for Dusty?" Bella asked a Trent an unnecessary question.

The pain that crossed Trent's face was all the answer we needed.

"Does he lock his door?"

Trent tensed. "Yeah, and I don't have a valid reason to pick it. To question him, yes."

"You don't," I shot back.

Trent leaned forward. "You don't either and do I have to remind you, you're in a fucking police station. You can't just go around picking fucking locks in plain view of police officers, essentially breaking and entering into the fucking sheriff's office. Again, in plain fucking view of police officers."

"Where does he keep the backup key for emergencies?" Nothing was going to deter me from getting the information I needed to find Alex.

"I knew you were fucking crazy but dammit Dean, the sheriff's office? And anything you find won't be admissible in court. You have no cause to enter his office. So where the fuck would that leave us with Alex?" Trent crossed his arms.

Fucking logic sucked. How to get around it?

Bella's grip on my hand tightened. "When's the FBI going to get here? Do you have their contact number? Can they give us the authority to enter?"

Hope lit Trent's face at Bella's words. "Castor never gave anyone the FBI contact information. He said it was a buddy of his, and he'd handle everything since it was his detective missing." Trent shuffled papers around his desk. "If Castor took Alex, what fucking reason could he possibly have?" He lifted a piece of paper. "Found it. Give me a second. I'm going to give the local FBI branch a call."

"Do you think the FBI will give Trent the authority to go through the sheriff's office?" Bella asked.

"Yeah." I tugged her closer as I realized Castor's actions may have hindered the investigation more than we initially thought.

She leaned into me. "What?"

I scanned her face, wondering how much more she'd be able to handle. "I don't think Castor ever called the FBI. I think the FBI is going to be here in a matter of hours once Trent gets off the phone with them."

She face planted into my chest.

I wrapped my arms around her and leaned down to whisper, "Hang in there, Bella."

She lifted her head and nodded.

Trent's phone bounced in the cradle as he mumbled under his breath, "Fuck me." Then he turned to the bullpen and addressed his fellow officers. "I need your full attention."

Bella's weight lifted from me as she turned to take everyone in.

The room quieted, and with everyone's attention on Trent, he advised, "As of this moment, the FBI has given me the authority of Feldspar Police Department. If Sheriff Castor returns to the police station, he is to be taken into an interrogation room and held there until the FBI arrives and assumes control. I don't have time to explain, but I hope I have your full cooperation for the next few hours."

Bella's hand tightened around mine. She knew that meant Castor had never contacted the FBI and that we'd lost two full days of looking for Alex.

Puzzled looks were exchanged, but no one spoke out against Trent.

Trent nodded once and turned to me. "Let's go break into the sheriff's office."

We were making our way to the sheriff's office when Donny piped up. "What can we do to help?"

Trent's stride didn't falter. "Set up conference room two for an investigation. Bring boxes to the sheriff's office to transport files. Then I want you to pull Alex's file and work it without any of Castor's restrictions."

"Sure thing." Donny jogged out of the room.

Gordon was the next to offer assistance. "What do you need me to do?"

"Get Blake King back into interrogation and see if you can't find out what the root of the beat down was the night of the Winter Formal. Then bring in Leonard Evans and grill him about everything." Trent kept moving toward Castor's office as he barked out orders. "Then I want you to go over Richard Coleman's death with a fine-tooth comb. Go back to the night he was arrested at Shackles and what his ramblings were about. Don't leave anything out. While you're at, pull the report on the Hall's accident from ten years ago and any other accidents on that stretch of road for the week prior to theirs. This time look at each word written, each piece of evidence collected or not, each person involved as suspect. Don't assume anything at face value. While you're at it contact the lab and get a rush put on the evidence Alex sent them."

"On it." Gordon lifted his phone to begin on his list.

At Castor's door, Trent turned to Bella. "I'm sorry, Bella, but I can't let you in the room. You're a civilian and linked to all of these cases."

She nodded. "I figured, but is it okay if I just stand right outside the door? I can't... please don't make me leave." She whispered, fear in her words, on her being.

"Sure," Trent agreed.

Bella

My stomach was in knots. They pulled box after box of files out of Sheriff Castor's office, and I wanted to get in there and dig into it all. Somewhere in all those papers was the answer to why Richard and Bruce had beat up Blake, why Emily had left Feldspar, why Richard had died, why Bruce had been attacked, who had taken Alex, and why my parents had died. Castor had had the answers at his fingertips this whole time and because of his need to protect his daughter, we had nothing but questions.

Both Trent and Dean headed out of the office.

"Let's go." Dean grabbed my hand as he got to me.

"What? Where are we going?" I didn't want to go anywhere without the files.

He didn't answer as he followed Trent to the conference room. They both stopped outside the door.

"I'm going to let you in here for ten minutes. Ten minutes only. After that, I can't let you anywhere near any of this, and if anyone asks, I will deny I let you in here. Do you understand me?" Trent stared at me, waiting for my reply.

My heart pounded. "Yes."

Trent, Dean, and I entered the conference room with all the boxes and files spread throughout. I walked over to the table and moved some papers toward me. "He has just about everything I have on my accident." Moving more documents around, I noticed Sheriff Castor's scribbles on the sides. "Did you notice the notes he made in the margins? They're pretty darn close to what I've been saying all these years." To knowing I was right.

Trent and Dean's "yeahs" were simultaneous.

The silence stretched as we sorted through papers, read through the notes, and processed everything Castor had gathered on me and Alex since my parents' death.

"Is it just me, or is it a little creepy that the sheriff has a comprehensive file on his daughter's life?" I asked Trent and Dean. I looked at the pictures of Emily leaving work, having drinks with her friends, weeding her flower bed, and having breakfast *in* her kitchen. Did she know her father was watching her every move?

"It's not creepy. It's fucking psycho," Trent stated the obvious.

Dean rumbled his agreement. "This is fucked up. What dad stalks his grown daughter?"

"Look at that." Trent slid a paper toward Dean and me.

I picked up the paper and looked up at Trent. "That's my admission paper to Granite Creek." He tossed another at me and I scanned it. "That's Emily's admission paper to Granite Creek. We were there at the same time. I don't understand. Why was she in the hospital? I thought she moved there because her aunt needed help?"

Dean pulled the paper out of my hand and scanned it. He glanced up at Trent. "Did you see?"

At Trent's nod, I asked, "What? What did you see?"

Leaning into Dean, I reread the paper. "No! Oh my, poor Emily. I know Bruce and Richard are major assholes, but..." I swallowed. "They wouldn't rape Emily, would they?"

Dean wrapped an arm around my shoulders, pulling me into him. "Originally, I would have said no." Shaking the paper in his other hand, he continued, "Now, I'm not so sure."

"It doesn't state who the culprits were, but one and one are easily adding up to two," Trent added.

"Why didn't she press charges? Why didn't Castor arrest them? It doesn't make sense, and what does it have to do with my parents' death?" I gave Dean more of my weight as I held onto the side of his shirt.

Trent and Dean exchanged a look before Dean cupped my face. "You have no fucking clue how thankful I am that you don't know what Emily went through that night. But, if I'm right, can you imagine what she was feeling after that? How much of a mess she would have been? And then got behind the wheel of a vehicle to escape?"

As his words penetrated the fog in my brain, I tensed. Barely getting the words out, I breathed, "Emily killed my parents?"

Dean's hold on me tightened. "Before we jump to that conclusion, how about we have another conversation with Emily?" He waited for my agreement.

My nod was slow—the implications of everything we'd discovered filtering through my brain.

"Bella, I know you're getting some big news right now, but when we speak to Emily, you need to let Dean and me handle the questioning. Whatever information we get from Emily needs to be admissible in court."

Sucking in a breath, I squared my shoulders and looked Trent in the eyes. "I want... to say that I want her to pay." I rocked between justice and sympathy. "But did she already pay that night?"

"Bella..." Dean's arms flexed around me.

Turning in his arms, I cut him off. "No. I'll follow your rules." To an extent. "But we have to follow this through. I need answers, and I want Alex back."

Trent reminded me, "Everything we get has to be admissible in court. We don't do any shortcuts."

"Then let's go find out the truth." I wanted it admissible in court as well, but I wasn't going to stand by anymore. Fuck that.

"What do you mean by that?" Dean's voice was weary.

"It means if Emily isn't home, *I* don't need a search warrant to *search* her home." I looked over at Trent. "Pretend you didn't hear that."

"You're going to sneak around Emily's home?"

"Yes." I attempted to walk toward the door.

Dean held onto my arm. "You're not doing any sneaking around."

"Yes, I am." I dared Dean to stand in my way.

"No, you're not. Have you lost your mind?" His anger was barely leashed. "You may not need a warrant to search her home, but it doesn't mean you can't be arrested for trespassing or breaking and entering. Not to mention the fact Castor may be there or the fact you've never snuck around and searched someone's home."

I kept my mouth closed. Dean was right, not that I was going to let that stop me. "I won't get caught." Looking over at Trent, I implored him, "We're talking about Alex."

"Dammit, Bella." The space between his eyes crinkled as his frustration mounted.

I didn't say anything. I wasn't turning back, no matter what.

"If she's not home, it won't stop you, will it?" Dean stared at me.

"No."

Dean's "Shit" was resigned. "You'll follow my lead. If I say run, you'll run. No hesitation. No backtalk."

"As much as I want you two to get the answers we need, I can't let you guys question Emily." Trent held his hand when he saw me open my mouth. "Without me." I snapped my mouth shut. "I'm heading over to the sheriff's house first. He's unraveling, and I might get lucky and find something at his place."

Dean turned his head toward Trent. "Take Markson with you. If Castor is truly losing it, then you'll need backup—and an impartial witness."

"Will do. I'm going to contact Granite Creek PD and let them know what's going on. It won't hurt to have them on notice if anything goes down," Trent included.

I stepped back and grabbed my purse. "Let's go." My bones ached with the knowledge I was going to find Alex soon.

Trent shook his head. "Bella, Castor's house first, then Emily."

I bit my lip. I couldn't agree to that.

Dean tugged me into his arms. "You're going to take off the second we turn our backs, aren't you?"

I looked to the side. Yes, a bathroom escape seemed imminent.

Dean sighed. "We'll meet you at Emily's, Trent."

My head snapped up at Dean. *Yes!*

"Shit. Don't do anything before I get there." Trent's resignation was loud and clear.

CHAPTER TWENTY-SEVEN

Bella

"W HY ARE WE JUST SITTING HERE?" I ASKED DEAN FOR THE millionth time.

Dean and I sat in his truck, staring down the street at Emily's house. Well, I was inching toward bouncing out of my seat with anxiety. Something inside of me pushed me to get inside Emily's house. That if I waited any longer, it'd be too late.

"To give Trent time." He rested his arm on the back of my seat. The epitome of someone with no care in the world.

"Do you think Sheriff Castor is here?" Smoothing my sweaty hands down my jeans, I looked around Emily's neighborhood.

Dean checked his mirrors. "No, I don't see his truck."

I bounced in my seat and pleaded, "Then why are we sitting here? Let's go!"

"Patience, Bella," Dean said with *all* the patience in the world.

Both Dean and Trent knew what they were doing, so Dean's advice to be patient was sound and logical. The problem was that feeling inside of me was getting stronger. Pushing me to move and the fuck with patience.

Before Dean could stop, I opened the door and climbed outside. "I'm sorry, but I can't. I *have* to get inside."

I didn't wait for his response. I marched my way over to Emily's house, but before I could pound on her front door, Dean yanked me back by my belt loop.

He whispered low in my ear, "I'll spank your ass later for this little stunt, but until then, you will follow my lead. It is non*fucking*negotiable. Do you understand me, Bella?"

My acquiescent was immediate. "Yes." Just get us into the house. Now.

Dean's arm extended past me to the doorbell, the whimsical sound no longer soothing as we waited for Emily to open the door. What was taking her so long? What was she doing?

Dean's other arm slid around my waist as I vibrated with frustration. "Calm down."

Fuck calm. I pushed the doorbell again and chanted over and over, "Open. Open. Open."

Dean rubbed circles on my side as we waited.

"Her house isn't that big. What's taking her so long?"

"She may not be home, Bella," was Dean's calm—*how was he calm?* — response.

I looked up at him. "Well then, pick the lock. Get us in there."

He smiled, but I didn't see anything to smile about. "Don't move."

Dean was a seriously talented man. To anyone else, we looked like a couple in a lover's embrace from behind. He utilized our position to pick the lock without anyone being the wiser, and within seconds we were standing inside Emily's house.

It looked the same as it had the day we'd originally visited.

Dean kept his hand on me, forcing me to stand in position at Emily's front door. With his other hand, he tilted my chin up to his face. Once he had my eyes, he lifted his finger to his mouth, letting me know to stay quiet.

I nodded once to convey I got his message, but I didn't know how he could hear anything. My heart beat frantically in my ears, so it was the only thing I heard.

A few more seconds, then Dean walked around me and pointed at me to stay behind him. Again, another quick nod from me. Anything to get us going.

Now that we were inside, the urge to press on escalated. My body vibrated with the need to *move*.

I grabbed onto Dean's back belt loop to restrain myself from pushing past him and racing through Emily's house. Dean was slow and methodical in checking each room we passed. From my observation, nothing was out of place, but since I hadn't explored it the one time we visited, I couldn't be sure.

By the time we reached the backdoor, my stomach rolled. I gave Dean's belt loop the slightest tug to get his attention. Quietly, I let Dean know, "He's here. I can feel him."

Bless the man, Dean didn't question my sixth sense. "Alex?"

I nodded.

Dean inched the curtain on the window on the back door to the side and peeked.

I held my breath, waiting.

He turned and leaned down to my ear. "It's not a big yard, but we're going to be exposed in some areas. Stay behind me as we make our way to the shed."

I gave Dean a little shove in response and bounced on the balls of my feet. I guess I expected the door to creak and give us away, but it was eerily silent. Even the birds were quiet.

Emily's backyard was just as tidy as her front yard. Manicured lawn, flowers everywhere, trees providing a decent amount of shade, and one neat medium-sized shed in the corner.

I propelled forward at the sight of the shed, completely ignoring Dean's earlier instructions. My legs jellified with each step that brought me closer to the door.

"Dammit, Bella!" Dean whispered-yelled after me.

The screech of the shed door as I opened it reverberated throughout the backyard, killing any hope of a stealth search. Not waiting for my eyes to adjust, I'd barely stepped into the shed when I was yanked in, my arm jabbed up behind me, and a hand covered my mouth.

Someone rumbled something into my ear, but I wasn't paying attention—not with Emily and Leonard in front of me. My eyes bugged out. What the actual hell?

Pain radiated up my arm, and I tried to grab the hand on my mouth to scream.

"It's Bella. Let her go," Leonard said.

The pain in my arm immediately alleviated as the person behind me released me.

I pulled my arm forward and tucked it to my front rubbing where it hurt. At the same time I started to turn around to give whoever grabbed me a piece of my mind when I heard, "Well, isn't this convenient?"

Shit. Sheriff Castor. He sauntered in taking us all in.

I was pulled behind arm dude when he replied, "I don't know if *convenient* is the word I would use."

Alex.

"Really, what word would you use? Fortunate? Lucky?" The sheriff's smirk was beyond creepy.

Emily took a small step forward. "Dad, what are you doing here?"

"Covering for your stupidity, *again*." He aimed his furious eyes at Emily.

Pain tore through Emily's face. "*My* stupidity? *You're* the one running around killing, beating, and kidnapping people."

I sucked in a breath.

With a gun in his hand, the sheriff swung his arm around the room. "Because of your stupidity." He began pacing in the small doorway. "All those years after your mother died and you ran amuck through town. Who do you think covered up your messes?" He thumped his chest with the gun. "Me! That's who. Not once did you stop to think about how your reckless behavior would affect me. The sheriff. Instead, I had to manipulate reports, turn a blind eye to misdemeanors—all so charges wouldn't be pressed against you. Not including the bribes to have your record sealed. How would that look to have the sheriff's daughter with a record?" He stopped and waved his gun at Emily again. "Did you ever stop to think how that reflects *on me?*"

Anger slowly replaced Emily's pain the more the sheriff spoke. "Yes, *Dad*, I did. It was the only way to get your attention."

As they argued, Leonard stepped closer to the wall of gardening tools.

Castor noticed and swung his gun to Leonard. "Stop. Do you think I don't know why you're here? Why after ten years, you started calling and visiting my daughter? Trying to get Emily to speak up against me?" He thumped his chest again. "She owes me. I've done everything for her."

"She didn't ask you to kill Richard, beat my brother up, or kidnap Alex." Leonard faced off with the sheriff. "Your pride got in the way. You couldn't handle the fact Richard mouthed off at Shackles about how you didn't do anything ten years ago and how you can't do anything about it now. That was *your* pride, not Emily's asking." He leaned toward Castor, ripping with anger. "Bruce didn't do anything to you. He wanted to make it right. He wanted peace and to change his life. He found love."

"Shut up!" Castor yelled. "Richard was a piece of shit. He should have kept his big mouth shut. I would have let it go, but he bragged to the men who work *for me* that he got something over on me. I couldn't let that go. What would they think that the sheriff didn't and couldn't handle someone as repugnant as Richard?"

All this time, I'd thought Castor had called in his favors to have Emily's indiscretions swept under the rug out of love for his daughter. Instead, they were based on his need to appear sanctimonious.

His pacing grew more erratic, and each step showcased his jerky movements. "So, I did what I had to do. I killed him and staged it to look like a drunk driving accident." He swung his maniacal gaze to Alex and me. "I thought it was fitting to have it where you crashed ten years ago. I knew Bruce would get the message and keep his mouth shut."

My stomach dipped, and I grabbed Alex by the shirt. Castor had confirmed Richard and Bruce were connected to my accident, to my parents' deaths. Did he mean it was their vehicle involved in what happened to me?

"*You* were the big game Bruce wanted to catch at his cabin. He wanted you exposed so he could live his life with a good woman and not keep looking over his shoulder." Leonard jabbed a finger at Castor. "*Your* ego wouldn't let it go. You beat him and left him on the verge of death because you couldn't let it go. Why didn't you let him just be?"

The sheriff jolted as he came out of his thoughts. The crazed look in his eyes chilled me as he turned to Leonard. "Your brother in love? Ha! Like any good woman would want anything to do with him. He thought I would believe such a thing." He jerked his head side to side. "No. Bruce was just like Richard. Trying to one-up me. I couldn't let him say anything. No one could know."

Leonard faced Emily. "When I visited you the other day, you said you didn't know anything. You acted shocked when I told you everything that was happening. Did you lie?"

"No, I didn't lie. I had an idea, but I didn't know for sure." Tears gathered in Emily's eyes.

Alex shifted to his left, blocking me from the sheriff's view. "Is that why you hid me from your father the day I came to visit you? Because you had an idea he was behind everything?"

Emily's nod was meek. "Yes. My father is big on his public appearance. The timing of everything was too coincidental. So after Leonard's visit, I contacted my dad to find out the truth. We made plans for him to visit me on the same day you were here. I didn't want you here when he got here, but you wouldn't leave. I didn't know what else to do, so I overdosed your coffee with my anxiety medicine. I figured you'd be out of for a while—at least until my dad left. So I dragged you back here until I could figure out what to do."

"Why didn't you tell me when I was here? Dean and I would have helped you," I asked Emily.

Emily drooped. "I was scared. I didn't know what to do." Fear crossed her face when she looked at her dad. "My dad can be unpredictable, but I...love him. He has protected me in his own way."

In a demented sort of way, sure.

"Yes, I have, and this is the thanks I get." Sheriff Castor pointed his gun at Alex and me. "You kept him hidden from me. So I searched his house trying to find any clues to what he was doing, to where he could be, and to how close he was to finding everything out. Now, instead of having to get rid of one body, I have three to deal with." Sheriff Castor shook his head in resignation. "You never did think things through."

I squeezed Alex's shirt at the sheriff's words.

Emily went back on a foot. "Dad, are *you* thinking? You're talking about killing three people—one of them a police detective. There is no way you can keep this quiet. This will be all over the news."

"I'm the sheriff. No one will say anything. I'll keep putting off the FBI, and my men know not to go around me." He straightened his shoulders.

I tightened my grip on Alex's shirt.

The sheriff didn't miss my reaction. "Trent contacted the FBI, didn't he?"

Alex blocked me from the sheriff's gaze again.

Castor began his maniacal pacing again. "It can still work. Dusty is an excellent leverage piece in keeping Trent in line. He can call the FBI back and let them know it was a false alarm." He stopped pacing and fixed me with a determined look. "Where's Dean? He hasn't left your side since this all started. Between Dean, your nosey neighbor, and Raquel, getting close to you or your apartment has been a serious nuisance for me. Even when I busted your lightbulbs hoping to use the cover of the dark someone was always there. Why can't they ever leave you alone?"

"I don't know." Although it was a great fucking question. Why wasn't Dean coming to save the day? I mean we already figured out it was Castor busting my lights and Castor was right—Dean hadn't left my side so where was he now? He had to be close.

The sheriff aimed his gun at me. "This isn't a good time to lie to me, Isabella."

I shook my head. "I'm not lying. I don't know where he is." But any time now would be an excellent time for Dean to pop up and come to the rescue.

Alex shifted once more, placing himself in the line of sight of the gun and drawing attention away from me. "What was Richard trying to get over on you, Sheriff, and how was the site of the accident a message?"

"Richard raped me at the Winter Formal."

Emily's quiet words dropped a bomb in the shed.

Sheriff Castor dropped his arm. "Shut up! We don't ever speak of it!"

"Not speaking about it doesn't erase it, Dad."

Alex's head swiveled to Emily. "That's what you were going to tell me when your dad showed up."

She nodded but didn't take her eyes off her father. "It's the real reason I moved here ten years ago. My aunt threatened my dad she'd make *everything* public if he didn't let me live with her. I spent time at Granite Creek Hospital being treated for my physical injuries and my mental health." Emily's face softened. "I was there the same time you were, Isabella."

Pieces fell together at her admission. "That's why your dad always visited me when I was there. He was there checking on you."

"He was checking to see if you remembered what happened."

My eyes shot to Leonard as he took a step back.

"Remember what?" I asked.

"Your accident," Alex added. "Our parents' death. That's how Bella and I fit in this, isn't it?"

Emily nodded as tears streamed down her face. "After Richard raped me at the Winter Formal, I was a...mess. I wasn't thinking straight. I wanted to get as far away from Richard, the Winter Formal, everything as possible. So I got in my car and drove. It was the wrong thing to do, but I wasn't thinking clearly. I just needed to get away."

The air in the shed pressed into me as she spoke. Having confirmation of what happened to Emily weighed on me. The suffering she must have endured all these years. My hand hurt from clenching Alex's shirt.

"I never meant to hurt you or anyone. I...I'm so, *so* sorry for all the pain I've caused you." She sucked in a shallow breath. "I couldn't see where I was driving, and then by the time I did, it was too late. I hit the back of your car. Your dad braked so hard you guys skidded across the road. He tried to correct it but it was too late. You went off the side of the road. I tried to get down to you, but the terrain was too dangerous. I couldn't get down to you."

Finally knowing why my dad had swerved didn't abate the pain or loss. Years of pain freshly assaulted me.

"I called my dad for help. I always called him for help. I thought he'd get everyone out there to save you, but..." She sucked in another breath. "He pulled me away. Told me to let you all die so no one would know what really happened. I didn't know he was mentally unstable then."

"Enough! I'm finally going to put an end to all of this. It's ten years overdue." Castor aimed his gun at Alex.

It all happened at once.

A chorus of "No!" reverberated in the shed as everyone scrambled for the gun.

Emily shot forward to tackle the gun away from her father. Leonard grabbed a shovel and swung at the sheriff. At the same time, Dean appeared behind the sheriff and joined Emily and Leonard in their struggle against the sheriff.

Alex maintained his position in front of me as a human shield, and I utilized my measly grip on Alex's shirt to shove him out of the way.

Grunts echoed through the shed as everyone fought with the sheriff for control of the gun. I saw an opening, the sheriff's gun hand visible between the gap in their bodies. My forward momentum faltered as Alex yanked me back, and the deafening sound of the gun being fired had me staggering.

Everyone froze at once, and the horror on the faces around me let me know the sheriff's aim had been true after all. Terrified at the thought of losing Alex, I turned to him.

"Shit!" Alex cursed. "Bella, I got you."

He pulled me down to the ground, and I asked, "Did he get you?" I tried to lift my hand to scan his torso, but there was a weight on my arm—making it impossible to raise it.

"No, Bella. He didn't get me." Alex's eyes roamed my face.

"Bella." Dean wrapped his hand around my neck.

His eyes were concerned too. I tried to speak, to ask him what was wrong, but something was clogging my throat. I struggled to clear it, but it hurt; my chest, my lungs.

"Stay with me, Bella." Dean squeezed my neck.

I wanted to tell him I was right there, but my voice didn't work.

I was so tired. I just wanted to take a nap.

The last thing I remembered was Dean yelling, "Don't you fucking go!"

CHAPTER TWENTY-EIGHT

Bella

I'D HAD SOME STRANGE DREAMS, BUT THIS ONE RANKED RIGHT UP there with the night of my parents' death. I'd fought with the sheriff in his daughter's shed while attempting to rescue my brother.

The most worrisome part of the dream was the look on Dean's face as he told me I'd be all right as he gave me the sweetest kiss before leaving. It was so sad—his expression, the kiss, the goodbye.

I had difficultly shaking the feeling off, sluggish and slow as if I'd been drugged. What I needed was caffeine to wipe the cobwebs out of my mind.

In my attempt to roll over and get out of bed, I was hit with such agony from my torso. The scream that escaped me unavoidable.

"Shit. Don't move Bella."

Alex gently pushed me back down on the bed.

"Easy. Slow breaths in and out."

His calm, steady voice penetrated my pain-fogged brain, and I listened to him to talk me through breathing—one slow, agonizing breath at a time.

I carefully opened my eyes and saw Alex hovering over me. "Better?" he asked.

"Depends." My throat was raw.

Alex reached behind to the table and grabbed a cup with ice chips. "Open a little—this will help with your throat."

Yeah, that soothed my throat.

"Better?"

"Yeah."

"It's good to see you, Bella." My brother was worried.

"It's good to see you too, Alex." I scanned the room and realized I was in the hospital. My eyes shot back to Alex, who was shoving aside the blankets next to my hand, looking for something. That's when I noticed the bandage on his forehead.

"There it is." He held up a nurse's call button.

"Your head... Are you okay?"

A small smile from Alex. "That's my question."

"Well, you're the one who was kidnapped by Psycho One and Psycho Two, and you have a bandage on your forehead."

A shrug. "A small bump. You... fuck, Isabella, what were you thinking? You tried to attack *a* man *with* a gun."

"So, it wasn't a dream?"

"No, it wasn't."

I was afraid of that. "Me? What happened to me?"

"I've been wondering that since you were born." A small smile graced Alex's mouth.

"Jerk." I grinned letting him know I didn't mean it.

"A jerk you love."

"Yes, and you're avoiding answering. Just give it to me."

"Oh, you're awake. How are you feeling?" Nurse Booby asked me even though her eyes devoured Alex. If I knew laughing wouldn't hurt, I would have. Alex look repulsed.

Alex unclenched his jaw. "You didn't answer her."

"Was she speaking to me?"

His eyes narrowed, and I really, *really* wanted to laugh.

"Anything you want me to *look* at? Any pains you need me to *handle*?" The last word breathed as if she was already handling him.

This wasn't fair. Me, unable to laugh, and a live, in-your-face comedy happening right in front of me.

I took pity on my brother and got Nurse Booby's attention. "I'd like to speak with the doctor on duty. Would you mind getting the doctor for me?"

"I'll let Dr. Gleason know you want to talk to him."

She sashayed out the door without another word or backward glance.

"She's so full of sunshine." My words dripped in sarcasm.

"You're such a pain in my ass."

"Yes, but you love me anyway." I threw his words back at him.

"Bella?" Alex's somber tone replaced our earlier humor.

"Yeah?"

"Don't do that again."

"I'll make you a deal. Don't get kidnapped by crazy people, and I won't tackle those crazy people." He knew he wouldn't get any other answer from me because he loved me just as much as I loved him.

"Deal."

"All right, you've avoided the question enough. Tell me what happened before the doctor gets here."

Alex looked back at the closed door. "If he's not here in five, I'll go find himself."

"I don't know if that's safe. Nurse Booby might corner you in the storage closet."

"Nurse Booby?" His lips twitched.

My eyebrows shot up. "Do I need to explain that one?"

A shake of his head.

"Stop stalling."

Alex shoved a hand through his hair. "When you decided to intervene with the good Sheriff, he fucking shot you. Depending on how you want to look at it, he wasn't aiming, so he missed all the vital organs. But that doesn't mean he didn't do damage. Fuck, Isabella, do you have any idea how fucking lucky you are? He could have killed you!"

I reached for Alex's hand. "He had you. He was going to shoot you. I didn't have a choice."

"What would I do without you?" His face softened.

"Ditto."

The swoosh of the door alerted us to a visitor.

A nod from the doctor at Alex. "Detective Hall." He focused on me. "Miss Hall, nice of you to join us. I'm Dr. Gleason. How are you feeling?"

"Like I've been shot."

"Well, getting shot will do that to you."

Alex's calm and serious voice matched his expression. "I'm sorry, Dr. Gleason, my sister is a smartass when she's cranky. Isabella, be a good girl and answer the good doctor's question *politely*."

"You're lucky I'm laid up in this bed, immobile."

The pissy mood slid out of Alex. "Yeah, I am."

God, I loved my brother.

Turning back to the doctor, I told him, "It hurts to move. Sharp pains in my torso. Mostly just tired, but I guess that's a combination of the medicine and my body recuperating."

"That's good to hear. Now, I don't want you to move because I don't want you to tear anything open. The bullet didn't do you any favors while inside you, and I don't want to take any chances we might cause any unnecessary damage. You should have a full recovery, and there shouldn't be any lessening in functionality."

"That sounds good. Do you have an idea of how much longer I'll have to be here?"

"A few more days. I want to make sure you're all good."

"Thanks, Dr. Gleason." Alex shook the doctor's hand.

"No problem." He turned back to me. "I'll check in on you a little later."

Alex turned to me. "Why do you have to be such a pain in the ass?"

"You'd be bored if I wasn't." I couldn't put it off any longer. "What happened to Sheriff Castor? Emily? Leonard? Dean?"

Dean was who I was mainly interested in. Sheriff Castor could rot in jail for all I cared. Emily's penance came that night in so many forms. And she's been trying to right her mistakes all these years, even if she did go about the wrong way in the end. Leonard—I wasn't sure about. I needed time to process all of it before I decided where I stood on our friendship.

He hooked his foot on the leg of the chair and pulled it next to the bed before he sat down.

"Well, shortly after you blacked out, the local authorities arrived with the FBI. They arrested Emily, who didn't resist. She recounted the same story to the FBI that she mentioned in the shed. I'm not sure how the feds will proceed with her in regards to our parents' death, but she's ready to face whatever punishment is dealt to her. Leonard was released shortly after because he wasn't an active participant in any of this. He had some inkling about things but no concrete proof of anything, so the feds let him go. As for Sheriff Castor—well, Dean hogtied him right after he shot you, and before that, Dean was outside recording our little engagement for evidence. Everything was turned over to the feds, who have Castor in custody and are now taking the lead on the entire investigation."

"Wow. It's still so hard to believe. The whole time I thought Castor did everything he did for his daughter out of love for her. It turns out he's just a little psycho."

Alex sighed. "Yeah. Working for Castor had its moments, but I didn't see this coming. He kept that side of himself under pretty tight wraps."

"Was she trying to help you or him? I don't get it. She kept you hidden for days. Dean and I had been to see her, asked about you. She could have told us she had you. We would have helped her while saving you. She never said a word." Just for that, she deserved some substantial time in a four-by-four cell.

"You gotta remember Bella; she's been under Castor's thumb for years. Doing her best to live up to his expectations. And as twisted as it sounds, she loves her dad. He may have gone off the rails and did some horrible things, but in his own twisted mind, he did them out of love, to protect her."

"That may be, but I was there when she said he did those things to protect his image, his ego. Love or not, it was wrong." My fear of almost losing Alex wouldn't let me easily forgive Emily.

"I agree, but it's not as simple as that. What I didn't tell you is that

Emily also collected her evidence against her dad during my brief stay with her. And with the new analysis of the evidence from your accident that I had sent in before my disappearance—it all backs Emily's collection. That includes the auto repair guy confirming Castor did what he always did—bribed the guy to fix Emily's car and keep it quiet. Of course, she didn't want to use it or turn against her dad, but as you saw at the shed, he gave her no choice. When it comes down to it—love, it fucks with people." He stood up. "Enough talking. Don't think I didn't notice your eyelids drooping and the yawns you've been trying to hide. We can talk about this later."

Of course, a huge yawn cracked wide open. "That sounds good. Alex?"

"Yeah?"

"I'm glad you're okay."

"Love you too."

I might have been tired and recovering from a gunshot wound, but that didn't mean I didn't notice Alex hadn't mentioned Leonard.

Or the fact Dean wasn't there.

THE NEXT SEVERAL days went by at a snail's pace. It was eat, sleep, and pain meds. I was beginning to believe this was a new form of torture.

Visitors came and went. Rocky, Emma, Brooke, Margie, Ava, Parker. Everyone came bearing gifts, gossip flying around town, and well wishes for my speedy recovery. It made me realize how lucky I was to have such great friends. It also hurt that, while the entirety of Feldspar rotated through my hospital door, Dean was absent. Not a text—and I checked a million times daily—not a message—again, another million checks—nothing.

My casual attempt at questioning Alex about Dean's whereabouts gave me nothing. Dean's wrapping up a new case, or he's working on a new case, or he's coloring his hair. Okay, he didn't say the last one, but he might as well have.

Dean was avoiding me. I was laid up in a hospital bed recovering from a bullet wound, and he'd skipped out on me. I'd known it would happen. Alex rescued, and the bad guys behind bars; I didn't need his protection anymore. Therefore, he didn't need to be around me anymore.

I tried not to let it hurt, and for the most part—while I was being tortured by the hospital staff—I was able to accomplish that. Otherwise, I failed miserably. I mean, I knew we would never be, it was impossible, but my stupid, stupid heart didn't want to believe it. When I slept, I dreamt of my time with Dean. How he'd held me, looked at me, the way he'd made me feel. I know he hadn't meant to, but the little bit of resistance I'd created between a possible future with him, he'd crushed. I was exposed in a way I knew I couldn't get past. I didn't have a choice.

"Hey, what's the gloomy look for?"

Alex was the best brother ever with the most horrible timing.

"I just finished some stretches, and it's lingering."

"You didn't overdo it trying to recover faster?"

I wasn't going to answer that honestly. "The doctors say discomfort is normal."

"Uh, huh."

"Tell me that delicious smell is from Harper's Corner and that it's all for me."

"Of course, it's from Harper's, but I don't know if I should share with someone who stretches the truth."

"Occupational hazard."

"What?" Alex tilted his head in question.

"My brother's a detective. I learned to be creative to survive his interrogations."

He threw his head back and laughed. Then he pulled the tray closer to me and laid our meal out.

"Mmm...this is delicious."

"Yup. Now, you want to tell me what's up?"

I almost choked on my bite of food. "Nice, stealth attack."

A shrug. "What can I say? I've been watching out for my baby sister for years, and I *am* a detective."

I pointed my fork at him. "Touché."

He chewed his food and gave me his *I'm waiting* look.

"I don't know if I want to have this conversation with you. It's about a boy."

"You mean Dean."

I semi-shrugged so I wouldn't hurt myself. "Who else?"

"You know, I love you both, but right now I want to kick both your asses."

This time I was confused. "What? What'd I do?"

"Both of you can't see past your own nose when it comes to each other." He shook his head.

"What?" I was too hungry and tired to put any effort into frowning.

"I thought I would be happy you two finally hooked up. Not happy you hooked up but that you both finally got your fingers out your ass and saw what was right in front of you. Now, I'm not so sure."

"What?" I felt like a broken record.

"Even after, you're both still clueless."

"What?" What was he talking about?

He pointed his fork to my cornbread. "You going to eat that?"

"Wha... Touch my food and prepare to lose a finger. Now, go back to what you were saying and explain to me what you're saying."

"Isabella, you love Dean."

I wasn't hungry anymore.

He took hold of my hand. "Listen to me, Bella. You've loved Dean your whole life, and it may have taken Dean a little longer to figure it out, but he does loves you too. When he finally got a clue, he did what he'd been doing—ignoring it."

"I hate to break it to you big brother, but I spent a lot of time with Dean and he doesn't feel the same way. If he did, he'd be here right now." And the pain I was feeling had nothing to do with the gunshot.

Alex ignored my comment and continued, "Unfortunately, it took me getting kidnapped to throw you two together in a way I hoped would be permanent. However, Dean's a stubborn ass, so I have to interfere with my sister's love life. And I can't believe I just said that and didn't convulse." Alex shivered in revulsion.

I threw my cornbread. It would've hit him square in the face if he didn't have quick reflexes.

"Shame on you, that's Harper's."

I ignored him. "If what you're saying is true, then why isn't he here now?"

"Because Dean's got his head up his ass and I expect you to stop waiting for him to get it out." His hand went up before I could get a word out. "Yes, I know you're laid up right now, but you do have a phone, and you won't be laid up in forever." The fun-loving tease left his voice. "Isabella, don't fuck this up. Don't let him slip through your fingers. You'll regret it if you do."

My brother could be serious when the situation called for it. He was mostly an easy-going guy who made sure life's ups and downs didn't stress me. So when he was serious, I paid attention. But I had an inkling this wasn't all about Dean and me. Who was it my brother had loved and lost?

He squeezed my hand. "Promise me you'll try."

"Promise." Although I had no idea how I was going to do that. "Don't think I didn't notice you haven't given me my cornbread back."

He released my hand, smiled, and took a bite of *my* cornbread.

CHAPTER TWENTY-NINE

Bella

STARING OUT THE HOSPITAL WINDOW, I THOUGHT OF HOW I'D slept, rested, and eaten my way through all the directives the hospital staff had given me. I was over it. I wanted out. I wanted to get to Dean, scream at him, shake him, and make love to him with or without a doctor's approval. Not necessarily all in that order. But I had to wait for the doctor's release, and if I had anything to do with it, and I would, I'd be released later this afternoon.

Leonard's barely there, "Isabella?" reached my ears.

I turned my attention to the man who'd been a fantastic friend to me for the last ten years. Who helped me get through one of the most challenging times in my life, and I wondered if I'd ever truly known him.

"I'm surprised you came."

He stepped fully into the room, closing the door behind him. "I wasn't quite sure if you wanted to see me or what I would say to you when I did."

"Honestly, I'm not sure either." Even though I was sitting in my bed exhaustion was settling in.

We stared at each other—the quiet of the hospital room weighing down on us.

"Was it all a lie?" Was our friendship a lie?

He took a tentative step in. "No." He paused, looking for his next words. "Our friendship, that was true."

"Really?" I cocked my head.

He made it to the chair across from me and sat. "Absolutely." Sincerity poured from him. "When we first met, I about peed my pants."

A chuckle burst out of me. "What?"

A small smile graced Leonard's mouth before disappearing. "You were—*are* so beautiful. All the guys wanted to be your friend. Well, they wanted in your pants but with Alex, Dean, and Trent around there was no way they'd approach you. Forget even waving at you—that trio had everyone living in fear of what they'd do to them. So when we literally ran into each other, I kept looking over your shoulder, waiting for Alex to jump out."

Smiling, I shook my head. "I wondered why I could never get a date. I mean, I assumed Alex put the fear of himself in all the guys, but I didn't realize it was the three of them."

Leonard rested his forearms on his knees. "I wouldn't say it was bad. It was more like hell at Feldspar High, Alex, Dean, and Trent style." The humor fled Leonard's face. "But it wasn't them I was most worried about. You were so...you, and then after the accident, you had this invisible shield around you. You didn't trust anyone, but I had to know."

"You had to know if I knew your brother had something to do with me? My parents' death?" My heart sank further.

"Yes. No." A shake of his head. "I knew Bruce was home with me, so he wasn't physically responsible for your accident, but—was he a cause? I wanted, needed to know if Bruce was responsible. I needed to know if my brother would go that far. If he could be as ugly as our parents. You know home was horrible for me, us growing up. Bruce stepping into to protect me from them, telling me to get out, do more, escape."

He stopped, lost in his thoughts.

"The night of the Winter Formal, I saw Emily speed out of the parking lot. She was crying, her makeup smeared. I thought maybe her date, who was Richard by the way, had done something to upset her or even Bruce, who was everywhere Richard was. I didn't overthink it because I was more focused on getting to Bruce. We had to be home in twenty minutes, and I didn't want our parents catching us out after curfew. I was in a hurry, rushing through the gymnasium looking for Bruce. It wasn't until I got to..." He squeezed his eyes closed and reopened them. "I found Richard and Bruce. They were pounding on Blake. I thought they'd killed him. He wasn't moving. I screamed for them to stop, and when they didn't, I tackled Bruce."

Leonard stopped. "I'm not proud of what I did, but we beat it the hell out of there. We were barely going to make our curfew, and I didn't want to give our parents any reason to go off on us. Not that they needed one." He paused and sucked in a deep breath. "It wasn't until the next day when I overheard Bruce and Richard on the phone that I knew something was wrong. Bruce was beyond pissed at Richard, more than usual. He told Richard he'd seriously fucked them and that Bruce wasn't going to go down because Richard was fucking psychotic. I didn't understand what Bruce was talking about because I'd seen Bruce wailing on Blake too, so it couldn't have been that. When I questioned Bruce about it, he told me to mind my own fucking business, and he made it clear life at home could be a lot worse if I decided to pursue anything."

He rose from the chair and began pacing. "Then I saw the news about your accident, and I thought maybe... I couldn't, didn't want to believe Bruce was responsible for any of it. I mean we were running to get home so I knew he couldn't have been there when you crashed. But a part of me kept thinking it was all related." He ran his hand through his hair. "Then something Bruce said to Richard on the phone back then clicked when you came to see me the other day. Bruce said, '*Emily's won't. . .*' and then I remembered seeing Emily speeding away from the Winter Formal."

He stopped to face me. "But that was just it. The only thing I saw was Emily upset driving away from the dance and Richard and Bruce beating Blake up. I convinced myself none of it was related because I was scared—a chicken. I was more worried about what my parents would do to me if Bruce wasn't there because he was tougher. He could take what they dished out, and he stayed even after he graduated to make sure they wouldn't touch me, and by then, he was bigger, stronger than my dad. So, I kept my mouth shut."

He looked at me, pleading with his eyes to understand, to forgive him.

"I don't know what to say. You lied, by omission, but still lied. I..." It was my turn to shake my head, to try to clear the thoughts bouncing around. "You could have told me this back then or anytime in between."

"I know. I've kicked my ass so many times these last ten years." He sounded dejected.

"Why did they beat Blake up? Did he see Richard rape Emily?" This one piece still didn't make sense.

Leonard sat back down across from me. "Blake saw Emily running out of the room. He went to investigate and saw Richard fixing his belt and smiling, looking smug. Bruce was tearing into at Richard when they saw Blake—you know they weren't the nicest to him throughout high school—they ensured he wouldn't think of snitching."

"How do you know all of that? Blake's sister, Ava, didn't even know. She assumed it was Richard and Bruce, but Blake never admitted it. Nor did Blake confirm it when Trent, Dean and me questioned him a few days ago." Had Leonard kept this a secret too?

Leonard's sigh was heavy with his burden. "Bruce woke up during your admission to the hospital. Trent's been by to question Bruce about the attack, and once Trent confirmed the sheriff was in custody, Bruce confessed to it all. How Richard raped Emily, how Bruce and Richard kicked Blake's ass afterward to ensure he didn't open his mouth. Well, Bruce admits he beat Blake because Bruce was an asshole, and he didn't want him to snitch on Richard and, by default get himself in trouble." Leonard paused. "You know Bruce met someone recently. It caused a rift between Richard and Bruce. One night at Shackles, Bruce backed out of some plans he'd made with Richard to be with this woman. Richard, already drunk, upped his drinking game and his doucheness by threatening Bruce to go to the sheriff about Bruce's part in Emily's rape ten years ago. Which, according to Bruce, was walking in at the end when they were both righting their clothes. By then, the police were already there and Sheriff Castor overheard Richard and—you've recently learned he doesn't take to having his image publicly varnished—killed Richard and tried to kill Bruce."

Stunned silent. I tried to process everything Leonard just told me. My parents were dead because one teenage asshole had raped the psychotic sheriff's daughter, and his best friend had been too psychologically traumatized from the abuse of two people who were supposed to protect him unconditionally. All these years, all the secrets, all the hurt because of assholes.

"Bella, I'm so sorry. If I could take it all back, I would. If I could prevent any of it from happening, I would. I would do anything to turn back the hands of time. To prevent you from the world of hurt you've endured over the last ten years, I would. In a heartbeat." His shoulders dropped. "I'm so fucking sorry."

"Bella?"

Both Leonard and I turned to see Rocky and Alex standing in the doorway.

Leonard walked toward them. "Bella, I hope one day you can forgive me and maybe, we can be friends again. Our friendship was never a lie."

Squeezing passed Alex, who hadn't moved, Leonard didn't wait for my response.

"You okay?" Rocky asked.

"I don't know. Everything Leonard said makes sense, but I don't know if I can forgive him." I gave Rocky an honest answer full of my confusion.

"Take your time. There's no rush." Alex bent down and kissed for my forehead.

I looked up at him. "Did you, Dean, and Trent scare away guys in high school?" I asked him for the answer I already knew.

Plopping down in the seat Leonard vacated, Alex admitted without remorse. "Yes."

"Alex! Do you know how hard it was for me to get a date?" I didn't hide my irritation at his answer.

"Yeah." He smiled a very smug and satisfied brotherly smile.

"You guys were getting laid left and right, and you couldn't even throw your sister a guy smiling at her." Rocky came to my defense for their intentional cock blocks.

Alex's smile never waivered. "Hell no."

Lying back in the bed, I warned Alex, "I think it's time I instituted little sister payback." I gave him my best innocent smile. "I feel the need to randomly show up when you're on a date and cock block you."

"Oh, I want in on this." Rocky sat at the edge of the bed.

"Don't you two have anything better to do than run amuck in my sex life?" Alex narrowed his eyes at us.

I pretended to gag. "You win, no more talk about you and your sex life."

"You're giving up too easily. This is gonna be fun," Rocky persisted.

He ignored Rocky. "You ready to go home?"

"Oh, yeah." Understatement.

"I bet. Hospitals always give me the creeps. All the sick people and dying people. Do you know they have dead bodies just a few floors below us?" Rocky shivered and looked around the room. "For all we know, someone's ghost could be standing next to us. Watching us."

Staring at my friend, I wondered where the heck she came up with this stuff. "Yeah, Rocky, let's talk dying people and ghosts to the woman who was just shot."

She shrugged. "How can you not think about it? You *are* in a hospital."

It was my turn to ignore Rocky. "Tell me about what's going with Sheriff Castor and Emily," I demanded from Alex.

"They're not telling me a whole lot for obvious reasons. Castor's still in federal custody. Emily's in our jail cell pending the outcome of their investigation. Bruce is still laid up in the hospital, so he's not going anywhere, and there is still a police officer at his door. Blake was released from custody since he should never have been behind bars. It's amazing when police work is done properly that everything falls in line." A muscle ticked in Alex's jaw as he clenched his teeth. "Fucking Castor."

"There's a lot I didn't get with all of this, but why was Castor trying to pin your disappearance on Blake?"

Alex shook his head. "Trent mentioned Castor wanted Blake out of the way since he *might* know something. Castor didn't know what Blake knew or didn't know about what transpired at the Winter Formal, so he was covering his bases. Plus, he figured if Blake took the fall for my disappearance, then everything would be wrapped up, and people would move on."

My mouth dropped open. "I never would have let it go."

Alex smiled. "Yeah, Castor admitted to the feds that you were becoming a problem, and he was trying to get into your apartment to find out what you knew." He chuckled. "He was pissed because every time he came near your apartment, Mr. Stewart would see him. So he kept busting your lightbulb so Mr. Stewart wouldn't be alerted to his presence."

"Is there more?" *Please tell me no.*

"That's all you need to know."

After everything that'd happened and everything I'd learned, I thought I agreed with Alex. Except. "Are you in any trouble?"

"Fuck no."

The wicked sheriff was detained, my brother was safe, and the love of my life was incommunicado.

Two out of three.

My odds were getting better.

CHAPTER THIRTY

Bella

HOME.

Finally.

The doctor agreed if I promised to follow his instructions to the T, I could go home. I, obviously, readily agreed to get my freedom. Alex was not happy about it. He thought I should have stayed so I could have twenty-four-hour care while I recuperated. If I stayed another night, I might have stabbed Nurse Booby with the plastic fork that came with my meals.

"I gave your apartment a once-through yesterday when I learned you were being released. Your cupboards and fridge are stocked, clean linens on the bed, and in the hall closet. I even prepared a few slow cooker meals so you can just pop them in the microwave. Nothing too stressful, but still delicious." Rocky emptied my duffel bag from the hospital. She was the best friend any girl could have.

"Thanks. You didn't have to do that."

"I know you're recovering, but don't make me hurt you." Rocky's words would have scared anyone who heard her if it wasn't for the smile on her face.

I sat down on my couch and aimed a fake annoyed look at Rocky. "Fine. I'm not thankful for you."

"Are you sure you don't want to stay with me? I can take some time off work." Alex interrupted us with practiced ease.

I shook my head. "No. You've already missed a ton of work staying at the hospital with me. I'll be fine. I need to get back to my life." A life I was going to convince Dean he wanted to be an intimate part of.

"I'm not happy about you staying here by yourself." Alex's understatement rubbed at my guilt. Here I was putting him in the position to take care of me again.

"I haven't been by myself for over a week. My guess, the next several days I will have so many visitors I'll be calling you asking to move in just for some quiet alone time."

I meant it as a joke, but I wasn't so sure it was. My hospital stay was more like a social hour at the local country club. Visiting hours were hectic with everyone popping in to check on me. I was looking forward to peace and quiet.

"Call me the second you need me." He bent and kissed my forehead.

"Will do."

"Rocky, take care of our girl."

As soon as Alex closed the door, Rocky turned to me. "I've been quiet, but I gotta ask. How're you doing?"

"I really am good. Just a little sore and tired."

"That's good, but not what I'm talking about." Rocky sat next to me. "Don't. Don't keep it to yourself and pretend there's nothing wrong."

I knew she would only let it go for so long. It wasn't like I was trying to avoid the conversation about Dean.

"I'm not trying to. I...just don't know what to say."

Rocky gentled her tone before asking, "Has Dean called you?"

"No." The tears I didn't know I was fighting now clogged my throat.

"Yeah, being laid up in the hospital bed from a *gunshot* would make it a little difficult to reach out to anyone." Rocky's sarcasm came through loud and clear.

"Listen. I don't know what's going on with Dean. I haven't seen or heard from him since I woke up in the hospital." The deep breath I took did nothing to loosen the pain.

"What did Alex say? Has he spoken to Dean?" Rocky inquired.

"He didn't say anything, but I promised him I would try. That's all." Nothing difficult at all.

Rocky wasn't so convinced. "Why is it up to you? You're the one who was laid up. He's back to business as usual. Like he never had you in his bed."

"Rocky!"

"What? Am I lying? He can't even pick up the phone to say, 'Hey, glad you're not dead from being shot.' Uh-uh. No, the man just goes back to work and acts like his best friend's little sister didn't nearly croak. The woman he had his in bed for a week. No way." She turned fully to me. "I'm sorry. I know you love him, and there was a time where I wanted him for you. But this—it's a dick move."

Opening and closing my mouth, I didn't know what to hone in on. "It is a dick move, isn't it?"

"I'm sorry, Bella. Guys can be such douches." Rocky gave me a one-arm side hug.

"How about we stop talking about jerky guys and eat some of the delicious food you packed into my kitchen? It's time for my pain meds, and I have to have it with food."

It wasn't my smoothest transition, but I wasn't lying either. The pain was less and less as the days went on, and I was getting stronger with all the physical therapy that was being jammed down my throat, but I'd moved a whole lot today in my excitement to get out of the hospital and home. The slow ache was there, and it screamed at me to listen. I needed food, a painkiller, and a nap. Then I could tackle the many things on my to-do list.

It was close to six when Rocky left. Probably because I fell asleep on her while watching a movie. I tried to stay awake, but I'd had a full day, full belly, and some powerful pain medication. I could only resist so much.

It was little past seven now, and I was wide awake. My mind kept playing over and over the time I spent with Dean. How he'd been with me. How Alex insisted I not give up.

I knew my feelings for Dean blinded me. I knew my years of obsession clouded my reasoning. No, my reasoning *had been* clouded. It wasn't now. No, now, I clearly understood how Dean and I were, and we were not how he was other women. Don't get me wrong, Dean treated all of his lady friends with care and respect. He was never cruel to any of them even when he ended things. But I was different—unique.

I wasn't making it up to rose color the situation to my advantage. My thinking was clear. I wasn't another conquest. I wasn't someone to pass the time. I was more.

So Alex was right, I owed myself and Dean the chance to make this right. It was up to me to make sure it happened. I had to come up with a plan.

I told myself to wait until the morning to see him, but I knew I was just putting it off.

So, I jumped at the opportunity to act when the two beautiful German Shepherds puppies were delivered to me fifteen minutes ago. A few years ago, I'd helped a breeder deliver a litter of puppies when the mother was in distress. At the time, the breeder said if I ever wanted one, they'd give me a deal for coming out and giving them a hand. All these years later, I'd decided to take them up on their offer.

Dean needed a puppy or two for his home, something I'd told him and something he agreed to when we talked about it later. I figured this would be the best way to break the ice with him since we hadn't spoken in over a week. He couldn't be mad at me with two fur babies.

What I didn't account for was he might have company. I didn't know whose white SUV was in the driveway, and I couldn't back out and drive away because I couldn't keep the puppies at my apartment since it was a no pet zone, and I didn't want Mr. Stewart to snitch on me. So here I was sitting outside his house with the puppies and no place to go.

I didn't have a choice. I had to take the puppies to Dean.

They were small but heavy. Plus, their crates and necessary supplies the breeder provided made it so I was stretching the limit of my wound by carrying everything to Dean's door. I didn't care. It was now or never.

The doorbell sounded a lot louder to my overly anxious nerves, and I prayed I appeared as calm as the deceptively angel-like puppies next to me.

The door opened, and there he was. Dean looked as breathtaking as ever with no shirt, pants, and bare feet. God, he was gorgeous.

"Isabella, everything okay?"

I forced my gaze from his pants and stammered, "What? Oh, yes."

"What are you doing here?" I saw the change come over him. Guarded.

It hit me then. Dean called me Isabella. *Isabella*. Not Bella. And it physically hurt.

I swallowed to moisten my now dry mouth. "Can I come in? I was hoping we could talk?" That we could be together but I didn't say that.

"Now's not a good time."

With each word he spoke, the hope I held onto was dying. "I promise I won't take a lot of your time."

"Isabella..."

"Dean, everything all right?" From behind Dean, a beautiful blonde woman wrapped in his bathrobe put her arm around his waist and leaned to the side to look at me.

Everything in me shattered.

The puppies, however, chose that moment to let out a pitiful bark.

"Oh! How cute are they!" She bent to peek into their crates.

I stood there, staring at where she'd been wrapped around Dean.

"Can I take them out and play with them?"

I moved my eyes to Dean. "I... They're for you."

"Dean! They're so cute. What are their names?"

"Brutus and Penelope." My eyes never left his.

Dean raised his hand to me. "Isabella."

A strike, that's what my name felt like. As if I had been struck.

I took a step back. If Dean touched me, I would break, and I couldn't do that in front of him. In front of her.

I looked down at the puppies and their supplies. "They have everything they need to last about a week. They'll need a checkup in a few days. You should call and get an appointment with a vet of your choice." Not me. "Sorry, I interrupted you..." More steps back. "Enjoy your evening."

I turned and ran. I didn't care what it said about me, but I was barely holding on. I needed distance before I shattered.

"Isabella!"

Bending into my car, I looked up at Dean, who was tangled in the puppies and the woman. His face etched with worry.

Uh-huh. No way. All this time and *now* he was worried. Now he wanted me to wait for him. While he had a woman in his bathrobe playing with *my* puppies.

What was I thinking coming out here to make him see reason that we were meant to be together? I knew better. I wanted to believe he felt what I felt.

God, I was *so* stupid.

I didn't wait for him. I flung my car into reverse and flew down his drive. I didn't look back. I just kept driving. Away from them.

My phone rang, but I didn't reach for it. I let it ring. It took all my concentration to drive. Everything was blurry, my body trembled, and I needed every last ounce of focus I had to make it home in one piece.

And I did.

I lay in my bed, curled in a ball, with the covers surrounding me like a cocoon. Except I wasn't sheltered. My eyes and wounds were wide open. No, they were blown open. There was no way I could shore them back up. It was a huge fucking black hole sucking everything in its path in.

Pain radiated with every involuntary shake of my body. My breath was short, torn out of me. The sobs...they hurt. I hurt. There wasn't a single part of me, physically, emotionally, that didn't not hurt.

It felt like my wound was pulling, stretching with the force of my shaking. I tried to press against it; to secure the stitches so they wouldn't rip prematurely. Except I couldn't get my hands to work. They shook so hard they rubbed against the stitches, aggravating my wound more.

Then I felt Rocky's warm body wrap around me, doing its best to hold me stable.

"Shh. Bella, you're going to hurt yourself."

Wrong. I was past being hurt.

"You've got to get a hold of yourself. You're going to rip open your stitches."

Like I had a choice.

"I'm going to fucking kill him."

"Ddddooonnn't." The shakes made me stutter.

Rocky tightened her grip around me. We lay there like that for a long time. Me, trying to pull myself together, Rocky holding me tight. Eventually, the aches, the hurt, and the exhaustion lulled me into sleep.

CHAPTER THIRTY-ONE

Bella

"You're awake."

I rolled to my side. "Yeah." I sounded like I'd had acid poured down my throat.

"Get up. Get cleaned up. I'll make you some food and get you something for the headache, throat, and aches."

Rocky left before I could agree or object. Not that she was giving me much of a choice.

I cleaned myself the best I could without a full-on shower, applied ointment, a fresh bandage to the incision site, and had pulled on my yoga pants and sweatshirt when Rocky yelled, "Food's ready."

I didn't feel like eating. I didn't feel like doing anything. I knew if I didn't, Rocky would call Alex to help force-feed me, and then they'd drive to Dean's and shoot him. I couldn't allow that. One because I loved Alex and Rocky, and I didn't want to visit them for the next fifty years behind bars. Dean, I loved him too, and I didn't want to visit his gravesite for the next fifty years either.

Rocky set my plate on the bar counter and stepped back with her dish, shoveling food in her mouth. I took my seat and looked at the omelet she'd made me with a side of country fried potatoes, toast, orange juice, and coffee. Next to it sat my antibiotics and pain pills the doctors had prescribed when I was discharged.

Scooting my behind on the barstool, I picked up my fork and took a bite. Rocky was an excellent cook. I loved her cooking. Today, I couldn't taste a thing, but I ate it so she wouldn't force me to. The faster she left me to my misery, the better.

"How did you know to come to me?"

I'd wondered that when I was cleaning up. Rocky didn't have a reason to be here.

"Dean."

I looked up from my plate to her. "Dean?"

"Yeah."

"What do you mean Dean?"

"Dean called me last night after you left his place." She set her plate on the counter.

I stared at Rocky. I wasn't sure how to take the fact Dean had called Rocky after I left his house in an obvious emotional mess *after* interrupting Dean with *another* woman.

"Want to tell me what happened?"

"He didn't tell you?"

"No."

Hmm. I didn't know how to take that either.

"Bella, what happened?"

"Nothing."

"Bella." Her eyes narrowed in warning.

"Nothing happened." That wasn't a total lie. "I gave him Brutus and Penny, then I left." With my heart shattered.

"Brutus and Penny?" Her eyebrows shot up.

I hadn't told anyone I'd picked out two German Shepherds for Dean. "German Shepherds."

"Bella, you're going to have give me more than one-word answers if you want me to follow you." Her chest expanded with a deep breath in her search for patience. "I'm trying to be patient and understanding, but you make it difficult."

Shit. I didn't want to tell Rocky. I didn't want to discuss it with anyone, but I couldn't hurt her. "Promise me first you won't do anything that will harm you."

She visibly tensed. "Why?"

"And you won't tell Alex, so he doesn't do anything either."

"What the fuck happened last night?" She leaned toward me.

I echoed her position. "Promise me."

We went into a mini-stare down before Rocky backed off, literally and figuratively. "I promise not to do anything that will harm me."

It wasn't the best, but it would do.

"Well, you know Alex told me not to give up on Dean, but I didn't know how to approach him. Then I remembered when I stayed with him that he needed a dog or two. It screams doggie heaven with all the land and nature. I told him too and he agreed with me. So, I thought getting him a dog would be the best way to break the ice. A way in."

I took a deep breath. The next part hurt.

"I finally got my nerve up, and the puppies were getting loud, and I don't have an animal lease. I couldn't keep them with me overnight or Mr. Stewart would call management on me. It was a hassle I was trying to avoid. So I packed Brutus and Penny up and headed over to Dean's."

What a mistake that had been.

"I got there, saw another car parked out front, and the light on. I knew." I shook my head. "I was there, so I thought, one clean swipe, like a band-aid." It was so much worse than a band-aid. "He opened the door. He tried to tell me it wasn't a good time, but I was there with Brutus and Penny and all of their supplies." My throat was closing up on me. I had to forcibly swallow to moisten it. "He didn't have a shirt on, pants partially buttoned, barefoot. I should have taken his warning and left." A shake of my head. "Then she... she came around Dean, hand around his waist, in his robe."

Rocky walked around the counter to me.

"Brutus and Penny wanted out. She loved them. I left."

I was in Rocky's arms, her warmth wrapped around me, keeping me safe like she had after my parents died. Tears silently streamed down my face into her shirt.

"I didn't think I had any more tears in me." I looked up at her.

Rocky looked down at me. "I'm gonna fucking kill him."

"No! You promised."

"I promised I wouldn't do anything to harm me. Killing Dean is not going to harm me."

"No! Killing him puts you in prison. That's harming you."

She shook her head. "It's not. It'll make feel fucking fantastic."

"Rocky, you can't. I can't lose you." My broken heart didn't warrant this. I'll get past it. Eventually.

"What am I going to do with you, Bella?" Rocky watched me.

"Stick around by not going to prison. You could start with that."

Another shake of her head. "All right, I won't kill him."

Whew! I relaxed. "Thank you."

"I'll just get creative with my punishment," Rocky mumbled. "Alex is a police detective, so he should have some tricks up his sleeve."

"No! Just leave it alone. I'll work through it. You, just be your normal self with Dean. I'll be fine." Eventually.

"Mmm-hmm." Rocky's noncommittal response didn't soothe me. "Well, I know your fridge is stocked, so how about we binge-watch some kickass flicks and gorge ourselves with chocolate?"

I'd lucked out with Rocky as a best friend, but her capitulation was too easy. "I'm serious, Rocky. Stay out of it."

She released me and grabbed the remote. "How about the baking channel? Or do you want action where the assholes are being blown up?"

I eyed Rocky as she flipped through the channels and continued to ignore me. After all these years, I knew no amount of pleading would turn Rocky around on something. So if that meant she read Dean the riot act, then so be it. He wasn't mine to worry about anymore.

"Action. I want to see some ass-kicking."

Dean

I stared at the paper in front of me, not seeing it. Instead, I was haunted by images of Bella unconscious, drenched in blood. It didn't matter how loud I yelled at her to stay with me, she didn't open her eyes.

I wanted to kick my own fucking ass for not being able to protect her. I'd known sleeping with her would lead to this. I fucking knew, but I couldn't resist her.

"For a smart man, you are behaving like such a stupid dick."

Rocky's anger blasted me out of my pity.

I leaned back in my chair. "What can I do for you, Rocky?"

"You mean Bella, right? Because that's who you should really be with. Instead, you're sitting behind your desk working."

Keeping my composure proved difficult. "Bella has a team of doctors tending to her and you and Alex to handle any other matters she may need assistance with."

"You're right. Bella has a phenomenal group of people surrounding her, but you know who is missing? *You!* You're supposed to be there carrying it all for her, *not* leaving it to her brother and me. What the hell is wrong with you?"

Pain shot through me. Rocky was wrong. I didn't deserve the right to be at Bella's side. I'd failed to protect her.

"Bella doesn't need me anymore. Besides"—I pointed to the papers scattered on my desk—"I have a ton of work I need to catch up on."

Rocky stared at the papers. "Are you serious?"

Absolutely. I'd proven that when Bella was shot. "Rocky, as you can see, I'm busy. If there's nothing else I can do for you, I need to get back to it." To focus on anything other than my abject failure.

Rocky leaned forward and hissed at me, "I thought Carson was the Douche King with his lying cheating ways, but I was wrong. You beat him and any other possible contenders for the spot."

While I'd failed at protecting Bella, I wasn't anywhere near the league of Carson. "Careful, Rocky."

"Fuck careful. You know Bella's been in love with you for years. You knew the second you crossed that line with her there would be no turning back for her, but you did it anyway. And, don't give me that bullshit that she's a grown woman and knows the score. Fuck that! She'd crawl over broken glass if it meant she got a chance with you. But you know all that, and you still went there."

I sucked in a breath. "I'm not having this conversation with you." Because I'd had it with myself nonstop for the last week, and I didn't need anyone else kicking my stupid ass.

"You fucking are. What kind of man willingly takes a woman to his bed knowing she's loved him for years, walks away without an explanation, and then plants another woman in her place?" Rocky pointed at me. "A fucking dick. I never expected you to make such a dick move, much less with Bella."

I drew in a deep breath. It didn't matter Bella and Rocky were wrong. There was never and never would be anything between Samantha and me, but I knew the picture we'd painted the night Bella showed told something else. "I don't owe you an explanation."

Rocky's midsection bowed from my unexpected verbal strike. "You asshole," she breathed.

"If you're done assaulting me, I have to get back to my work." I glanced at the papers on my desk, knowing I wouldn't get a single thing done after Rocky left.

Slowly she closed her eyes, and I could see her trying to rein in her anger. She opened her eyes, and I braced because she wasn't angry anymore. "Bella loves you. She'll push through for Alex, for me. She'll paste a smile on, laugh at the appropriate moments, but she won't be alive. Bella was shot, but you killed her."

And with that, Rocky walked out of my office, leaving me bleeding.

AFTER ROCKY LEFT, I received a phone call from Alex. I wasn't surprised. I'd expected it. What I didn't expect was his calm composure. He thanked me for everything I'd done and for protecting Bella while he was indisposed. Nothing unusual about it. Then he ended our call stating he never knew me to be a coward, and he was disappointed to find out I was.

Rocky and Alex's verbal throw downs coupled with my own thoughts spun in my head all day. One thing stuck out in all of it—I loved Bella. No matter the distance or time, I was going to love Bella forever.

The thought struck me front and center, and I knew living without her wasn't possible. So I gathered up Brutus and Penny and headed over to see Bella.

Brutus and Penny were little demons on four legs. There wasn't a place in my house they hadn't thoroughly explored, a corner they hadn't tried to piss in or a boot they hadn't tried to tear to pieces. I had imagined raising them with Bella—together—because that was my first thought when she mentioned them before. Now, I was done with them taking over. I needed help.

At least it was the excuse I was using to get Bella to open the door to me.

I pounded on her door and hollered, "Bella, open up."

No answer, but I could hear her moving inside.

I pounded again. "Bella, don't make me leave the puppies on your doorstep." On cue, Brutus and Penny let out tiny barks.

Bella's door opened and she hissed, "You can't leave them here. I don't have a pet lease."

She knelt to give them rubs, and the little terrors immediately acquiesced under her attention.

"I don't care. They're constantly getting into everything, and they don't listen to me. I can't leave them unattended to get anything done without them tearing my house apart." I left off the part where I purposely didn't put effort into training them because I wanted Bella training them with me.

She gave them another pet before standing back up to face me. "Of course you can't leave them unattended. They're puppies. The same goes for them not listening. They need training." She flushed with exasperation and anger.

"I didn't ask for them. The least you could do is train them." I pushed, wanting Bella to corner herself into helping.

She opened and closed her mouth. My point was valid and bullshit. The training wasn't an issue. I just wanted Bella.

"No. There are plenty of qualified dog trainers in Feldspar or Granite Creek. Hire one of them." She stepped back to close the door, and they whined. They knew we needed her too.

She hesitated and looked at them, looking torn.

"No," I told her.

Bella's eyes bugged out. "I can't keep them. I have a no pets clause in my lease, and Mr. Stewart would turn me in a heartbeat."

I didn't miss a beat nor the opportunity. "Then you'll have to move with me. Pack a bag. We'll come back later and get the rest after we get them settled."

"What?"

I moved closer to Bella and cupped her face. "We miss you. We can't sleep without you. We're unhappy when you're not around. We want you back." I stared into her eyes, hoping she saw the truth. "I'm sorry, Bella. For everything. I never meant to hurt you."

Bella's mouth dropped open at my touch. "What?"

"I want you to move in with me because I love you. I'm sorry for everything. For being stupid and hurting you. I let my friendship with your brother get between us. I made a foolish mistake, and I promise you I won't ever do it again. I love you, Bella. Please forgive me." My heart was in my throat as I waited for Bella to respond.

"I love you, too, but I don't know if I can forgive you." A single tear slid down her cheek.

My stomach roiled. "Tell me what I can do to make it up to you. To make it right."

"I can forgive the fear of losing me. I can forgive your caveman ways. But I can't forgive the other woman." More tears followed as she stepped back from me.

I stepped forward. "There is no other woman. The woman at my house is Samantha, Lily's cousin. She needs my help as a private investigator. She couldn't find me at the office because I was with you, so she tracked me down at my house. She was baking and the cake popped, or whatever that shit does when it goes wrong, all over us, the kitchen, everything."

"Why not go to Lily? Why go to your house and why was she baking?" Bella raised her eyebrows in disbelief.

"She doesn't want Lily to know what's going on and she's a pastry chef. Supposedly baking helps her focus. So, she baked." How it calmed her I didn't know and didn't care. "I haven't been with anyone since you. You're the only person I want."

Brutus and Penny barked in agreement.

Bella glanced down at them.

"Miss Hall, after an apology like that from a man of Mr. Cannon's stature, I highly recommend you accept it." Mr. Stewart dropped his vote as he entered his apartment with his laundry basket under his arm.

Bella blinked at Mr. Stewart's closed door.

I utilized her distracted state to step farther into her apartment. I closed the door with my foot and let Penny and Brutus free. Moving in close to Bella, I wrapped her in my arms. "I love you, Bella. Say you forgive me."

"You can't ever do that again. If this is going to work, we have to talk about where we're at. No more leaving me thinking you're protecting me." Hope lit her face up.

"I promise you, together."

"Together."

EPILOGUE

Rocky

In between watching Bella and Dean the whole night make lovey-dovey eyes at each other, I'd been doing my best to evade Kevin. After all these years of participating in her many Dean-attention-grabbing scenarios or staying up late plotting out their happily ever after, I was beyond thrilled she was finally living those dreams *with* him.

However, I couldn't fully embrace my glee because freaking Creepy Kevin was doing everything in his stalkerish way to stay close to me. To insert himself into my every conversation, every drink—which I conveniently always spilled because I did *not* trust an open glass around him—everything. Even the bathroom was not safe. I visited the bathroom so many times to escape Kevin that Doc Jameson pulled me aside to let me know cranberry juice was an excellent remedy for a bladder infection and if it didn't clear up before Monday, to make an appointment with him. Embarrassing didn't even cover it.

I hoped Mayor Dixon enjoyed his party because I sure wasn't. But as a business owner, a female business owner of a predominately male business, I had to make my appearance. Let the public know I was a respectable, professional business owner, even though I had breasts. It didn't help freaking Kevin was doing everything in his power to shove Feldspar back into the Mayberry era with his antiquated views of gender roles.

To boot, it looked like the people of Feldspar were eating it up. Surprised because there were so many working moms in residence, but at the same time, the backlash of what Sheriff Castor had done was still rippling through the community. People wanted to hold onto the old town feel. To not be thrust into what they called city folk prob- lems.' *Feldspar? Why those big-city problems don't happen here.'* Nowhere was immune, but Kevin used the sheriff's scandal to his advantage. He used their fears in an attempt to keep Feldspar bubbled around old- school values and traditions.

This was bad for many reasons. One because I was a female busi- ness owner in a male business. Two, seriously, we were *not* Mayberry, and no way were we going to revert to caveman tactics. You, man, hunt. Me, woman, stay. Umm, no thank you.

Unfortunately, Kevin had turned his sights on me as his June Cleaver, and no matter my subtle or not-so-subtle rebukes, he wasn't getting the message. I was getting worried I was going to have to report him, which, however you looked at it, would probably backfire on me.

"Rocky, why does it look like you're not enjoying this fine celebra- tion in honor of Mayor Dixon?"

Turning to my best friend, I answered, "Not everyone has the man of their dreams swooning over them, Bella."

"Dean does not swoon. He melts my panties."

"Yeah, yeah, yeah. Swoon, melting. I'd just like a good orgasm not induced by BOB."

"Oh, I don't know. BOB can make it interesting." Bella's smile turned naughty.

"Argh. Enough, I can't take it."

Bella's laugh lit up the night.

"Not funny. It seems the only man throwing his hat in is the one who wants a stay-at-home woman who darns his socks, while barefoot and pregnant." I shuddered at the thought. "No, thank you."

Bella scrunched her nose. "Yeah, I hear you, but remember you promised me you wouldn't close all the doors." She placed her hand on my arm. "He's out there, Rocky. Don't give up. I know it seems impossible right now, but if my dream can come true, yours can too."

Dean slid an arm around Bella's waist. "What other dreams do you have that I need to fulfill?"

Bella's words were lost to me as she leaned into him. Not that I needed to hear them. No, the love radiating out of them was nauseatingly apparent. Even if they weren't standing next to each other it wouldn't be hard to miss. They pulsated with so much joy and love a blind person would *feel* it—sight not necessary.

I forced my eyes away from the lovebirds and took in the room thinking once more that I too wanted that same soul drenched type of love. That no matter where my other half was anyone and everyone would *know* he was mine and I was his.

Like Bella and Dean.

God, jealousy was a bitch.

I was a bitch.

The End